Francis Charles Montague

Life of Sir Robert Peel

Francis Charles Montague

Life of Sir Robert Peel

ISBN/EAN: 9783337060916

Printed in Europe, USA, Canada, Australia, Japan

Cover: Foto ©Raphael Reischuk / pixelio.de

More available books at **www.hansebooks.com**

STATESMEN SERIES.

LIFE OF
SIR ROBERT PEEL.

BY

F. C. MONTAGUE.

LONDON:
W. H. ALLEN & CO., 13 WATERLOO PLACE,
PALL MALL. S.W.

1888.

PREFATORY NOTE.

THE materials for the life of a statesman are in part the same with the materials for the history of his State. It would be affectation to try to give a list of the principal sources of English history in the first half of this century. They are extremely copious, and they are accessible to everybody.

For what relates more particularly to the career of Sir Robert Peel, his speeches and memoirs must take precedence of other authorities. No complete collection of his speeches has ever been made; but everything which he said in the House of Commons has been reprinted in four stout volumes. Peel's memoirs are disappointing. They are not an autobiography, but a collection of materials for the justification of the author's conduct at three of the most memorable periods in his life—the period of Catholic Emancipation, the period of his first Administration, and the period of the repeal of the Corn Laws. They fell flat upon the public, which had long since passed on to other topics of interest; but they are valuable to the biographer, because we have so little except speeches from Peel himself.

Previous lives of Peel afford little help to the writer of a new Life. Sir Lawrence Peel's sketch contains some interesting particulars respecting the family, but does not tell much about the hero. Lord Dalling's sketch is brilliant and appreciative, but rather a criticism than a biography. M. Guizot's study of Sir Robert Peel is able, but errs in giving undue consequence to transactions in which Guizot was personally concerned, and which he wished to justify to his countrymen. Beside these and other sketches of Peel, two voluminous Lives have been published. Doubleday's *Life of Sir Robert Peel* is the work of an industrious writer just acute enough to be eccentric. Cook Taylor's *Life of Sir Robert Peel* is a wordy narrative, which tells next to nothing, and is swollen to a dropsy by interminable quotations from *Hansard*.

Many scattered facts respecting Peel may be gathered from the Lives of other statesmen more fortunate in their biographers. Among such Lives one may mention that of Liverpool, by Yonge; that of Althorp, by Le Marchant; that of Melbourne, by Torrens; that of Palmerston, by Bulwer; that of Cobden, by Morley; and especially that of Bentinck, by Disraeli. Still more information is to be gathered from such publications as the *Greville Memoirs* and the *Croker Papers*. The

Greville Memoirs tell us more about Peel than do all the published Lives of Peel put together. They give us that which is so valuable, the successive impressions of an acute and well-informed contemporary, who was neither superior to his age nor yet enslaved by its party spirit. The *Croker Papers* contain many letters which throw the strongest light upon certain critical moments of Peel's career. To prolong the list of less useful authorities would need much more space than can be afforded here.

But the most precious of all authorities for the life of Peel as yet remains unused. Peel preserved every letter which he received and a copy of every letter which he wrote. His entire correspondence is now in the hands of the Peel trustees. But the huge size of the collection has defeated the collector's purpose. The selection from its contents, so long promised to the public, is still delayed from year to year. In the meantime, the papers remain inaccessible. The present sketch is offered to the public as a candid summary of the facts hitherto ascertained respecting Sir Robert Peel.

F. C. M.

CONTENTS.

CHAPTER VIII.
PEEL'S SECOND ADMINISTRATION.
1841–1846.

CHAPTER IX.
LAST YEARS AND DEATH.
1846–1850.

CHAPTER X.
CHARACTER AND ACHIEVEMENT.

LIFE OF
SIR ROBERT PEEL.

CHAPTER I.

EARLY YEARS.

1788–1809.

The Peel family—The first Sir Robert Peel—Birth of Robert Peel—
His Early Education—His School Life—His College Life—His
Election as Member for Cashel.

THE ancestors of Sir Robert Peel had long been prosperous people in the middling walks of life. Their
original home was in East Marten, in the district of
Craven and county of York. About the year 1600
William Peel left this home to settle near Blackburn, in
Lancashire. He was accompanied by three brothers and
an aged father, and family tradition says that troubles
arising out of religious diff·rences led to their change of
abode. About forty years later, Robert Peel, the grandson of William, is known to have been a thriving manufacturer of woollen cloths at Blackburn. His great-
grandson, Robert, founded the greatness of the family of
Peel. Robert Peel, who was educated at Blackburn
Grammar School, married, in 1744, Elizabeth Haworth,

1

a descendant of the ancient family of that name. At first he gained a livelihood by farming, eked out by handloom weaving. It was not till he had reached middle life that he set up as a manufacturer and printer. His brother-in-law, Mr. Haworth, is reputed to have been the earliest calico-printer in Lancashire. Having mastered the business in London, Mr. Haworth returned to Lancashire and entered into partnership with Robert Peel, who mortgaged his land in order to raise the neces- sary capital. But finding their joint resources all too little, they took into the concern a Mr. Yates, who is said to have kept the " Black Bull " at Blackburn, and thus established the eminent firm of Messrs. Haworth, Peel, and Yates.

The firm printed the fabrics of its own manufacture, and established a warehouse for their sale in Manchester. Robert Peel had an inventive talent, and did much to improve the machinery used in the trade. But the premises were wrecked and the machinery was smashed by a riotous assemblage of handloom weavers, in whose eyes its perfection was its worst fault. Robert Peel used to repeat that, with allowance for accidents, a man might be what he chose. So without yielding to despair he removed from Blackburn to Burton-on-Trent, in Staf- fordshire, where he built three new mills ; and in order to supply one of them with water, cut a canal, at a cost of £9,000 sterling. He was an excellent man of busi- ness, plain in his speech, and simple in his ideas, but shrewd and reflective. When he walked the streets of Burton, his abstract air, and eyes fixed upon the ground, drew the attention of the common folk, who dubbed him the Philosopher. Towards the close of his life he re- moved to Ardwick Green, then a pleasant suburb of Manchester, and there he died, in September 1795, at the age of seventy-two years. A few months later his wife followed. Their grandson, the future Prime Minister, who often came to Ardwick Green while yet a child, always remembered them with reverence and affection.

Old Mr. Peel's third son inherited his name, his energy, and his abilities. Whilst yet very young he joined his maternal uncle as a partner in the firm of Haworth and Yates. Haworth retired, and Robert Peel became supreme in the management. When his innovations called forth remonstrance, Mr. Yates would reply, "The will of our Robert is law here." He was indefatigable in labour. "He would rise at night from his bed, when there was a likelihood of bad weather, to visit the bleaching grounds, and one night in each week he used to sit up all night, attended by his pattern-drawer, to receive any new patterns which the London coach, arriving at midnight, might bring down—for at first they were followers and imitators of the London work. But they soon aspired to lead their masters, and it was soon apparent to the Londoners themselves that their trade would desert them and flow into these new channels."* Such men are made to achieve success, and success in the Lancashire of one hundred years ago meant unspeakable opulence.

When thirty-six years of age, the second Robert Peel married Ellen (the daughter of his partner, Mr. Yates), who bore him six sons and five daughters. Robert, their eldest son, but their third child, was born on the 5th of February 1788, it is said, in a cottage close by the family mansion of Chamber Hall, near Bury, which was then undergoing repair. This event was equally grateful to the father's affection and the rich

---

* "Life of Sir Robert Peel," by Sir Lawrence Peel, p. 34.

man's pride. When first he heard that he was the father of a son he fell on his knees in his closet and returned thanks to Almighty God, vowing at the same time he would give his child to his country. For somewhat of a nobler ambition tempered the practical nature of Robert Peel. A near relative has told us that what many great men have owed to their mothers the statesman owed to his father—the inspiration of an early faith, a bent, a purpose, and an aim. Anxious to form the boy's mind, the father, although no scholar, kept him under his own supervision. Young Robert's progress in learning may have been as much hindered as assisted by this precaution. But his eager and aspiring mind was early directed to the toils and glories of a public career. Almost too early he was taught to be an orator. Whilst he was yet a very little fellow his father would playfully lift him on to a small round table which stood beside the breakfast-table, and encourage him thence to recite some childish lesson. When he had reached the age or twelve years his father, each Sunday, would call him into the study and make him repeat all that he could remember of the sermon. He was taught not merely to repeat the discourse, but to give the substance of it in his own words, to ask questions, and to obtain solutions of any difficulties which it might suggest. By these exercises his memory, his command of words, and his dialectical power were developed to an unusual degree. But his political ambition was still more strongly developed by the conversation and example of his father, who was now a member of the House of Commons.

Mr. Peel had always taken a lively interest in public affairs. In 1780 he published a pamphlet designed to prove that the National Debt was favourable to national prosperity; in 1790 he was elected by

Tamworth and entered Parliament, where he uniformly supported His Majesty's advisers, and in 1797 his firm subscribed £10,000 towards the voluntary contributions for the war with France. These services were rewarded in 1800 with a baronetcy. The good done by the first Sir Robert Peel in originating the two earliest Factory Acts has gained him a purer and more lasting honour. He was an active and spirited member of Parliament, but he was a vehement Tory. Like so many other men of that time, he had been frightened into violent reaction by the violence of the French Revolution. The long war completed what the French Revolution had begun, and for him blended inseparably the dislike of change and the love of his country. He was religious, also, according to the somewhat rigid and narrow piety of his class, and to him the maintenance of the Catholic disabilities was a fortieth article of faith. He revered Mr. Pitt as the perfect type of a great Minister. But the Pitt whom he reverenced was not the Pitt of earlier years, the sober and rational reformer ; it was the Pitt of later years, Pitt hardened and blinded by the war with France and the struggle against French ideas.

To young Robert Peel all the prejudices of the time of reaction came thus recommended by the authority of a tender and loving father, a man irreproachable in all private relations, and generous and beneficent to his fellow citizens, a man of acute and vigorous understanding and of untiring energy. All these prejudices the boy welcomed to his mind ; yet his was not the mind that could rest content with them. He, like his father and grandfather, was too restless to remain for ever in the bondage of routine. He was destined to put forth in political life the inventive qualities which they had exercised in business. He was as quick as they had been to seize the ideas of a time of change. Nature had made him a great administrator, and circumstances were to make him a great reformer. But how painful was that forty years' struggle of nature and of circumstances with the habit of thought and feeling which circumstance had made almost as strong as nature ! How often amid the tearing of party ties, the loss of private friends, the passionate invectives of those who thought that he had betrayed them, and the stinging compliments of those who congratulated him on reaping where they had sown, how often must that proud man have regretted that he had entered on political life with a creed to which events almost daily gave the lie ! It is thus that the fondest parents twine crowns of thorns for their children to wear.

Nor was the perversion of his intellectual development the only disadvantage of his early training. It had in one respect an unfortunate effect upon his character. As he had no childhood, he never possessed the unlaboured charm of those who have once been downright children. He was good and gentle, docile and studious, observant and thoughtful ; but he was morbidly sensitive, shrank from the rough ways of his equals in years, and preferred the society of his elders. He thus acquired a certain formality and stiffness, as of a self-conscious child, which remained with him all his life, and led those who did not know him to think that he had no heart. He also developed an egotism rather superficial than essential, such as we often see in persons who have been tenderly reared and carefully trained under the eye of loving parents, and away from the brusque democracy of school. With these failings he had, however, the virtues which redeem them. If he was formal, he was ever courteous ; if he was sensitive to pain, he was slow to inflict it upon others ; if he was somewhat of a pedant, he was correct in his morals and refined in his tastes. For these good qualities a good home is the best nursery. And after all, when we lay stress upon Peel's domestic training we must remember that he had the training of a public school and university as well.

Rather later than usual young Peel was sent to school at Harrow. He brought with him no extraordinary store of knowledge, nor did he display any miraculous powers. He did not endear himself to the schoolboy mind by feats of strength or daring, nor court a painful pre-eminence by original breaches of discipline. He disliked games, and had a habit of taking walks by himself. He was as quiet and industrious as he had been at home. The capacity for taking pains, which made him one of the first men in England, made him one of the first boys in Harrow. Everybody remembers Byron's character of Peel : that he always knew his lesson and was never in a scrape. Byron thought that he had been quite equal to Peel in general information, and superior to Peel in acting and declaiming. Lord Dalling tells us that Mr. Mark Drury, his school tutor, whose pupil Peel had formerly been, preserved many of Peel's exercises, and would refer to them to show how tersely and how clearly Peel had expressed himself both in English and in Latin.

Peel left Harrow in the summer of 1805, when he was in his eighteenth year, and in October entered as a gentleman commoner at Christ Church, Oxford. That great foundation was then at the zenith of its fame. Cyril Jackson who had been Dean when Canning was an undergraduate, continued to be Dean during Peel's academical career. At Oxford, Peel, as so often happens, grew somewhat younger, indulged himself in boating and riding, and dressed like a man of fashion. But he did not abate either his industry or his decorous behaviour. He was one of those admirable undergraduates who play no pranks, have no adventures, give no trouble, are always punctual at chapel, and never fail to be ready for an examination. With his tutor, the Rev. Charles Lloyd, who afterwards became Bishop of Oxford, Peel formed a close friendship, which continued unbroken till Lloyd's death. In the Michaelmas term of 1808, Peel achieved the distinction of a double first class in classics and mathematics. In the mathematical first class he stood alone. This double honour had not yet been gained under the modern system of examinations, which was then comparatively new. It was, no doubt, easier of attainment before the progress of knowledge and the fever of competition had enlarged the studies of the several schools. Still Peel's performance was a brilliant one. As he already had a great name among his fellow students, a numerous audience came to hear his examination, but did not disturb his uniform serenity. But who shall describe old Sir Robert's pleasure at this, the first achievement of his darling son? For a long time he could not speak of his son's degree without shedding tears. Young Robert had justified his hopes, had repaid his anxiety, and was certain to prove a second Mr. Pitt. Children so generally disappoint the fond unreasoning hope of their parents, that even now one dwells with satisfaction on the joy and pride of the worthy old gentleman.

Nothing remained except to provide Robert with a seat in Parliament. Sir Robert Peel looked round for a snug borough, and saw the ancient Irish city of Cashel with a constituency of twelve electors, in the patronage of Mr. Richard Pennefather.   A bargain was easily concluded.   Robert was elected member for Cashel in the April of 1809, and took his seat in the House early in the session of that year.   Richly endowed by nature and by fortune, tall, strong, and handsome in person, in mind vigorous and highly cultivated, with all the reputation that a youth can acquire, and with all the resources of inexhaustible wealth at his command, Robert Peel found himself on the highroad of power and of glory, at an age when most clever lads are beginning to think that it is almost time · to choose a means of earning a livelihood.

CHAPTER II.

POLITICAL APPRENTICESHIP.

1809–1819.

The House of Commons in 1809 — Peel's future Colleagues and
Opponents—Peel's First Year in Parliament—Peel seconds the
Address in 1810—Peel becomes Private Secretary to Lord Liver-
pool—Peel Under-Secretary for the Colonies—The First Bullion
Committee—Peel Chief Secretary for Ireland—His Merits and
Defects as Chief Secretary — The Irish Constabulary — Irish
Education—Agitation for Catholic Emancipation—Quarrel with
O'Connell—Peel Member for Chippenham—Peel Elected by the
University of Oxford—Peel's high reputation—He resigns the
post of Chief Secretary and holds aloof from Office — Peel
Chairman of the Second Bullion Committee—Resumption of Cash
Payments.

WHEN Peel entered the House of Commons there was
no lack of eloquence and statesmanship among its
members. Pitt and Fox, indeed, had been dead three
years, and no man had been able to take the place of
either. But on the ministerial side, Canning was in the
full flush of renown. Tierney, Sheridan, and Grattan
were still numbered among the Opposition; and they
were soon afterwards rejoined by Plunket. Althorp first
distinguished himself in this very session. Brougham
did not enter the House until the year following, and
Mackintosh was still in India; but Romilly and Horner

represented the cause of calm and philosophic reformation. Among the younger men whose names were to be
linked with those of Peel, William Lamb, afterwards
Viscount Melbourne, was now thirty years of age, a
promising member. Lord Palmerston, a few years older,
and Lord John Russell, a few years younger than Peel,
had scarcely yet attracted public notice. Outside the
House, Wellington, now in his fortieth year, was engaged
in driving the French out of Portugal. O'Connell was
a prosperous and Copley a promising barrister. Stanley
had reached the beginning and Graham the close of
school life. Richard Cobden was a little boy of five,
and Benjamin Disraeli was slightly younger. Lord
Aberdeen had risen high in the diplomatic profession,
and about this time had the honour to be laughed
at by Byron.

During his first year in Parliament, Peel spoke
seldom and never more than a few words at a time. He
was regular and close in his attendance, and devoted
himself to acquiring that knowledge of the House and
its business, in which he at length surpassed all other
men. Industry and influence brought him to the notice of
the ministers, and he was chosen to second the Address
in reply to the Speech from the Throne at the opening
of the Session of the year 1810. The occasion was not
a happy one. In the preceding year the whole naval
strength of England had been exerted in vain, and a
gallant army, such as might have supported a struggle
for freedom in North Germany, or might have carried
Wellington in triumph to the gates of Madrid, had
perished uselessly in the marshes of Walcheren. The
genius and fortune of Napoleon had gained their last
decisive triumph on the field of Wagram, and Europe
had sunk back into uneasy rest. Only in the Peninsula

the British and the Portuguese still stood at bay.
Incompetence and discord had put an end to the
Duke of Portland's ministry. Perceval became Premier; Canning and his friends went out of office;
Lord Liverpool succeeded Lord Castlereagh at the
Colonial Office; and Lord Palmerston became Secretary
at War. So weak a ministry has rarely governed in a
crisis so perilous. Under these circumstances the
youngest orator could scarcely rise to glowing eloquence;
the most skilful orator could scarcely do more than veil
in neat, plausible phrases the follies of the late, and the
mediocrity of the present, ministers. This Peel did
with a modest assurance, which was the more conspicuous by contrast with the nervous embarrassment of
Lord Barnard, the mover of the Address. Biographers
tell us that this, his maiden speech, assured preferment
to Peel; but maiden speeches seldom obtain anything more than praise from the ladies of one's own
family. When Lord Liverpool chose Peel to be his
private secretary, he doubtless rested his good opinion
on grounds more solid than this speech affords.

In this post Peel attracted the favourable notice of
George III., who had not forgotten old Sir Robert's
loyalty. Lord Liverpool was so well satisfied with his
secretary, that he promoted him to be Under-Secretary
for the Colonies. Soon afterwards there came before
Parliament the first of those great questions on which
Peel began by siding with the party of resistance, and
ended by carrying out the ideas of the party of reform.
This was the question of the resumption of cash payments, a question which then shook the scientific and
the commercial world. Its intimate connection with
Peel's career makes necessary a brief sketch of its
history before the year 1811.

When Great Britain engaged in war with France in the year 1793, her currency included, besides coin, the notes issued by the Bank of England and by the numerous country banks. At that time nobody contemplated the suspension of cash payments. But in 1796 the Government borrowed largely of the Bank of England, and then postponed payment of its debts. The Bank was thus reduced to contract its circulation of notes. About the same time, the rumours of a French invasion led to a run on the country banks. These, in turn, made large demands upon the Bank of England, and by the 27th of February 1797 the specie held in reserve at the Bank had fallen to £1,000,000 sterling. In this emergency, an Order in Council forbade the Bank to make any further payments in specie until the will of Parliament should be made known, and an Act passed the same year confirmed and continued the prohibition. By subsequent Acts the prohibition was continued until the expiration of one month after the close of the war.

During the twelve years following the prohibition of cash payments, the inconvertible paper was issued with such discretion that it was not at all depreciated in value. But in the year 1809 the value of bank-notes and of their nominal equivalent in gold began to show a divergence so marked as to attract the attention of Parliament. In the year 1810 a Committee of the House of Commons, since known as the Bullion Committee, and comprising many of the most eminent statesmen, economists, and financiers of the day, was appointed to investigate the subject, and produced an elaborate report recommending the resumption of cash payments within the space of two years. On the 6th of May 1811, Mr. Horner, who had acted as Chairman, moved a series of sixteen resolutions embodying the conclusions of the Committee. These resolutions gave rise to a brisk debate. The change from an inconvertible to a convertible currency, although salutary, must always be painful, since most of the transactions which have been made in the depreciated currency are thrown out of gear by the attempt to restore its value. A powerful opposition amongst men of business was supported by the Government, still engaged in a terrible war, and afraid of impairing its resources. Mr. Horner's resolutions were rejected, and in their stead, Mr. Vansittart, Chancellor of the Exchequer, moved and carried three resolutions, affirming, amongst other things, the gross and palpable falsehood that the currency had undergone no depreciation. It is thus that governments restore confidence. On this occasion young Peel voted with his father and the Ministers—a fact which he was never allowed to forget.

Always equal to his work, and never above it, Peel, whilst he was yet little known to the public, had firmly established himself in the good opinion of those who held power. The murder of Perceval in May of 1812 led to a remodelling of the Cabinet, which opened up new prospects to Peel. Lord Liverpool became Prime Minister, and Peel rose with Lord Liverpool. The place of Chief Secretary for Ireland, which had been offered to Palmerston and declined by him, was accepted by Peel, who held it for six years, under three successive Viceroys, the Duke of Richmond, Lord Whitworth, and Lord Talbot. Important though the place was, it was then, as now, the most disagreeable in the gift of a Premier.

During his tenure of it Peel displayed some admirable qualities. In a jovial court, and at a time of life when men are rarely averse to dissipation, he was punctual, methodic, and laborious. He was upright himself, and he discouraged jobbery in others. Inventive and practical, he was the first to establish an efficient police in Ireland. His claim to the invention may be disputed, for it has been ascribed to Sir Arthur Wellesley, when he organized the Dublin police. He cannot be denied the praise of ingenious adaptation. No country in Europe needed a police more. Wide tracts of bog and mountain, the scarcity of good roads, the want of education, the prevalence of misery and discontent, all contributed to make certain offences easy and certain offenders difficult of capture. In default of a civil police the military were often called in. At every turn the soldiers were called upon to seize an illicit still or to arrest a criminal. For such duties soldiers are ill suited, and the performance of such duties is unfavourable to the excellence of the soldier in his own profession. It wears out his spirits, relaxes his discipline, and lessens his credit with the people. These considerations led Peel to introduce, in 1814, a Bill which empowered the Lord Lieutenant in Council to appoint stipendiary magistrates for the disturbed districts, and to place under their orders a regular constabulary. When passed, this measure was applied to parts of the counties of Tipperary, Louth, Clare, and Cavan. It answered its purpose, but was partial in its operation. In the session of 1817 Peel introduced a new Bill for the extension of the constabulary system, which may therefore be dated from that year, although some time elapsed before it became universal in Ireland.

When we turn from Peel the administrator to Peel the statesman we must abate something from his praise. Those who blame him severely forget the

character of the school in which he had been reared,
and of the party to which he belonged. It is unreason-
able to expect that a young man of twenty-four years
should break loose from the prejudices of his education
and take his own way, regardless of the opinions of his
chiefs and of his friends. But from so young a man
we might have hoped more sympathy with the people,
and from so sagacious a man more insight into the
causes of their misery. Upon one subject of grave
importance Peel did indeed entertain far-reaching
views. He was strongly impressed with the deplorable
ignorance of the people of Ireland, and their ardent
desire for a better education. A few months after taking
office he said in the House of Commons :—

> Many instances evincing the thirst of knowledge felt by the Irish
> peasantry, such as must arouse the warmest feelings in every generous
> mind, had come within his knowledge. It was a thing quite frequent
> for working people to deprive themselves of all advantage from the
> labour of their children, in order that they might have their whole
> time devoted to literary acquirements ; and he knew one parish in which
> there were no fewer than eleven evening schools, where adults used
> to repair after the toils of the day, in order to procure that culture
> which had been denied in their earlier years.

In the discussion of the Irish Budget of the year
1815 he returned to this topic and added :—

> He was convinced, and he avowed it without hesitation or reserve,
> that the only rational plan of education in Ireland was one which
> should be extended impartially to children of all religious persuasions ;
> one which did not profess to make converts, one which, while it im-
> parted general religious instruction, left those who were its objects
> to obtain their particular religious discipline elsewhere.

This was a striking anticipation of the principles
subsequently adopted in organizing the National School
System. In the next Session he again took occasion

to dwell on the necessity of popular education for
Ireland :—

It was the peculiar duty of a government that felt the inconveniences
that arose from the ignorance of the present generation, to sow the
seeds of knowledge in the generation that was to succeed. It was
because he felt strongly the many excellent qualities of the Irish
character; it was because he saw, even in the midst of extravagances and
errors which were to be deplored, qualities of the highest description,
capacity for great exertion and aptitude for great virtue, that he
entertained on this subject an anxiety which he could not describe.
The attachment to that country which the many excellent qualities of
its inhabitants had created in him would long survive any political
connection he might have with it.

But upon the other great questions affecting the
Irish people Peel was scarcely more liberal than Lord
Eldon would have been. It was rather his misfortune
than his fault to be the instrument of an administration
which ruled less by its own impartial might than by
allowing a faction to trample on the rest of the people.
Peel, however, was more than the instrument of Protestant ascendancy; he thought it a good thing, and
struggled to confirm it. He thus earned the nick-
name of Orange Peel. He had, indeed, no particular
love of Orangemen. Insolence and violence were not
congenial to his nature. Such countenance as he gave
them was no more than must have been given by anyone
who was resolved to keep the Catholics in subjection to
the Protestants.

Peel was a resolute enemy of Catholic Emancipation. Resistance to Catholic Emancipation was sancti-
fied to him by the example of his father and his king.
At first some hesitation may be discerned in his treat-
ment of the Catholic question. In February of 1812,
when resisting Lord Morpeth's motion for a Committee
on the state of Ireland, he pleaded the reluctance of

2

the Catholics to allow to the State any, even the least influence, in their ecclesiastical arrangements. He referred to the project of a veto on the appointment of Catholic bishops, to be exercised by the British Crown, a project which had been long and eagerly discussed and finally rejected by the Catholics of Ireland. But he added that, in giving his vote on that occasion, he would by no means pledge himself with regard to the general maintenance of Catholic disabilities.

In the debate of May 1815 Peel took a more decided tone. During the interval the agitation had been steadily gaining in strength. For the first time it was conducted by one who had no interest distinct from the interest of the whole body of Irish Catholics, by a Catholic Irishman whose hopes of fame and power were inseparably bound up with the improvement of their condition. O'Connell had long cherished and always continued to cherish, the bitterest dislike for Peel. Peel's smile, he said, resembled the plate on a coffin. The precise and formal Peel returned O'Connell's dislike in full. Referring, in 1815, to a Bill which had been introduced two years before, he quoted certain of O'Connell's unmeasured expressions in order to show that no compromise would satisfy the Catholics. In return O'Connell resolved to fix a quarrel upon Peel. At a meeting held in support of the Catholic cause he took occasion to express himself as follows :—

I said at the last meeting, in the presence of the note-takers of the police who are paid by him, that he was too prudent to attack me in my presence. I see the same police informers here now, and authorize them carefully to report these my words, that Mr. Peel would not dare in my presence, nor in any place where he was liable to personal account, to use a single expression derogatory to my interest or my honour.

A very pretty quarrel grew out of these remarks. Peel sent his friend, Sir Charles Saxton, to O'Connell, not to deliver a message, but to say that Peel would be happy to receive one, if O'Connell thought that he had reason to complain of Peel's language. Mr. Lidwill acted as O'Connell's representative. But Mr. Lidwill and Sir Charles Saxton could not agree as to which party should send the challenge. Saxton said that Peel was quite ready to waive his privilege, and to answer for anything he had said in Parliament. Lidwill replied that if Peel felt aggrieved, it lay with him to take the first step. As neither principal would move in the matter, the seconds contradicted in the newspapers their several versions of the negotiation, and thus assured to themselves, at all events, the pleasures of a duel. They agreed to meet at Calais. In the Catholic press the whole affair was represented as an evasion on the part of Peel. Peel thereupon sent Colonel Browne to O'Connell with a direct challenge. O'Connell accepted, but was arrested and bound over to keep the peace. Then they resolved to go abroad. But O'Connell and Lidwill were arrested in London on their way to the Continent, and were bound over to remain in the country. Peel and O'Connell returned to Ireland, and the duel between the seconds proved a harmless affair. Peel tried to make out a right to fight Lidwill in lieu of O'Connell, but, as his claim was not admitted, the squabble ended in nothing worse than general laughter. If ridicule kills, it is no wonder that the duel has died out.

Peel was now regarded as the most promising young man of the orthodox Tory party. At the general election of 1812 he had relinquished his seat for Cashel and had been returned for Chippenham, in Wiltshire. He

2 *

was soon invited to offer himself to a more illustrious
constituency. Towards the end of the session of
1817, Mr. Abbott, the Speaker of the House of
Commons, retired on a pension, and was raised to
the peerage by the title of Lord Colchester. By
this event a seat for the University of Oxford
became vacant. To sit for that University had long
been a darling object of Canning's ambition. As
a distinguished Oxonian, the boldest and most original
of living statesmen, the most accomplished and eloquent
of living orators, Canning had claims which would have
been irresistible but for his unsoundness, his half-dis-
guised Liberalism, his frank advocacy of Catholic Emancipation. Aware that he was disqualified for Oxford,
Canning had to be content with representing Liverpool.
Lord Eldon and Lord Stowell employed all their University influence in behalf of Peel, who was returned
without a contest. If Canning were vexed at such a
compliment paid on such grounds to a man far younger
and less eminent than himself, he had the sense to
conceal his vexation and the magnanimity to congratulate Peel in his most cordial and dignified manner. But
Peel's election by Oxford was the first of the incidents
which suggested the belief that he was at deadly feud
with Canning.

What opinion was entertained of Peel at this time we
learn from the diaries and correspondence of John
Wilson Croker. Croker was twelve years older than
Peel, Secretary to the Admiralty, and a literary man of
considerable reputation. Although favourable to the
Catholic claims, he was nearly as correct a Tory as Peel,
and for some time an intimate friendship had subsisted
between them. They had contributed, in conjunction
with Palmerston, to the *Courier*, and other minis-

terial papers, and of their satirical effusions, "The Trial of Henry Brougham for Mutiny," was by Peel. They had visited Paris together in the July following the battle of Waterloo. In July of 1818 Croker writes to Peel :—

I must now mention to you more seriously (because it has been mentioned more seriously to me) what I have heretofore touched lightly upon, namely, your taking office. I do assure you upon my honour that I have never begun any conversation on the subject, but that in those companies where I have been, composed of very different classes of society, your acceptance of Van's (Vansittart's) office and your ultimate advancement to the highest of all have been wished for warmly and unanimously. . . .

I went yesterday to dine with Yarmouth, and as I came early, I found him alone. After a little talk on general matters, he said, " Croker, I have been thinking of what I have twice already mentioned to you, and we must have Peel Minister. Everybody wishes for him, everybody would support him. Lowther, Apsley and myself, who are heirs apparent of some weight in votes at least, would join him heart and hand. I like him personally, I have no other motive than personal liking and public respect, and I should be glad on every account to see him at the head of affairs."

It is seldom that a man of thirty years is sounded by friends as to whether he would like to be Prime Minister. Still more rarely is a man at that time of life so prudent or so cold as to meet these gentle insinuations with blank refusal. Peel replied to Croker that he was as anxious to be emancipated from office as the Papists were to be emancipated into it. He was, in truth, weary of the Secretaryship, which he resigned at the end of the summer. He then took a lengthened holiday in the Highlands. As he obstinately refused either to resume his old or to accept a new office, there went a rumour that he was about to retire from public life altogether. In reality he was recruiting his strength, and watching the course of events. The Liverpool Cabinet was so weak that it must either fall to pieces or be re-constructed, and Peel knew that in its reconstruction he could not be overlooked. Merely to be a member of the Cabinet in its decrepit state would not advantage him. Meantime he was called to preside in a weighty discussion. The Legislature was obliged once more to consider the resumption of cash payments.

During the interval between the rejection of Horner's resolutions and the close of the war with France, the depreciation of our inconvertible paper had gone farther and farther until, in the year 1814, it amounted to 25 per cent. With the conclusion of peace in the following year an improvement began, and in the year 1817 the values of gold and of paper spontaneously returned to a perfect equality. The resumption of cash payments was still delayed by successive Acts of Parliament. But the Bank voluntarily undertook the redemption of its one-pound and two-pound notes dated prior to the 1st of January 1816, and finding that very few persons took advantage of this offer, it went farther, and offered to pay gold for notes of every denomination issued by it prior to the 1st of January 1817. The making of this offer was followed by a reappearance of the premium on gold, and a consequent drain upon the Bank, which have been variously explained, but, at all events, made necessary the interference of the State.

Secret Committees of both Houses of Parliament sat to investigate the causes of the financial crisis, and Peel was chosen chairman of the Committee of the Commons. The First Report of this Committee, dated the 5th of April 1819, recommended the prohibition of all further issues of bullion from the Bank. The Second Report, dated the 6th of May, dealt at

length with the resumption of cash payments, and in
its arguments and recommendations was based upon
that Report of Horner's Committee of 1811 which the
Government and its supporters had declined to adopt.
It was drawn up chiefly by Peel, whose conversion is
ascribed to the influence of David Ricardo. A strong
party in the City and the Bank of England itself were
hostile to the views expressed in the Report. On the
very day on which the Report was taken into consideration by the House of Commons, old Sir Robert Peel,
who had abated no whit of his former persuasion, presented a petition against the resumption of cash payments. In presenting it he said, with grave simplicity,
that he was sorry that his son should have strayed into
wrong paths, but that he knew him well enough to
feel sure he would not long wander there. When the
time came for going into Committee of the whole House
on the Report, young Robert Peel stood up to make
his first great and characteristic speech. He frankly
owned his error in former years, he paid a handsome
tribute to the talents of the late Mr. Horner, he lamented
the public necessity which compelled him on this occasion to differ from an authority to which he had always
bowed with deference, and he recapitulated with force
and skill the alternative courses which had presented
themselves to the framers of the Report, as well as the
motives which had determined them in making their
choice. He concluded with four resolutions providing
for the gradual resumption of cash payments. The next
day the resolutions were carried without a dissentient
voice. Unanimity in the decision of such a matter was
regarded as so desirable, that the few dissentients were
persuaded to withdraw their opposition. Additional
resolutions provided that the full resumption of cash

payments should take effect as from the 1st of May 1823; but the Bank of England, of its own motion, anticipated this date by fully two years.

Few persons will now question the necessity of the resumption of cash payments. It was, however, attended with some injustice and some inconvenience. Debts which had been contracted in the depreciated, were now to be paid in the restored currency. In many instances, therefore, creditors were enabled to claim, and debtors were forced to pay, more than the original debt. Those who objected to the resumption declared that the depreciation of paper as measured in gold gave no adequate idea of its depreciation as measured in commodities. They declared that Peel's Act caused a disturbance of commerce infinitely more serious than he would acknowledge. Some went so far as to ascribe to the resumption of cash payments the greater part of the distress which was chronic in England from the Peace of Vienna until the Repeal of the Corn Laws. In Doubleday's *Life of Sir Robert Peel*, the resumption of cash payments appears as the incurable, the fatal blunder, the consequences of which pursued the hero more implacably than the Furies ever pursued Orestes. None of Peel's measures was more frequently or perseveringly attacked in Parliament. In the country it was the familiar theme of demagogues and agitators. Problems relating to the currency are difficult to solve, but easy to put into a form which excites passion.

CHAPTER III.

IN THE LIVERPOOL CABINET.

1820–1827.

Death of George III.—Change in Public Opinion—Peel still remains
out of Office—Ministerial Changes—Peel's Marriage, June 1820
—He becomes Home Secretary, January 1822—His Relations
with Canning—Peel's Reform of the Criminal Law—His other
Legal Reforms.—His opposition to the Catholic Claims—He
wishes to Resign in 1825—Dissolution of the Liverpool Cabinet
in 1827—Peel's Relations with Canning—Canning's Premiership
and Death—Lord Goderich becomes Premier—He is dismissed.

GEORGE III. died on the 29th of January, 1820.
Although he had long been incapable of exercising
power, his death marks the close of one period of English history and the opening of another. The reaction
brought about by the violence of the French Revolution
had well-nigh spent its force. The liberal ideas of the
eighteenth century once more began to have currency.
Almost thirty years had passed without a single reform
of importance. Now reform began slowly to come into
fashion again. Public opinion grew more and more
favourable to tolerance in matters of religion, reform of
the House of Commons, freedom of commerce, the
abolition of slavery, and the mitigation of the penal

code. At first the change was slow and obscure in its
working. But insensibly it spread and modified the
temper of statesmen before it altered their measures. Its
first effect was not to restore power to the Whigs, but to
transfer power from the fanatical to the moderate Tories.
The influence of such men as Eldon and Sidmouth
dwindled almost without notice from themselves or from
anybody else, whilst the influence of such men as
Canning and Huskisson grew insensibly but steadily.
Between these groups Peel remained in mental solitude,
attracted to the one by his own constitution of mind,
fettered to the other by education and by early ties. A
letter from Peel to Croker, written about this time,
admits us to some knowledge of his political medita-
tions.

> Do you not think that the tone of England—of that great compound
> of folly, weakness, prejudice, wrong feeling, right feeling, and news-
> paper paragraphs, which is called public opinion— is more liberal—
> to use an odious but intelligible phrase—than the policy of the
> Government? Do not you think that there is a feeling, becoming
> daily more general and more confirmed, that is independent of the
> pressure of taxation or any immediate cause, in favour of some unde-
> fined change in the mode of governing the country? It seems to me
> a curious crisis, when public opinion never had such influence on
> public measures and yet never was so dissatisfied with the share which
> it possessed. It is growing too large for the channels that it has been
> accustomed to run through. God knows it is very difficult to widen
> them exactly in proportion to the size and force of the current which
> they have to convey, but the engineers that made them never dreamt
> of various streams that are now struggling for a vent.
> Will the Government act on the principles on which, without being
> very certain, I suppose they have hitherto professed to act? Or will
> they carry into execution moderate Whig measures of reform? Or
> will they give up the Government to the Whigs and let them carry
> those measures into effect? Or will they coalesce with the Whigs and
> oppose the united phalanx to the Hobhouses and Burdetts and
> Radicalism? I should not be surprised to see such a union. Can we
> resist—I mean not next session nor the session after that—but can we
> resist for seven years Reform in Parliament? Will not—remote as is

the scene—will not recent events in Spain diminish the probability of such resistance? And if reform cannot be resisted, is it not more probable that Whigs and Tories will unite and carry through moderate reform than remain opposed to each other?

All the particular anticipations in this letter proved wrong, but its general drift is noteworthy.

By remaining out of office at this time, Peel gained the same advantage which Canning secured by going abroad, the advantage of not being in any way concerned in the quarrels of that repulsive pair, the King and Queen of England. Peel entertained no illusions about the merits of Queen Caroline, but he disapproved of the inconsistency of excluding her name from the Liturgy whilst she was yet Queen. In the course of the proceedings against the Queen, Lord Liverpool's Government became yet more unpopular, and in the December of 1820 Canning resigned for fear of having to take part in any further discussion of the Queen's affair. His resignation left a vacancy at the Board of Control, which for the moment was supplied by Mr. Bathurst, the Chancellor for the Duchy of Lancaster. Lord Sidmouth too, was desirous of resigning the office of Secretary for Home Affairs. Lord Liverpool thought of securing Lord Melville for the Home Office and Peel for the Board of Control. Lord Melville accepted the offer, not because he wished it, but because the King and Lord Liverpool forced it upon him. Peel was more difficult and coy. He told Croker that Lord Liverpool had sent for him and had made a general offer of Cabinet office, couched in strange, shuffling, and hesitating language. Peel answered this vague offer in terms equally vague. He understood Lord Liverpool to offer the Board of Control, and the Board of Control he was determined not to accept. When he at length re-

ceived a distinct offer of it, he replied with assurances
of his loyalty to the Government, but pleaded anxiety
about his health, inability to be of use in such a post,
and other considerations of a like nature.   Lord Liverpool wrote to the King on the 10th of June 1821, to inform him of Peel's refusal, and to suggest that the Board
of Control should be offered to Mr. Charles Wynn, a
man of much less ability but of much greater family.

During the course of these negotiations, as frequently in later years, Peel's caution and reserve gave
rise to charges of unbounded ambition and cunning.
But his conduct is easily explicable under the circumstances.   We have seen that about this time he
was unsettled in his own opinions, and doubtful as
to the future course of the Liverpool administration. This being so he preferred to wait, as by waiting he could lose nothing.   Already he was held in
the highest esteem; already men talked of him as a
probable premier.   He was in the prime of life, and
although nervous about his health, was equal to the
severest labour.   Time was certain to bring all that the
largest ambition could hope, whilst the present was
full of private happiness for Peel.   The sordid anxieties
which had, preyed upon so many of our greatest statesmen were unknown to this excellent man of business,
the son of one of the richest manufacturers in England.
He enjoyed with equal relish the pleasures of field-
sports and the pleasures of literature and art.   Success
in love came to crown his felicity.   On the 8th of June
1820 he married Julia, the youngest daughter of General Sir John Floyd, who had done distinguished service
in India.   Peel was singularly happy in his married
life.   He was a faithful and affectionate husband, and
Mrs. Peel was an amiable and devoted wife.   In the

enjoyment of so much felicity a young man might well be slow to take a post which the public would regard as rather below than above his deserts.

At this time Lord Liverpool was in hopes of recovering Canning's assistance. He had intended that when Melville went to the Home Office, Canning should take Melville's place at the Admiralty. But in this intention he was baffled by the King. Whether it was that Canning's refusal to take an active part against the Queen, had wounded the King in his tenderest part, his domestic hatreds, or whether it was that the King suspected Canning of certain Liberal tendencies, he had resolved that Canning should never more be one of his ministers. Canning, on the other hand, was in no hurry to return to office. He knew that his time would come, and he was too proud to sue for pardon. Lord Liverpool was still anxious to bring Canning into the Cabinet. He begged the King to reconsider his refusal, and declared that Canning's services were essential to the Government. But he was forced to content himself with an understanding that Canning's exclusion should not be perpetual. He therefore gave up the plan of moving Lord Melville from the Admiralty to the Home Office, which he now offered to Peel. Peel accepted it, and entered the Cabinet on the 17th of January 1822.

For some time it seemed possible that Peel might be the leader of the House of Commons, as well as Secretary for the Home Department. It was felt that only he or Canning could be leader. Canning had been excluded from the Government by an over-ruling power, and the precise Tories would have been heartily glad to replace him once for all with Peel. Even when Lord Londonderry's death had left the Cabinet so weak as to make Canning's adhesion almost a vital matter, Croker, who was the friend of both statesmen, wrote to Peel in this strain : "If Canning does not come in, can you carry on the business of the country in the House of Commons? First, without him; second, against him? Everybody says Yes to the former, and *almost* everybody to the latter." It is thus that the friends of great men insist on making them rivals. Huskisson went so far as to tell Croker that there could be no question as to Peel's being leader; that the only question was whether Canning was needed to second him. But Canning did not accept Huskisson's view. Canning said that at his age he could not long stand in Peel's way, and could not with honour accept an inferior situation. Peel probably felt the force of these arguments. In any case, he was too wise to be led by pique into hindering his colleagues from securing the assistance of a statesman whom they thought indispensable. There is no evidence that he felt piqued; no evidence that he acted unfairly. Canning wrote to Croker in the April of 1822 that he could not do sufficient justice to Peel for having shown a frankness and straightforwardness beyond example. Charles Greville tells us in his *Diary* that Peel shared with the Duke of Wellington all the credit of having persuaded the King to consent to Canning's return to office. The Ministers managed to soothe the vindictiveness of George IV. and the pride of Canning. Canning took the Foreign Office and the lead of the House of Commons, and entered on the latest and most glorious period of his unequal career.

The merit of a Minister must be judged partly by his contribution to the general policy of the State, partly by his conduct in his peculiar department of affairs. As a Home Secretary, Peel was admirable. Not content

with the punctual discharge of routine, he was ambitious of the honours of a reformer, and in a few years
did reform the criminal law, the law relating to prisons
and transportation, and the law relating to juries. The
reform of the criminal law was the most needed and the
most extensive of these. But whilst we praise Peel for
this reform we must remember that Peel was not the
first to conceive it, nor even one of the first to adopt
the principles of the reformers. He merely moved with
the most enlightened public opinion of the time. He
had an instinctive preference for large views, and the
practical ability to embody them in legislation.
Romilly had begun the struggle for the reform of the
criminal law, and Mackintosh had maintained it when
Romilly fell. In March of 1819, whilst Peel was out
of office, Mackintosh had carried against the Government a resolution for appointing a select committee to
inquire into so much of the criminal law as related to
.capital punishment. In June of 1822, when Peel was
Home Secretary, Mackintosh carried against the
Government a resolution binding the House at an early
period of the next session to take the criminal law into
consideration with a view to increase its efficacy by
diminishing its rigour. But when Mackintosh returned
to the attack in May of 1823 and concluded an eloquent
oration by moving new resolutions in favour of miti-
gating the criminal law, Peel met him half-way, and,
whilst opposing the resolutions, admitted their principle.
He made good his professions of sympathy with Mackintosh by introducing in the course of that very session
five Bills to amend the criminal law. By these Bills
nearly one hundred felonies were removed from the list
of capital crimes; courts of justice were empowered in
all cases other than cases of murder to abstain from

pronouncing the capital sentence if the culprit appeared
deserving of mercy, and the indignities formerly practised on the bodies of persons who had committed
suicide were abolished.   So rapid had been the progress of humane ideas that Peel's Bills encountered no
serious resistance, and hardly any serious criticism in
either House.

In the session of 1825 .Peel introduced another Bill
which put an end to some curious anomalies.   It
gave to a pardon under the sign-manual that effect
which had hitherto belonged only to a pardon under
the Great Seal, and thus restored to persons whose sen-
tences had been commuted the full enjoyment of their
rights as citizens.   Formerly such persons, when dis-
charged from prison, found themselves without their
"credits and capacities," and therefore unable to give
evidence in a court of justice.   The same Bill provided
that clergymen, upon a first conviction of an offence
which had benefit of clergy, should no longer be dismissed
with impunity.   In the following session Peel enlarged
the scope of his labours.   Cruelty was not the only
vice of our old criminal law.   The procedure in criminal
trials had gradually become so technical as to defeat the
ends of art, and to make the result of a trial depend
almost as much upon accident as upon the merits of the
case.   Peel, therefore, brought in a Bill to amend the
administration of criminal justice.   But the substance
of the criminal law was hardly so faulty as its form.
Special Acts had been passed to repress special offences
which happened at any time to arrest attention.   Many
offences totally distinct from one another were often
dealt with in one Act.   Criminal enactments were thrust
into Acts which for the most part had nothing to do
with the criminal law.   For the punishment of some

offences no provision whatever had been made. A tenant who robbed a furnished lodging was held to have committed a grave offence; but a tenant who robbed a furnished house was not held to have committed any offence at all. The statute punishing the destruction of fish in streams referred only to streams passing through an estate, and was silent respecting streams which flowed between estates. No adaptation to one another or to any uniform principles could be discovered in the criminal statutes. The consolidation of the criminal law had often been suggested by jurists, but was first taken in hand by Peel. In this session he brought in a bill to consolidate the law of larceny. This bill had to be withdrawn. But in the next year it was introduced anew, and with it a bill to consolidate the law relating to injuries to property, a bill for amending the law of damages, and a bill for the repeal of the statutes which would become useless on the passing of the consolidation bills.

In the same session in which he undertook to soften the rigour of the criminal law, Peel carried a measure for amending and consolidating all the existing statutes relative to gaols and houses of correction. In the following year he caused all the statutes relative to the transportation of offenders to be similarly revised and consolidated. In the year 1825 he brought in a second time, and carried, a bill consolidating no less than sixty-six old Acts relating to the constitution and function of juries. This measure did away with such legal antiquities as the attainder of jurymen who took bribes or gave improper verdicts. A juryman so attainted became infamous for life, forfeited his goods and the profits of his lands, and was driven out of doors with his wife and children. Of course, no instance of this punishment had

3

been known for many generations. The provisions of
Peel's bill, which enabled merchants and bankers to serve
on special juries, and persons other than freeholders to
serve on petty juries, illustrate the change then passing
over English society. All these measures were praise-
worthy in execution as well as in design. In the preparation of his bills Peel received the assistance of many
professional men, notably of Lord Chief Justice Tenter-
den and of a certain Mr. Gregson, a barrister on the
Northern Circuit. But the speeches in which he introduced the bills to the House show that he had studied
their subject-matter, and could discuss it with an accuracy and a fulness seldom shown by laymen in discussing
legal topics. In the session of 1826 he threw out a
suggestion for the appointment of a public prosecutor,
which was not carried into effect until many years after
his decease. In the session of 1827 he recommended
the revision of the entire body of the statute law—a
useful and noble work, late taken in hand, and even now
far from complete. His own contribution to that work
was not unworthy of a great Minister. Shortly after his
return to power, in 1828, he was able to inform the
House that in his first tenure of the Home Office 278
Acts relating to the criminal law had been repealed, and
their useful provisions embodied in eight new Acts. Yet
so late as 1826 this open-minded, intelligent man could
argue against George Lamb's motion to bring in a bill
enabling persons accused of felony to make their defence
by counsel.

In his own office, Peel was strong and successful, but
in the Cabinet he was insecure and ill at ease. An incurable schism condemned the Government to weakness.
Although decidedly adverse to Catholic Emancipation,
Lord Liverpool, knowing no adequate administration

could be formed out of those public men who agreed
with him on that subject, had not made resistance to the
Catholic claims a condition of entrance into his Cabinet.
The Cabinet accordingly consisted of two factions; the
faction of Canning, friendly to the Catholics and Whig
in everything but their dislike to Parliamentary reform,
and the faction of Eldon, hostile to the Catholics and
averse even to such change as the soundest Tory might
with consistency accept. Upon most topics, Peel inclined to agree with Canning. Beginning with a deep
veneration for Eldon, he had gradually slid into the less
rigid Toryism of Liverpool. Then he outgrew Lord
Liverpool and approximated to Canning. A short time
before Lord Liverpool's last illness, Peel told an intimate
friend, that in council upon any matter of importance,
he generally found his own views forestalled by Canning,
who advanced the very arguments which had convinced
him, only clothed in better and more forcible language.
Happy had it been for Peel and for Canning, still
happier for their country, had this concord been flawless
and entire. But upon the most momentous, the most
pressing question of the day, Peel was set in sharpest
contradiction to Canning. Peel was as strongly convinced as ever that it would not be safe to remove the
Catholic disabilities. Alone among those members of
the Cabinet who had seats in the House of Commons,
alone among the young men of political promise, he
maintained a stubborn resistance to the Catholic claims.
His obstinacy moved the wonder and regret of those
who knew and admired his fine gifts.

I can forgive [wrote the genial Palmerston] old women like the
Chancellor, spoonies like Liverpool, old stumped-up Tories like
Bathurst; but how such a man as Peel, liberal, enlightened and
fresh-minded, should find himself running in such a pack is hardly

intelligible. I think he must in his heart regret those early pledges
and youthful prejudices which have committed him to opinions so
different from the comprehensive and statesman-like views which he
takes of public affairs. But the day is fast approaching, as seems to
me, when this matter will be settled as it must be.

In justice to Peel it must be said that if he took the
wrong side, he argued it on intelligible grounds, and
with the calm good manners of a gentleman. He argued
not as a theologian, nor as a fanatic, but as a politician.
Speaking in the House of Commons on the 28th
of February 1821, he declared that he had never viewed
this question otherwise than as a choice of evils, and had
never been satisfied with the alternatives proposed. But,
he said, the difficulty had grown out of an anomalous
state of society which they had found, not made. He
went on to argue that emancipation itself would not
satisfy the Catholics or induce them to acquiesce in the
existing constitution of Church and State. He had
outgrown at least one illusion, for he declared in a later
speech that safeguards such as the Veto were perfectly
futile. " If the great measure were once conceded," he
said, " he would infinitely rather place all its details
upon a principle of generous confidence, than fetter them
with a jealous and ineffectual system of restriction." He
objected even to that precaution which he subsequently
took himself, the precaution of disfranchising the forty-
shilling freeholders, and gave the curious reason that it
would favour the preponderance of the Catholics. In
support of this objection he quoted the opinion of
O'Connell.

Peel tells us in his Memoirs that he limited to the
walls of Parliament the opposition which he offered
to the Catholic claims. He never appealed to the
passion or prejudice of the multitude without. What-

ever might be the feelings of the masses, the feelings of
Parliament became more and more favourable to Emancipation. In the session of 1825, it seemed as though
the Catholics were on the very verge of success. Sir
Francis Burdett again brought in his bill for the removal of Catholic disabilities. In spite of Peel's opposition he had a majority of twenty-seven on the second
reading. A few days later Mr. Littleton's bill for the
alteration of the franchise in Ireland was read a second
time by a majority of forty-eight. Only three days
afterwards, Lord Francis Leveson Gower had a majority
of forty-three in favour of his resolution declaring that
it was expedient to make provision for the Catholic
clergy of Ireland.

Convinced that the removal of the Catholic disabilities
could no longer be delayed, Peel waited on Lord Liverpool
and said that he wished to resign his office. But Lord
Liverpool declared that Peel's retirement would involve
his own. As Home Secretary, Peel was in peculiarly close
relations with the Premier, and was chiefly responsible
for the affairs of Ireland. If he resigned, his place must
be taken by some friend of the Catholics with whom
Lord Liverpool could not have acted. Peel acknowledged
the force of these reasons, and consented to remain in
office. Long afterwards, his enemies trumped up a
story that he had intimated to Lord Liverpool a change
in his opinions on this subject, which he lacked the
honesty to act upon. For this story no foundation can
be discovered. The immediate stress of the Catholic
question was now relaxed. Sir Francis Burdett's bill
was thrown out by the House of Lords. New incidents
diverted the public attention, and Lord Liverpool was
allowed to die without having witnessed the triumph of
liberty of conscience.

Notwithstanding the perpetual embarrassment of the Catholic question, the later years of the Liverpool administration offer an agreeable contrast to its earlier period. Then everything had been rigid and immobile. Now a new breath of life was felt in every department of affairs. Whilst Peel reformed the criminal law, Huskisson enlarged the freedom of commerce, Robinson established order in the finances, and Canning transformed our foreign policy. It is incorrect to date the epoch of improvement from the first Reform Act. That act only quickened a process already begun. Had the throne been filled by large-minded and reasonable monarchs, instead of first a lunatic, and then a debauchee, the process of amelioration might have been carried much farther without agitation, tumult or disappointment. But England, fortunate in many things, was unfortunate in that power over her destiny was wielded by such men as George III. and George IV. They could not prevent, but they could hinder and trouble reformation.

Lord Liverpool had long been declining in health, when he was smitten with paralysis in February of 1827. Peel wrote word of the event to Canning, who was then ill at Brighton, and shortly afterwards visited him in order to discuss what should be done. From motives of delicacy they agreed to take no decisive step so long as there should be any lingering hope of the Premier's recovery. Lord Liverpool did not die, but he did not recover, and it became clear that he was dead to business and to power. Then a successor had to be found, and the attempt to find him disclosed the want of unity in the Cabinet. The King sent for Canning, and expressed his wish for an anti-Catholic Premier; whereupon Canning advised him to form a wholly anti-

Catholic ministry. This was more easily said than done, and the King was reluctant to part with Canning, who had disarmed his prejudice. Canning was tired of serving under inferior men with whom he differed, and would be Premier or nothing. Yet the King entrusted him with a memorandum to be communicated to the Cabinet, in which it was suggested that they should choose their own chief, as Mr. Percival's Cabinet had done after his assassination. Then the King, through Peel, empowered Canning to withhold the memorandum, so it was withheld. Many days elapsed before anything was done. Neither section of the Cabinet would consent to serve under a chief taken from the other section. Canning would not serve under Wellington, and Peel would not serve under Canning. Personal dislike and distrust for Canning helped to influence several of the anti-Catholic leaders. But Peel seems not to have entertained any such feeling. When it was finally decided that Canning should be Premier, all the anti-Catholics withdrew from the ministry. The other resignations came as a surprise, but Peel's was expected by Canning, who felt that Peel, having taken so decided a part upon the Catholic question, could not be expected to serve under the champion of the Catholics. They parted on cordial terms and with mutual respect.

Peel has been severely blamed for the course which he took upon this occasion. Envy and ambition have been alleged as the motives for his separation from Canning. It is impossible to deny positively that any man's motives in any action are bad ; for how often can we be sure that our own motives are good ? It must be allowed that, in this case, one or two circumstances lend a colour to harsh accusations. By the statements of both parties, it appears that upon every question but one Peel and Canning were in harmony. If Canning had been able to serve under a chief who held opposite views to his own upon that question, why should not Peel have done as much? Surely if Canning had tolerated Lord Liverpool, Peel might tolerate Canning. If he did not do so, the reason must have been that he wished to lead an opposition to Canning, and build his greatness upon Canning's ruin. This is plausible, but it hardly bears scrutiny.

Even when the Catholic question had not been a pressing one, even under a Premier who agreed with him, Peel's opinions had occasioned him much difficulty. How much more difficulty must he have experienced, now that the Catholic question was forcing itself upon everybody's attention, under a Premier who was the weightiest advocate of the Catholic claims? The very reasons which had made him an indispensable colleague to Lord Liverpool, would make him a useless, mischievous, impossible colleague to Canning. Peel, therefore, was right in retiring, he had no choice but to retire, nor was there anything factious or dishonourable in the manner of his retirement.

Peel said in the House of Commons, and his statement was not contradicted :—

The first person to whom I communicated my opinion that I should not be able to concur in the new arrangement was my right honourable friend himself, then Secretary of State for Foreign Affairs. I mentioned my intention to retire to him and to no other individual, and I knew not the intention of any other man. I acted under a sense of my own situation. The moment the subject was mentioned to me, I thought it did not become me to act with any reserve ; and having made up my mind, not to require that my answer should be postponed until the question had been formally and officially put. This I am sure my right honourable friend will do me the justice to admit. The 29th of March was the first time the subject was introduced ; and I then said to my right honourable friend, " I will tell you without reserve what are my feelings as to my particular situation; they dictate to me retirement from office, if His Majesty should select you to form an administration." I am sure he will recollect that I made this statement without any breach of the good understanding which has so long subsisted between us. That information I took care to convey to the highest quarter, for here again I thought that there should be no reserve. My resolution was not sudden—I acted upon long previous conviction. The step I took was in no respect precipitate; and no one ought to have been taken by surprise by it.

Yet if Peel was unable to act with Canning, he might have refrained from acting against him. Instead of so doing, he went into opposition along with the high Tories. Although he was uniformly moderate, his friends were extremely violent; and his brother-in-law, George Dawson, the member for Londonderry, was conspicuous for rancour against the ministry. Thus the breach between Peel and Canning daily grew wider. But Canning was not far now from that dark abode where neither love nor hate may enter, where the eloquent voice is silent, and the ambitious heart can ache no more. Forsaken by the bulk of one great party, and but doubtfully supported by the other, he maintained his place by the ascendancy of genius. The annoyances inseparable from such a position, joined with the cares of office, were more than could be borne by a constitution already undermined by toil and excitement. When he took office in April he was ailing; before the middle of August he was dead. The nation mourned for him as for one who had left no successor, and his friends soon discovered that without him they were helpless.

Robinson, now Lord Goderich, contrived to patch up a ministry. He had been a good Chancellor of the Exchequer; he proved a lame and impotent Premier. A

sound official, without a spark of genius, he had to
govern, unaided either by Whigs or Tories or by the
favour of the Court. The King seized the first tolerable
pretext for getting rid of Goderich, and he went out
just after the new year had come in.

————————

CHAPTER IV.

IN THE WELLINGTON CABINET.

1828–1830.

The Wellington Cabinet—Peel as a Statesman—Session of 1828—
Lord John Russell's Motion for the Repeal of the Corporation
and Test Acts—Compromise arranged by Peel—The Acts are
Repealed—Proposed Disfranchisement of Penryn and East Retford—Resignation of Huskisson and his Friends—State of Ireland
—Clare Election—Alarm of the Government—Peel resolves to
resign Office—Wellington's Embarrassment—Peel agrees to remain in Office—Obstinacy of George IV.—Peel resigns his Seat
for the University of Oxford—Session of 1829—The King's
Speech—Popular Excitement—Peel returned for Westbury—
The Bills of the Government carried—But the Government
greatly weakened—Observation on Peel's Policy with respect to
Catholic Emancipation—First Session of 1830—Peel as an Administrator—His Reforms in Law and Police—Second Session of
1830—Wellington tries to regain the Canningites—End of the
Wellington Ministry.

THE dissolution of the Goderich Cabinet opened a new
period in Peel's career. The King empowered the
Duke of Wellington to form a Government without im-
posing upon him any other condition than the exclusion
of Lord Grey. The Duke wrote to Peel to invite his
assistance, which Peel readily promised. He returned
to his old place at the Home Office, and he became the

Leader of the House of Commons. Hitherto he had never been more than a subordinate, although a subordinate highly placed; he now became a chief, second in consequence to Wellington alone. Hitherto he had displayed only administrative talent; it remained for him to show that he was a statesman; that he could originate a policy of his own, not merely give effect to the policy of others. In the course of the next three years he was put to a severe trial, the results of which were not entirely favourable. With all his energy Peel was constitutionally timid, and much more sensitive than befits a man of extraordinary powers. He took many years to emancipate himself from influences which were really uncongenial, and to learn that self-confidence without which he could not give play to his real nature. In youth Peel had been moulded by his father; in early manhood he had been dominated by Eldon and Liverpool, and even now he was influenced by Wellington to a degree unwarranted by Wellington's political ability. Wellington's political ability was not, indeed, so insignificant as it has sometimes been represented. In the course of the Peninsular War he had been exercised in civil almost as much as in military affairs, and had shown some of the highest qualities of a statesman. In settled times and under an effective monarchy Wellington might have been a great minister. But narrow sympathies and lack of ideas disabled him from understanding that revolution which he blindly felt to be in progress. A military training and a somewhat despotic temper unfitted him for the management of a machine so artificial and so nicely balanced as parliamentary government. So far as he himself was concerned, the defects of his intellect were redeemed by the solidity of his character. But for men of more insight and flexibility he was an unfortunate leader. Not until Wellington, partly by grave mistakes and partly by honest efforts to repair them, had excluded himself from the Premiership and from the command of the Tory Party had Peel a chance of showing what he could perform.

In following his fortunes as a member of the Wellington Cabinet we must separate Peel the Secretary for the Home Department from Peel the leader of the House of Commons and joint leader of the Tory Party. Peel's second tenure of the Home Office was as noteworthy as his first had been. But he now for the first time played a principal part in general politics. His share in removing the disabilities of Nonconformists and Roman Catholics has always attracted and always will attract more attention than the reforms which he effected in law and police. It is most convenient, therefore, to adopt in this chapter an order the reverse of that which we adopted in the last chapter: to trace the history of the Wellington Administration, which is the history of this part of Peel's life, and then to summarize Peel's labours in that department for which he was responsible, the labours of the administrator rather than of the statesman. The administrator was the more admirable, but the statesman was the more interesting of the two characters which Peel then sustained.

The Wellington Cabinet, like the Liverpool Cabinet, was formed on the understanding that the Catholic question should be left open. By this vain attempt to escape from encountering the great difficulty of the time it condemned itself to inward and incurable weakness; but it procured a momentary accession of seeming strength. It opened the door to the faithful followers of Canning. Huskisson and Charles Grant, Lord

Dudley and Lord Palmerston continued to hold under
Wellington the offices which they had held under
Goderich.   William Lamb, afterwards Lord Melbourne,
remained Chief Secretary for Ireland.   Lord Anglesea,
who was well known to be a warm friend of the Catholics,
became Lord-Lieutenant.   Even the stoutest Tories
did not insist on recalling Lord Eldon, in whose place
Lord Lyndhurst continued to be chancellor.   The
Chancellor of the Exchequer was Goulburn, Peel's
Achates or Horatio, interesting in nothing but his faithful devotion to a man greater than himself.   Such
a Cabinet offered little hope of lasting, even if luck or
dexterity should save it from having to answer that
tiresome Catholic question which persistently repeated
itself in tones growing ever louder and louder.

Scarcely had the session of 1828 opened when the
Government met with a severe defeat.   The Opposition resolved to press vigorously a grievance which had
long been agitated without effect.   On the 26th of
February Lord John Russell brought forward a motion
for the repeal of the Test and Corporation Acts.   By
these Acts all persons dissenting from the Church of
England had been excluded from civil or municipal
office.   But for many years past these Acts had been
regularly set at defiance, and Acts of Indemnity had
been annually passed for the protection of law-breakers.
The substantial injustice was thus lessened, but the
formal ignominy was perhaps enhanced.   Even if it
could ever be good policy to insult the feelings of a class
without breaking its power, the Test and Corporation Acts
were indefensible.   The disabilities of Protestant Dissenters, unlike the disabilities of Roman Catholics, could
not be coloured with any arguments of apprehended
danger to the commonwealth.   The Dissenters did not

form the bulk of a nation, they had no ecclesiastical chief outside the limits of the realm, they were divided among themselves, and some of their principal sects were not very remote in point of doctrine from the Established Church itself. Even upon a narrow and illiberal view of the subject, what could be said in favour of vexing loyal Protestants with humiliating laws at a moment when Catholic disabilities could scarcely be maintained, and discontented Catholics were threatening civil war? Peel cannot have been insensible to reflections such as these; but Peel was a member of the Cabinet, and the Cabinet was bound to satisfy, if not its own conscience, at all events the conscience of its supporters. Peel, therefore, spoke against Lord John Russell's motion. Never had he shown himself so bland, so plausible, so conciliatory. He declared that for the Dissenters he entertained the highest respect, the warmest feelings of personal kindness. He hinted that even success would lose most of its pleasure for him, since it must involve the disappointment of such worthy persons. It is not in this temper that persecuting laws can be effectually upheld. Lord John Russell's motion was carried by 237 votes to 193.

The ministry had thoughts of resigning upon this defeat. But when they considered the state of parties, and recollected the time of confusion which had followed Canning's death, they concluded that it was their duty to retain office. If they were to retain office they would have to hit upon some compromise which might satisfy the victorious Opposition without offending the Church. They therefore asked Peel to enter into a negotiation with the Archbishop of Canterbury and other prelates. In this negotiation Peel received valuable help from his old tutor, Lloyd, now Bishop of Oxford. Peel advised

that the Sacramental Test.should be abolished, and that
in lieu thereof persons entering on corporate or civil
office should make a declaration that they would not
attempt to subvert or injure the Church of England.
Lord John Russell had followed up his motion by
bringing in a Bill to repeal the Test and Corporation Acts. The Government refrained from opposing
it on the first or second reading, but Sturges Bourne
on their behalf moved an instruction to the committee in favour of requiring such a declaration. Lord
John Russell somewhat unwillingly consented, and his
Bill passed through the House of Commons. In the
House of Lords all the moderate Tories voted with the
Government. The declaration was made indispensable
in all cases, and was amplified by the addition of the
words "solemnly and sincerely, in the presence of
Almighty God, and upon the true faith of a Christian"
—words designed merely to make the declaration more
emphatic, but which, by accident, imposed a fresh disability on the Jews. In thus bringing about the removal
of a gross injustice and absurdity the Whigs gained a
brilliant victory, the more welcome because it was the
first after so many years of defeat and torpor. The
largest part of the honour must be given to Lord John
Russell. Peel justly gained credit for the temper and
tact by which he had done so much to soften the disgrace of his colleagues and to soothe the passions of the
bigots. But the Ministry as a whole had suffered, both
by their readiness to defend a bad cause and by their
agility in quitting the defence.

Before long the dissensions of the motley Cabinet
broke out into open schism. The particular matter in
dispute must appear trivial to a generation which has
twice seen a transformation of the constituent bodies,

twice seen the addition of two million fresh electors to the roll. It was simply the question whether the representation of a single rotten borough should or should not be transferred to one of the great towns which were wholly unrepresented. The boroughs of Penryn in Cornwall, and East Retford in Nottinghamshire, were famous for corruption. Bills had been brought in to transfer the franchise of Penryn to Manchester, and the franchise of East Retford to Birmingham. Huskisson and his friends were in favour of these Bills. The Tory members of the Cabinet did not deny that Penryn and East Retford deserved extinction, but they wished to merge them in the adjoining hundreds. Peel proposed to compromise the difference by throwing the one borough into the hundred, and by giving the representation of the other to a large town. As Cornwall had forty-two members, whilst Nottinghamshire had only eight members, the members of Penryn were to be given to Birmingham, whilst the members of East Retford were to be given to the hundred. But the arrangement relating to Penryn was defeated in the House of Lords. This rebuff decided Huskisson, Palmerston and Lamb to vote for the Bill giving the representation of East Retford to Birmingham. Peel and the other ministers who had seats in the Commons voted on the opposite side, and had a majority of eighteen votes. Huskisson and his friends went out of office. Sir George Murray succeeded Huskisson at the Colonial Office; at the Foreign Office Lord Aberdeen succeeded Lord Dudley; Sir Henry Hardinge went to the War Office in lieu of Lord Palmerston; and Lord Francis Leveson Gower replaced Lamb as Secretary for Ireland. A promotion more momentous, although less remarked, was the appointment of Mr. Vesey Fitzgerald to the Board of Trade.

4

The Ministry had no sooner purged itself of half-hearted members than it was forced to consider the Catholic question. The state of Ireland daily grew more alarming. Instituted once before, and once before suppressed by law, the Catholic Association was now more extended and active than ever. Shortly after taking office, the Cabinet had consulted Lord Anglesea as to whether they should procure the renewal of the Act of 1825, directed against unlawful societies in Ireland. Lord Anglesea replied that if the Act were renewed the Catholics would be certain to find means of eluding it, and if the Act were allowed to drop, might, perhaps, contain themselves within the bounds of moderation. The Chief Secretary supported the advice of the Lord Lieutenant, and the Cabinet acquiesced, not without misgivings on the part of Peel. This resolution was taken in April. On the 8th of May Sir Francis Burdett moved in the House of Commons " That it is expedient to consider the state of the laws affecting His Majesty's Roman Catholic subjects." After a long debate this motion was carried by a majority of six—Ayes 272, to Noes 266. The friends of religious equality had on several former occasions obtained a more decisive victory. But so weak was the Administration, and so menacing was the state of affairs, that Peel began to feel his part a hopeless one, and would have resigned but for his reluctance to leave his colleagues in such distress. A few weeks after this declaration of the sense of the House of Commons came the secession of Huskisson's party, the new appointments, and Vesey Fitzgerald's promotion to the Board of Trade.

When Fitzgerald took office he vacated his seat for the county of Clare. Everybody supposed that his

re-election was a matter of course. Fitzgerald was a
man of popular manners, a fair landlord, and a constant
advocate of the Catholic claims. But he belonged to a
Cabinet which was almost of one mind in resisting those
claims, and if he could be deprived of his seat, in spite
of all the personal considerations in his favour, the
weight of the blow would be all the more distinctly
felt. The leaders of the Association had no
sooner formed this conclusion than they resolved
to act accordingly. It was vital to prevent Fitzgerald's return for Clare; but where could be found
a more popular or more influential candidate? No
Catholic could take his seat in the House of Commons without perjuring himself. But a Catholic
might be elected to the House of Commons; and
to admit or to exclude him would be equally embarrassing. O'Connell offered himself as a candidate for
the county of Clare.

The election took place at the end of June. Fitzgerald and his friends, including Peel himself, were full
of confidence. But they could not make even a respect-
able struggle. Fitzgerald polled all the gentry and all
the fifty-pound freeholders. His own tenants and a
few of the tenants of one of his supporters voted for
him, but they were almost the only peasants who did so.
" All the great interests broke down," he wrote to Peel,
" and the desertion has been universal." " I do not
understand," he added, " how I have not been beaten
by a greater majority."

To those who look back upon this famous election it
may seem the most natural thing in the world. To the
Wellington Cabinet it was shocking and wonderful. The
forty-shilling freeholders had originally received the
franchise in order that they might swell the political

influence of their landlords, and hitherto they had fulfilled the object of their enfranchisement, but now they
had strangely resolved to vote according to their conscience and for the man of their choice. Their adhesion
had multiplied the strength and confidence of the
Association. Lord Anglesea reported to Peel that
it was powerful enough to lead the people into rebellion at any moment. From the Catholic populace
the spirit of revolt was spreading to the Catholic
soldiers—a source of danger more formidable than it
could be now, for fully half the recruits of the regular
army were Irishmen.

The Catholic question could no longer remain open ;
it must be answered one way or another. Either the
Catholics would have to be taught that their demands
could not possibly be conceded, or those demands must be
conceded fully and at once. The boldest partizans of
Protestant ascendancy advised the suppression of the
Association and the disfranchisement of the forty-shilling
freeholders. But neither the disfranchisement nor the
suppression could be accomplished without the approval of
the House of Commons, and the House of Commons had
lately shown that it would not approve of these measures
unaccompanied by relief to the Catholics. It remained
to dissolve Parliament and appeal to the country, but
there was no reason to think that the electors of Great
Britain would be more hostile to the Catholics now than
formerly, whilst there was every reason to think that
most of the counties of Ireland would follow the
example of Clare. The alternative of concession remained—an alternative equally disagreeable to a firm
spirit like Wellington and a sensitive spirit like Peel.
Although one may be justified in yielding, although it
may be one's duty to yield a position which one has

obstinately maintained for many years, against great
difficulties and in spite of solemn warnings, such a
retreat can hardly be glorious, and must always be
most painful, since it always draws down the reproach
either of rashness or of cowardice in the conduct of
affairs which call alike for courage and for prudence.

To legislate upon the Catholic question in the last
days of the session was clearly impossible. But when
Parliament had been prorogued, the Cabinet began to
consider very earnestly what they should do. Peel was
the first to form a resolution.

My intention [he writes] was to relinquish office; but I resolved
not to relinquish it without previously placing on record my opinion
that the public interests required that the principle on which the then
existing and preceding Governments had been formed should no
longer be adhered to; that the Catholic question should cease to
be an open question; that the whole condition of Ireland, political
and social, should be taken into consideration by the Cabinet pre-
cisely in the same manner in which every other question of grave
importance was considered, and with the same power to offer advice
upon it to the Sovereign.

I resolved also to place on record a decided opinion that there was
less of evil and less of danger in considering the Catholic question
with a view to its final adjustment than in offering continued resistance to that adjustment, and to give every assurance that after retirement from office I would in a private capacity act upon the opinion
thus given.

Soon after the close of the Session Peel went to recruit his strength at Brighton. On the 9th of August
the Duke wrote to him enclosing a memorandum which
gave an outline of the measures to be proposed for the
benefit of the Catholics. Peel replied on the 11th of
August to the effect that such measures could answer
their end only by being comprehensive, that he felt their
necessity, and would support them as a private member,
but could not originate them as a Minister, after so

many years spent in combating their principle. He therefore offered his resignation and promised his assistance. Wellington replied, promising to discuss the topics suggested by Peel when he should have more leisure. In the meantime Peel continued to discharge the functions of the Home Secretary.

As the autumn advanced the state of Ireland grew more menacing. In the counties of Tipperary, Clare, and Limerick meetings were held for the ostensible purpose of reconciling ancient local feuds. Among the thousands who came to these meetings many wore a sort of rude uniform, and often they marched to the rendezvous in military order, with banners flying and drums beating. Anglesea inquired of Peel whether he thought it advisable to forbid such meetings by proclamation. Peel replied in the affirmative, adding that six regiments of infantry and two of cavalry were held in readiness to embark for Ireland. The Catholic Association itself took alarm, and discouraged these gatherings by express resolutions, which were obeyed. The Lord Lieutenant, notwithstanding, issued his proclamation. But the Government was still so much afraid of the Catholic Association that they took the opinion of the law officers as well in England as in Ireland on the question whether it could lawfully be put down. The opinion given was so dubious as to stop any further proceedings.

Whilst the state of Ireland daily grew more alarming, the state of the Ministry daily grew more precarious. The Ministry had to solve the Catholic question or perish. It had no other strength but what it derived from the rigid Tories, on whom, in such a crisis, it could place no dependence. First among these Tories in rank and in power for mischief was the King himself.

Where the Catholic disabilities were in issue, the most undutiful of sons was obsequious to a father's prejudice, and the most dissolute of princes recollected that he was the Defender of the Faith. Upon the King the Duke of Wellington exhausted argument and persuasion in vain. As a last resource, the Duke addressed himself to the Archbishop of Canterbury and the Bishop of London and Durham. If these right reverend persons could be persuaded that it was necessary to yield, their authority might soothe even the delicate conscience of George IV. But the prelates agreed with the King, the House of Lords was known to agree with the prelates, and how was a Tory Cabinet to carry its measures against the combined resistance of the Sovereign, the House of Lords, and the clergy of the Established Church ?

Differences between the Duke of Wellington and Lord Anglesea completed the embarrassment of the Cabinet. Lord Anglesea had been indiscreet, but he was not unpopular. He was dismissed from the office of Lord Lieutenant, which was given to the Duke of Northumberland, an adversary to the Catholic claims, "a very good sort of man," says Charles Greville, "with a very narrow understanding, an eternal talker, and a prodigious bore." He dispensed a magnificent hospitality at Dublin Castle, and was not likely to be of any other use. Absolutely nothing, therefore, had been done in four months and upwards, and there seemed to be no chance of doing anything before Parliament re-assembled. All this while Peel had not withdrawn his offer of resignation, nor had Wellington decided to refuse or to accept it. Seeing his chief without one capable adviser or assistant, seeing the Ministry on the verge of overthrow and the country not far from civil war, Peel at length resolved to save the State and hazard his reputation. He brought himself to withdraw his resignation and to offer to take charge of the Bill for the removal of Catholic disabilities. He did not reach this conclusion without a struggle, for no man had a more anxious regard for decorum or was more sensitive to the opinion of his party and the world. Listen to his laboured apology for adopting a course which is now generally approved. It was written perhaps twenty years after the time of which we are speaking, but the writer's nerves were still quivering with fresh pain :—

I could not but perceive, in the course of my constant intercourse with him, that the Duke of Wellington began to despair of success. It had been his constant desire to consult my wishes as to the retirement from office, and to avail himself of the offer of my zealous and cordial co-operation in a private capacity. He well knew that there would be nothing in the resignation of office half so painful to my feelings as the separation from him at a period of serious difficulty. From the moment of his appointment to the chief place in the Government not a day had passed without the most unreserved communication personally or in writing—not a point had arisen on which (as my correspondence with the Duke will amply testify) there had not been the most complete and cordial concurrence of opinion.

The period was at hand, on account of the near approach of the meeting of Parliament, when a formal proposal must be made to the King in respect to the position of his Government and the consideration of the state of Ireland. I was firmly convinced that if the Duke of Wellington should fail in procuring the King's consent to the proposal so to be submitted to His Majesty, no other public man could succeed in procuring that assent and in prevailing over the opposition to be encountered in the House of Lords.

Being convinced that the Catholic question must be settled, and without delay—being resolved that no act of mine should obstruct or retard its settlement—impressed with the strongest feelings of attachment to the Duke of Wellington—of admiration of his upright conduct and intentions as Prime Minister—of deep interest in the success of an undertaking on which he had entered from the purest motives and the highest sense of public duty—I determined not to insist upon retirement from office, but to make to the Duke the voluntary offer of that official co-operation, should he consider it indispensable, which he scrupled, from the influence of kind and considerate feelings, to require from me.

Accordingly Peel wrote to Wellington on the 12th of January 1829, that if the necessary measures could not be carried in any other way he was ready to give every service which he could render in any capacity. Wellington replied on the 17th that he did not see the smallest chance of success unless Peel remained in office. Peel thereupon agreed to remain in office and to propose the measures contemplated for the settlement of the Catholic question.

A memorandum showing the necessity of liberal measures towards the Catholics had been appended to Peel's letter and obtained the approval of the Duke and all his colleagues, even the most anti-Catholic. The Duke submitted it to the King, and the next day each of the Ministers who had hitherto voted against the Catholic claims had a separate interview with His Majesty, in which they plied him with every argument that they could devise in support of the memorandum. But the joint eloquence of Peel, Lyndhurst, Wellington, Bathurst, Herries, and Goulburn could only induce the King to consent that the Cabinet should consider the state of Ireland and submit their views for his unpledged consideration. In a second memorandum Peel laid down the principle which should be followed in drafting the measure of relief. He advised the Cabinet not to risk the failure of their two great measures, the relief from civil disabilities and the regulation of the elective franchise by uniting them with an attempt to define the relation of the Catholic Church to the State, or an attempt to provide for the maintenance of the Catholic clergy. His colleagues accepted the suggestions of this memorandum also. The next step was to draft the Speech from the Throne. It contained a guarded statement of the intentions of the Ministry with respect to Ireland and the Catholics. Unwillingly George IV. granted his assent to this part of the Speech.

Parliament was to meet on the 5th of February, 1829. On the previous day Peel nerved himself to a sacrifice which he fondly hoped would prove the purity of his conduct and silence the voice of calumny. The University of Oxford had elected Peel without a contest; he had represented her for nearly twelve years; she was proud of his abilities, and he was equally proud of her confidence. He was now going to give effect to those opinions which had debarred Canning from the honour of a seat for the University. Feeling that he no longer faithfully represented Oxford he notified his resignation to the Vice-Chancellor, and let it be understood that he would not offer himself for re-election. But there are no friends like University friends; and Peel's Oxford admirers would not consent to lose him without a struggle. They resolved to nominate him without his consent. The anti-Catholic party chose for their candidate Sir Robert Inglis. The contest took place at the end of February, when Inglis polled 755 votes, as against 609 votes given to Peel; but among Peel's supporters were two-thirds of the professors and first-class men. Overwhelmed by myriads of country parsons, these intelligent electors at all events did something to save the credit of Oxford and to soothe Peel's vexation of spirit.

Although the Ministers had been so long considering what they ought to do, and had met with such obstacles to the execution of their plan, they had contrived to keep their secret fairly well. A speech delivered by George

Dawson at Derry in August had raised many surmises, but all vague and doubtful. It was not until the eve of the meeting of Parliament that anything was certainly known about the measures of the Government. Then, as custom required, copies of the King's Speech were sent to the leaders of the Opposition. The news spread fast, and the excitement was immense. The Whigs were exultant; the Tories were in despair. The Party which had so long lived in defeat and humiliation saw its policy suddenly triumphant. The Party which had so long enjoyed the monopoly of power saw itself deserted by its chosen leaders. From their friends the Ministers could scarcely expect mercy, and of all the Ministers Peel was singled out for the fiercest denunciation. That Peel, the pupil of Liverpool and the friend of Eldon; Peel, whom the Irish had dubbed " Orange " Peel ; Peel, who had challenged O'Connell, and had refused to serve under Canning ; that Peel should take a principal part in bringing forward a Bill to give the Catholics all that they had asked, and more than they had ventured to hope, was a surprise so unexpected and so violent that we can understand the rage which it excited and make some allowance even for the scurrility in which that rage found utterance. Scurrilous, indeed, and frantic was the abuse showered upon Peel. He was not merely a traitor to his Party ; he was an apostate from his Church. Peel knew that he had not deserved this denunciation ; but he did not feel it less, nor did he cease to feel it whilst life remained. Having set his hand to the work, he went on notwithstanding.

The necessity of finding a fresh seat brought home to him the extent of the popular indignation. Soon after the contest at Oxford had been decided in favour of Sir

Robert Inglis, a vacancy offered itself at Westbury. Westbury was a little borough which might be supposed exempt from the passions of the large constituencies. Peel secured the patron, a certain Sir Manasseh Lopez, but he could not conciliate the populace, who assailed the town hall whilst the election was going on. Peel was returned just in time, for immediately after he had been declared member a Protestant candidate arrived from London in a chaise and four. "Had he entered a few hours earlier," writes Peel, " it is probable that I should have fared no better at Westbury than at Oxford." So far as can be judged now, the masses were hostile to Catholic Emancipation. It was especially hateful to the people of Scotland and the members of the free churches. But the unreformed House of Commons was not a mirror of public opinion. The ministers and their trusty followers, together with the disciples of Canning and the Whigs could carry through the legislature anything on which they had determined.

Of the three measures resolved upon by the Cabinet, the Bill aimed against the Catholic Association was the first to be introduced. It was brought in by Peel on the 10th of February. Without naming any particular association, it gave the Lord Lieutenant power to suppress all such bodies as he might think dangerous to the public peace or inconsistent with the administration of the law. The opposition offered no hindrance to a bill which was temporary in its operation, aimed only at suppressing an association which had already done its work, and was necessary at once to salve the credit of the Government, to soothe the irritation of the King, and to appease somewhat the party adverse to those more weighty measures which were to follow. Accord ingly the Bill passed rapidly through the House of Commons, and on the 24th of February was read a third time in the House of Lords. It received the royal assent, and the Lord Lieutenant issued a proclamation in the exercise of its powers; but the Association had already dissolved itself, and the proclamation was little more than empty sound.

Everything was ready now for the introduction of the Bills dealing with the Catholic disabilities and the electoral franchise, when the King—who had been converted with so much expenditure of argument, and had allowed his ministers to announce these Bills in the Speech from the Throne—again changed his mind, and made a last endeavour to elude the necessity which lay before him.

On the evening of the 3rd of March, Wellington, Lyndhurst, and Peel received the King's command to attend him at Windsor early on the next day. On their arrival the King welcomed them cordially, but seemed anxious and uneasy in mind. He told them with how great pain he had assented to the proposals of the Cabinet, and asked them for a more detailed statement than he had yet received. Peel proceeded to give the King the desired particulars, but when he came to the alteration in the oath of supremacy, the King interrupted him eagerly, saying, " What is this? You surely do not mean to alter the ancient oath of supremacy? " He appealed to the other ministers, and all three tried to reassure him, explaining the Bill required from Roman Catholics the abjuration of the temporal or civil jurisdiction of any foreign potentate, and that to require more would be tantamount to refusing relief altogether. But no reasoning could reassure the King, who declared that in giving his

sanction to the proceedings of the Cabinet he had
entirely misapprehended their scope. He then asked
how the ministers meant to act under these circumstances. Peel replied that he must entreat the King to
accept of his resignation, and Peel's reply was echoed
by Wellington and Lyndhurst. The King, whilst re-
gretting their decision, owned that they could hardly
do otherwise. After an interview which had lasted five
hours he took an affectionate leave of the ministers,
who, on returning to town, found their colleagues at a
Cabinet dinner, and announced that the Government
had ceased to exist.

But a sudden change passed over the King. Later
on that very day he wrote to Wellington, owning
that he could not do without their services, request-
ing them to withdraw their resignations, and leaving
them at liberty to proceed with their measures. When
this letter was shown to Peel, he suggested that, after
what had passed, a mere permission to proceed was
not enough; that the Cabinet should be authorized to
assure Parliament of the King's entire consent and
approval. The King did not venture to refuse this
request, and Peel made the concession irrevocable by
the opening words of that great oration in which he
introduced the measure for the removal of the Catholic
disabilities. "I rise as a Minister of the King, and
sustained by the just authority which belongs to that
character, to vindicate the advice given to his Majesty
by a united Cabinet."

Peel spoke for more than four hours. The House
listened with profound attention, and the silence was
broken only by cheers loud enough to be heard in
Westminster Hall. It was natural that Peel's clear
exposition should fix an audience; still more natural

that men should hail with joy the approaching end of a thirty years' controversy, which ought never to have been begun. But to the modern reader this famous speech is even more disappointing than the generality of famous speeches. The manliest confession of defeat has something depressing about it. The elaborate enumeration of securities against Catholic aggression sounds vexatious and futile. We miss the profound insight which can raise a practical controversy into a philosophical discussion, the refined force of language which distinguishes the eloquent orator from the practised debater.

Upon the first reading of the Bill, the Ministers had a majority of more than two to one. Peel spoke again in the debate on the second reading, and concluded with a disclaimer of praise, and a protest against imputations, which remind us of his speech on another memorable occasion :—

One parting word and I have done. I have received in the speech of my noble friend the member for Donegal testimonies of approbation which are grateful to my soul; and they have been liberally awarded to me by gentlemen on the other side of the House in a manner which does honour to the forbearance of party among us. They have, however, one and all awarded to me a credit which I do not deserve for settling this question. The credit belongs to others, and not to me. It belongs to Mr. Fox—to Mr. Grattan—to Mr. Plunkett—to the gentlemen opposite, and to an illustrious and right honourable friend of mine who is now no more. By their efforts, in spite of my opposition, it has proved victorious. I will not conceal from the House that in the course of this debate allusions have been made to the memory of my right honourable friend now no more which have been most painful to my feelings. An honourable baronet has spoken of the cruel manner in which my right honourable friend was hunted down. Whether the honourable baronet were one of those who hunted him down I know not; but this I do know, that whoever did join in the inhuman cry which was raised against him I was not one. I was on terms of the most friendly intimacy with my right honourable friend, down even to the day of his death ; and I say with as much sincerity of heart as man can speak, that I wish he were now alive to reap the harvest which he sowed, and to enjoy the triumph which his exertions gained. I would say of him as he said of the late Mr. Perceval, "Would he were here to enjoy the fruits of his victory."

Tuque tuis armis, nos te poteremur, Achille!

I am well aware that the fate of this measure cannot now be altered; if it succeed, the credit will belong to others ; if it fail, the responsibility will devolve upon me and upon those with whom I have acted. These chances, with the loss of private friendship and the alienation of public confidence, I must have foreseen and calculated upon before I ventured to recommend these measures. I assure the House that in conducting them I have met with the severest blow which it has ever been my lot to experience ; but I am convinced that the time will come, though I may not live to see it, when full justice will be done by men of all parties to the motives on which I have acted: when this question will be fully settled, and others will see that I had no other alternative than to act as I have acted ; they will then admit that the course which I have followed, and which I am still prepared to follow, whatever imputation it may expose me to, is the only course which is necessary for the diminution of the undue, the illegitimate and dangerous power of the Roman Catholics, and for the maintenance and permanent security of the Protestant interests.

The majority on the second reading, less than the majority on the first, was still enormous. The companion measure for raising the Irish freehold qualification to £10 was distasteful to the Opposition, but was accepted by them for fear of delaying the abrogation of the Catholic disabilities. Both Bills, therefore, went through their remaining stages without difficulty. On the 31st of March the Bill for the removal of Catholic Disabilities was introduced in the House of Lords by the Duke of Wellington. It passed the first reading without debate, and the second by a great majority. On the 13th of April it finally passed the House of Lords ; the Bill dealing with the franchise had passed just

before. The King had exhausted his powers of contention, and assented to everything laid before him. The
great change which had seemed hopeless in the beginning of January was accomplished before the beginning
of May.

A period of such keen excitement is ever followed by
a period of total languor. The session closed without
any fresh events of consequence. But the triumphant
Ministry had inflicted upon itself a fatal wound. By
carrying the measures of an Opposition you neither conciliate nor weaken it ; you rather raise its credit and its
hopes. The people of Ireland reserved all their gratitude
for O'Connell, and the people of England were struck
with the prescience of the Whigs. By saving an extreme
party from the consequences of its own perversity you
no more gain its favour than you would gain the favour
of a child by snatching it from a precipice or a fire.
The high Tories never forgave the Government. Even
whilst the Bill was in progress, the Attorney-General,
Sir Charles Wetherell, had assailed his colleagues with
an intemperance which forced the Duke to dismiss him,
and Lord Winchelsea indulged himself in an imperti-
nence which forced the Duke to call him out. Lord
Winchelsea's pistol was not more deadly than Sir Charles
Wetherell's logic ; but they were specimens of a troublesome faction—the Richmonds and the Newcastles, the
Vyvyans and the Knatchbulls. In mere spite these
politicians joined with the Whigs, and acted as members
of the Opposition. Many others who would not go so
far had lost faith in their chiefs and in their cause, and
were of little assistance to the Ministry. It was clear
that the Duke of Wellington's Government could not
last long.

Bagehot has well remarked that history will call Peel

5

to account for having refused Catholic Emancipation so long, not for having yielded it at last. But Peel himself never saw the matter in this light. He was ever anxious to shield himself from the reproach of having played the coward or the traitor on this important occasion. It is curious to read in the memoirs which he composed in later years his passionate protest before Almighty God, to Whom all hearts are open, and from Whom no secrets are hid, that no sinister personal motive prompted him in proposing Catholic Emancipation. Obsequious to the prejudices of our own, we smile at the prejudices of another generation. But our merriment is checked by the reflection that in turn our opinions will look obsolete, and those who cherished them will be thought ridiculous. It is therefore wiser to put on a serious scientific air, and to try to understand our forefathers instead of laughing at them. It is also satisfactory to find an explanation of the conduct of an eminent man which enables us to believe that he was neither stupid, frivolous, nor dishonest, although he may have been most grievously mistaken.

We need to remember that Peel's resistance to Catholic Emancipation was grounded less on religious fanaticism or national pride than in considerations of political expediency and the safety of the State. Peel was disposed to respect piety even when manifested in forms which he disliked. For the silly and vulgar contempt with which some Englishmen have regarded the whole Irish nation Peel had no sympathy. When we read the many speeches in which he urged the rejection of the Catholic claims, when we consider his youth, his place in the foremost ranks of his party, the bitterness excited by the long controversy, and the unsparing invective so often employed by the leader of the

Catholics, we shall be surprised at the courteous and measured terms in which Peel expressed his convictions. We need to remember, too, that Peel was the son of a staunch Tory and staunch Protestant of the old school. We need to remember that he grew up in a generation inspired by the French Revolution with an almost frenzied fear of change. We need to remember that he began public life as secretary to Lord Liverpool. And even when we allow for all these extenuating circumstances, we can scarcely pardon the great man who contributed so powerfully to delay concession to the Catholics until concession had lost its grace and was regarded only as a sign of weakness.

At the same time, the reasons which led Peel to disapprove of Catholic Emancipation were not so childish as it is fashionable to suppose. Peel tells us that in Catholic Emancipation he saw danger to the Established Church of Ireland and the Legislative Union between the kingdoms. The bulk of his Whig opponents thought there was no danger to either. On this point the Whigs were wrong, and Peel was right. The most celebrated of Peel's successors in power has disestablished the Protestant Church of Ireland, and has consecrated his last years to the work of destroying the Legislative Union. No calm critic will suppose that either enterprise would have been attempted without the support of the Catholic Members of Parliament. It is true that at the present day we are all agreed on the indefensible character of the old Established Church of Ireland. It is equally true that the grant of perfect religious equality has attached to the Union, perhaps, a majority of educated Catholics in Ireland. Catholic Emancipation has been justified even as a matter of prudence. But the objections to Catholic Emancipation, founded

5 *

on the state of Ireland, were solid, although not convincing.

The session which opened in February of the year 1830, offered no surprises. It was dull and ineffectual. Abroad the policy of the Government had been feeble and commonplace, a sad contrast to the vigorous and liberal policy of Canning. At home, agriculture and manufactures were alike depressed. The labouring class suffered cruelly. Everybody was agreed that something ought to be done. Most people blamed the Ministers. Peel's Act for the resumption of cash payments was so unpopular, that the agitation set on foot for its repeal did much to prepare the way for Parliamentary reform. Although Wellington's Government had been unusually frugal, the public expenditure was the subject of long debates, in which Sir James Graham, Peel's future lieutenant, distinguished himself on the side of the Opposition. Little was done, although the Opposition grew daily in strength and hope. It had found a leader in Lord Althorp, who hated politics, and took them up really out of love of his country. The Ministers had been able to count upon the King; he died in June and his successor was less friendly to them. The death of George IV. occasioned a general election in which they lost heavily. One of Peel's brothers was beaten at Norwich, another was beaten at Newcastle-under-Lyme, and his brother-in-law, George Dawson, driven from Derry, was glad to be returned for Harwich. The Tories had still a slight majority, but part of this majority uniformly opposed the Tory government. Everything seemed to be going against Wellington and Peel.

From the errors of a falling Ministry it is pleasant to turn to the achievements of a successful administrator. Whatever might be thought of the Cabinet there could be only one opinion of the Home Secretary. Peel's second tenure of the Home Office was as notable as his first had been. Immediately on returning to power he had resumed the reform of the criminal law. In the session of 1828, he introduced a Bill dealing with offences against the person. The law of England, severe in punishing violations of property, has usually been lenient in the correction of personal violence. Its provisions under this head did not call urgently for mitigation. But in form, this part of the criminal law was as defective as any other. Provisions belonging to it were to be found in fifty-seven distinct Acts of Parliament, which were all consolidated by Peel's Bill. Another bill enabled Quakers and Moravians to give evidence upon affirmation in criminal as well as civil causes. In the same session he introduced a Bill to provide cheap and expeditious means for the recovery of small debts; but this he had to abandon on account of the opposition made by the officials of the Courts of Requests, institutions nearly useless themselves, yet an obstacle in the way of anything really useful.

Had not Catholic Emancipation been carried out in 1829, that year would have been remembered for Peel's reform of the police of the metropolis. The growth of crime in London had often claimed the notice of Parliament. Several committees of the House of Commons had sat to investigate its causes and to discover a remedy, but their reports had not resulted in any practical measure. No effective police had ever been organized for the vast city which contained so much misery and so much wickedness, so many temptations to the one and so many opportunities for the other. In the first year of Peel's first term at the Home Office, he had obtained another committee of the House of Commons. From

this report it appeared that the capital depended for
safety chiefly on the parochial police, although there
were special police establishments for certain large
districts, such as the City or Westminster, and at Bow
Street a police establishment which gave assistance
wherever it seemed most necessary. These organiza-
tions differed extremely in usefulness. The police of
the City of London was tolerably good. The police
of Westminster was indifferent. The various police
establishments of recent date were as useful as with
their limited means and jurisdiction could be expected.
The parochial police was everywhere bad, in most
places a mere imposture. Even within each parish
everything was confusion. In the parish of St. Pancras
alone there were eighteen different watch-trusts, that is to
say, eighteen distinct police establishments, without any
concert or common system of action. In the parish of
Lambeth there was no night watch at all. The parish
of Kensington, fifteen miles in extent, was guarded by
three constables and three head boroughs, officers
appointed by the steward of the manor and well-known
for their drunken habits. The parishes of Fulham and
Wandsworth were absolutely unprotected at night. Such
parishes as had watchmen sometimes paid them no more
than 2d. an hour, or chose them from the number of
their paupers. In the suburban parishes a night watch
was sometimes supported by voluntary subscription.
The watchmen were usually old, infirm, or otherwise
disabled in body. But if every parish had provided an
effective watch, the public would not have been properly
protected. The division of jurisdictions would alone
have hindered the police from acting. It was not unusual for one side of a street to be in one parish and the
other side in another. Outside the limits of his own

parish, a watchman or constable had only such powers of arrest as any private person possessed. Thus, a watchman standing on one side of a street, was bound to look on idly at a depredation committed on the other side of the street, so long as that depredation did not amount to a felony. Even on suspicion of felony he could not act out of his own district.

Under these circumstances, crime naturally increased. Between the years 1821 and 1828, the committals for trial in London and Middlesex increased by nearly forty-one per cent., whilst the population increased only by fifteen per cent. The inhabitants of Brentford and Twickenham went in constant fear for their persons and their property. Gangs of thieves posted themselves in open day at the corners of the streets of Spitalfields and robbed everybody who came that way. The frequency of crime delayed the mitigation of the law, and cruel punishments were supposed to supply the shortcomings of a useless police. Fortified by the report of the committee of 1828, Peel introduced a Bill to suppress all the police establishments then existing within the Metropolis and outside the City, and to replace them with a single force, effectively organized and subject to the control of the Home Secretary. Only a certain number of parishes were to be immediately transferred to the new police. It was to be first established in Westminster, and to be extended thence into the adjoining districts.

The London police remains in all essentials such as Peel made it. It has grown with the growth of London, and has furnished a model for the police of the other cities of the kingdom. It is now part of our habits; but it was not popular when first instituted. It was new; it was costly; it was an invasion of local self-government; it was an instrument of arbitrary power devised by a Tory Minister; it was to be armed with powers of espionage and of domiciliary visit; it was to be recruited with Irish Papists, and would ultimately place the Duke of Wellington on the throne of the Protestant and patriotic House of Hanover. Gradually it outlived its ill report, and proved its exceeding usefulness. Under the new police London grew safer as it grew larger, order and decency were promoted, and the reform of the Criminal Law was no longer retarded by the legislator's fear for his person or property. The inventor of the new police acquired a renown more general than had been enjoyed by any previous statesman, and his name still lives on the lips of thieves and schoolboys.

In the third session of the Wellington administration, Peel returned to the reform of the Criminal Law. The enactments dealing with the offence of forgery were scattered through 120 statutes, of which 61 ordained the penalty of death against forgers. Peel introduced a single Bill to consolidate these enactments, and to remit the capital penalty in most of the instances in which it had been provided. The Bill was cordially received in the House. Sir James Mackintosh proposed the total abolition of the penalty of death for this crime. To-day we all agree with Mackintosh; but Peel had proposed as large a reform as could be carried. When his Bill went up to the House of Lords, the party led by Lord Eldon amended it so as to restore much of the old harshness of the law, and Peel accepted the amendments for the sake of having his measure passed without delay. It had been his intention to bring in another Bill for the consolidation of the law relating to offences against the coin of the realm. Although he did not carry out this intention, he had already consolidated a great part of the Criminal Law. The endless list of capital felonies had been reduced to a few really serious offences—murder, attempted murder, arson, rape, burglary, housebreaking, highway robbery, cattle-stealing, coining, and certain kinds of forgery. Finding that the payment by fees of persons holding patent offices in the courts of justice was a main obstacle to the attainment of a simpler and less expensive procedure, Peel procured an Act of Parliament which directed that in future such officials should receive a salary equal to the average annual amount of their fees in the ten years preceding, or, in the event of the abolition of their offices, a pension equal to at least three-fourths of the salary. He thus did away with the conflict between the interest of officers and the interest of suitors. By another Act he did away with the separate judicature of Wales, consisting of eight judges, threw Wales into the same jurisdiction with England, and added one additional judge to each of the superior Courts of Common Law. All these measures tended to improve the administration of justice, and did honour to the sagacity of Peel.

On the 2nd of November the first Parliament of William IV. was opened amid the gloomiest forebodings. Seldom had there been more misery in the country; seldom had there been so much discontent and lawlessness. The Opposition had finally decided for Parliamentary Reform, and their decision was accepted by the Canningites, who thenceforward were merged in the Whig Party. In the course of the debate on the Address, the Duke of Wellington took occasion to make an unqualified declaration against any reform of Parliament. Brougham had given notice of a motion upon that subject, and the 16th was fixed for its discussion. But when the 16th of November came, it found a new Cabinet in power. The Duke of Wellington's Ministry had resigned, in consequence of their defeat on Sir Henry Parnell's motion relative to the Civil List, and the King had sent for Lord Grey. With short intervals, Robert Peel had held office for eighteen years. He was now to spend in opposition eleven years, broken only by one brief term of power.

On the 3rd of May, whilst Wellington was still in office, old Sir Robert Peel died at upwards of eighty years of age. He had lived to see his son fulfil all the hopes that affection could form. The child whom he had vowed to the service of his country had become a Minister and a leader of a great Party. If the younger Peel had failed to maintain the Protestant ascendancy, his father may have comforted himself by recollecting that Pitt had been in favour of Catholic Emancipation. By Sir Robert's death his son succeeded to the baronetcy, to an immense fortune, and to the mansion and estate of Drayton Manor, near Tamworth.

CHAPTER V.

THE LEADER OF THE OPPOSITION.

1830–1834.

Peel as Leader of the Opposition—Introduction of the first Reform Bill—Peel's Speech—His Caution—General Gascoyne's Motion—The Ministers appeal to the Country—Tory Losses in the General Election—The second Reform Bill passes the House of Commons and is thrown out in the House of Lords—The third Reform Bill passes the House of Commons—Negotiation between the Ministers and the moderate Tory Peers—Ministerial Crisis—Peel refuses to take Office—The Reform Bill becomes Law—General Election of 1832-3—Fresh Tory Losses—Peel and the new Conservative Party—Real Weakness of the Whigs—Session of 1833—Peel's skilful Strategy—Irish Measures of the Government—Peel's Growing Reputation—Session of 1834—Embarrassments of the Ministry—Secession of Stanley and Graham—Earl Grey Resigns—The King instructs Melbourne to form a Coalition Ministry—Peel declines to join such a Ministry and goes abroad.

FOR Peel the fall of the Wellington Cabinet was a piece of good fortune. Whilst his colleagues had lost he had gained in reputation. Acute observers declared that the Duke would never be Prime Minister again, but they foretold that all the Conservative interests in the country would gather round Peel and bear him back to power in a few years. Peel himself was not so sanguine. On the last day of November he assembled at his house forty official Members of the House of Commons, and after announcing that the Ministers had resigned, declared his intention of retiring into private life, or at least of giving up the leadership and offering no opposition to the new Government. At this time many Whigs hoped that Peel would join their party. With the Whigs he, perhaps, had more in common than with the Tories. But he had not the trenchant intellect which with one sweep of logic can cut through the influences of early life and the habits of later years. As he remained a Tory he had to remain the Leader of the Tories, for it was clear that without him they would have no leader at all.

Every day's experience confirmed their allegiance. "Men begin to look exclusively to Peel," writes Croker to Lord Hertford. "Peel plays with his power in the House," writes Greville, "only not putting it forth because it does not suit his convenience; but he does what he likes, and it is evident that the very existence of the Government depends upon his pleasure." With the sense of strength came the sense of enjoyment in its exercise. People noticed how cheerful Peel had become. To quote Greville again : " Peel is delighted ; he wants leisure, is glad to get out of such a firm, and will have time to form his own plans and to avail himself of circumstances which according to every probability must be in his favour." This last observation was too hasty. One circumstance was singularly adverse to Peel and his Party. By their persistent folly they had made popular the demand for Parliamentary reform. They had obstinately refused to make any improvement in the representation. They had wantonly declared that no such improvement was possible. And now their adversaries were in office,

pledged to a reform of Parliament and led by a statesman who had advocated reform for thirty years. The
Tories were thus bound in consistency to resist a change
which was desired by the people and could not be
defeated by them.

On the 1st of March 1831 Lord John Russell moved
the House of Commons for leave to bring in a Bill for
amending the state of the representation in England
and Wales. There was a general curiosity to know
what line Peel would take. It was said that the success
of the measure depended chiefly on his decision. Nor
was the saying so absurd as it may appear. Whilst
everybody assumed that Lord Grey's Government would
bring in a Bill for the reform of Parliament, very few
persons had any definite conception of the form which
such a measure would take, and still fewer expected a
measure so comprehensive as that which Lord John
Russell explained to the House on the motion for leave
to bring in a Bill. The House was first astounded,
then incredulous. As Lord John went on reading the
names of the boroughs doomed to disfranchisement, the
Opposition began to smile, and finally broke into loud
peals of laughter. An eminent member of the Whig
Party has recorded his opinion that if Sir Robert Peel
had stood up as soon as Lord John sat down, had
declared the Bill to be revolutionary, refused to discuss
it, moved the order of the day, and pledged himself to
bring forward a practical scheme, he would have had a
majority of at least a hundred. Perhaps so; but the
fact that such a Bill had been brought in by a Minister
of the Crown would have remained, and would have made
the success of the Tories, doubtful in any case, very
imperfect after all.

Strokes of this kind, which the philosophic historian

praises or blames, as they succeed or fail, it was not in
Peel's nature to execute.   He did not rise until the
third night of the debate, and he then made a temperate
and skilful speech.   In that speech he mingled, as
practised debaters do, the good arguments with the bad.
There never yet was speech made which could sustain
throughout the analysis of the impartial logician.   Nor
are such speeches needed.   Temperament and impulse
dictate the policy of large masses of men ; and for this
policy so dictated their leaders find reasons.   But what
could be said against the Bill was well said by Peel.
" I think," he said, " that in political speculation the
hazard of error is immense, and the result of the best
formed scheme often different from that which has been
anticipated."   Then he touched on the least popular
part of the Bill.   Under the old system of representation
the qualification for an elector had varied so much in
different boroughs that whilst some Members were
nominated by individuals, others were returned by nearly
universal suffrage.   The Bill established a uniform £10
qualification in all constituencies.   Peel dexterously
seized on this invidious provision.

I conceive the noble lord's plan to be founded altogether upon an
erroneous principle.   Its great defect in my opinion is that to which an
objection has been urged with great force and ability by the honourable member for Callington.   The objection is this, that it severs all
connection between the lower classes of the community and the direct
representation in this house ; I think it a fatal objection that every link
between the representative and the constituent body should be separated
so far as regards the lower classes.   It is an immense advantage that
there is at present no class of people, however humble, which is not
entitled to a voice in the election of representatives. I think this system
would be defective if it were extended further ; but at the same time
I consider it an inestimable advantage, that no class of the community
should be able to say they are not entitled in some way or other to a
share in the privilege of choosing the representatives of the people in
this House.   Undoubtedly, if I had to choose between two modes of

representation, and two only, and if it were put to me whether I would prefer that system which would send the honourable member for Windsor or that which would return the honourable member for Preston, I should undoubtedly prefer that by which the honourable member for Windsor would be returned; but I am not in this dilemma, and am at perfect liberty to protest against a principle which excludes altogether the honourable member for Preston. I think it an immense advantage that the class which includes the weavers of Coventry and the potwallopers of Preston has a share in the privileges of the present system. The individual right is limited, and properly limited, within narrow bounds; but the class is represented. It has its champion within your walls, the organ of its feeling and the guardian of its interests. But what will be the effect of cutting off altogether the communication between this House and all that class of society which is above pauperism and below the arbitrary and impassable line of £10 rental which you have selected? If you were establishing a perfectly new system of representation, and were unfettered by the recollections of the past and by existing modes of society, would it be wise to exclude altogether the sympathies of this class? How much more unwise, when you find it possessed from time immemorial of the privilege, to take the privilege away, and to subject a great, powerful, jealous, and intelligent mass of your population to the injury, aye, and to the stigma, of uncompensated exclusion!

Passing on to the consideration of the small boroughs which were to be disfranchised, Peel put forcibly the argument which since has become so familiar—the argument that to these small boroughs the majority of eminent public men had been indebted for their first admission to public life. After enumerating two-and-twenty of the most illustrious orators and statesmen of every party in the reign of George III., he showed that sixteen had first been returned to Parliament by boroughs now doomed to disappear. Lastly, confessing the anomalies of the actual representative system, he reminded the House that under it England had risen to an amazing height of power and glory, and had maintained her laws and liberties unshaken either by revolution or by military power.

Up to this hour [he said] no one has pretended that we shall gain anything by the change, excepting, indeed, that we shall conciliate the public
favour.   Why, no doubt you cannot propose to share your power
with half a million of men without gaining some popularity, without
purchasing by such a bribe some portion of goodwill.   But these are
vulgar arts of government ; others will outbid you, not now but at no
remote period, they will offer votes and power to a million of men,
will quote your precedent for the concession, and will carry your
principles to their legitimate and natural consequences.

It is curious to think that this prediction might
very well have been heard by the two men who were to
fulfil it.

But the tide of events could not be turned back.   After
the debate had lasted seven nights, leave to bring in the
Bill was granted, and the Bill was read a first time without a division.   The Ministerial party had displayed an
immense superiority in the debate.   Their success, however, was due chiefly to the sagacity of Russell, who,
seeing that a large measure was needed, had made it large
enough to excite popular enthusiasm.   Peel spoke again
on several occasions in the progress of the Reform Bill
for England and the accompanying measure for Ireland.
But the keener Tory partizans were much disgusted with
his moderation.   One of them complained bitterly to
Charles Greville of Peel's sluggishness and of the consequent want of union and tactical skill in their operations.   Croker wrote to Lord Hertford that "the real
cause of the success of this fearful measure is that our
leader neither has nor chooses to have the command of
his army."   Less prejudiced spectators were disposed
to echo these criticisms.   "He is, in fact, so cold,
phlegmatic, and calculating," wrote Greville, "that he
disgusts those who can't do without him as a leader ; he
will always have political, but never personal influence."
These criticisms did not grow milder when the Reform

Bill was read a second time by a majority of one in a House of more than six hundred members.

At last Peel found his opportunity. The Reform Bill proposed to reduce the representation of England and to increase that of Scotland and Ireland. Peel prevailed on the Ministers to pledge themselves to a division upon this provision of the Bill. He was so much elated by this advantage that he forgot his usual reserve. " Give us another month," he wrote to Croker, " and there is an end of the Bill, positively an end to it. It never could be carried, except by the dread of physical force." The point which Peel had suggested was raised by General Gascoyne's motion of the 18th of April, and upon that motion the Ministry was defeated. Finding that they had no prospect of carrying their Bill uninjured through committee, and, therefore, no prospect of carrying it at all through the House of Lords, they resolved to appeal to the country.

King William IV. had begun his reign with a favourable disposition to Parliamentary Reform, which was not yet exhausted. He readily consented to a dissolution, and hastened to prorogue Parliament without making any formal preparation. It was the 22nd of April. Sir Richard Vyvyan, one of the members for Cornwall, was inveighing against the Reform Bill, which, he said, would tear the crown from the head of the Sovereign, when the report of the first gun announcing the King's approach resounded through the House, and was answered by loud cheers from the Ministerial benches. Every fresh salvo had a like response, and laughter and cries of " Order " completed the confusion. Sir Richard Vyvyan had become inaudible for some minutes before he sat down. Then Sir Robert Peel, Lord Althorp, and Sir Francis Burdett all

6

sprang up at once. Immediately the tumult was redoubled. Shouts, groans, laughter, and cries of "Bar" greeted Peel, and were met by cries of "Order" and "Chair" from his supporters. He stood vainly gesticulating amid the din. So did Burdett and Althorp. At length the Speaker rose, and the hubbub slowly abated until he could make himself heard. By his interposition Sir Robert was allowed to continue his speech. He fiercely assailed the Ministry, taxed them with incompetence, folly, and recklessness, and was in the full current of denunciation when suddenly the Usher of the Black Rod appeared at the bar of the House and summoned its members to attend His Majesty in the House of Lords. The speech from the Throne announced that Parliament was prorogued with a view to its immediate dissolution, as the most constitutional means of ascertaining the sense of the people on the question of Parliamentary Reform.

At the general election of May 1831 Peel was returned for the borough of Tamworth, which had been so long represented by his father. The result of the elections was disastrous for the Tories. They lost above eighty seats, and with those seats their prospect of averting the reform of the House of Commons. A beaten party is always a difficult party to lead. The more ardent Tories renewed their murmurs against Peel's cold, calculating policy. Lord Lyndhurst, a much colder and more calculating man, said to a friend that Peel, if his opinion was not adopted, would take up a newspaper and sulk, and that if any friend or follower proposed to speak in a debate Peel would reply, not with encouragement, but with a dry, chilling "Do you?" These complaints were probably overcharged. But Peel suffered all through life from pride and awkwardness, and now, when he felt that he must be defeated in a cause which possibly did not command his entire devotion, he involved himself more than ever in impenetrable reserve. Yet his pre-eminence was never more conspicuous than in this winter of his discontent. Not only the Tories, but also the dissatisfied Whigs, looked to him as to their saviour. "He is our only resource," wrote Charles Greville, who never loved him, "and his capacity for business and power in the House of Commons place him so far above all his competitors that, if we are to have a Conservative party, we must look to him alone to lead it." Of the Tories, Greville says elsewhere, "There is nothing they are not ready to do at his bidding."

On the 24th of June Lord John Russell moved for leave to bring in the second Reform Bill, which differed from the first only in points of detail. Sir Robert reserved his strength for the debate on the second reading. On the night of the 6th of July he spoke with characteristic ability, but without the fire which would have shown confidence in his cause or rallied the courage of his fainting followers. On the division the Tories could muster only 231 votes, against 367, so that the Bill passed its second reading by a majority of 136. In committee Sir Robert ventured to move an amendment restoring a second member to each of the boroughs in Schedule B.; but he was defeated by a majority of 67, and the Bill passed through committee almost unaltered. On the third reading the Tory leader engaged hand to hand with Macaulay in a speech described by an opponent as the best which he had ever made. It was lucid in arrangement and skilful in argument; it was hardly so brilliant or so convincing as to justify the praise that it "cut

6 *

Macaulay to ribands." If the Ministers had only a
majority of 109 ou the third reading, the reason was
that their supporters regarded the battle as won. The
Bill went up to the Lords, and by them was thrown out
on the second reading.

Everybody knows how much excitement was caused
by the rejection of the second Reform Bill. Savage
riots took place at Bristol and Nottingham, and were
feared in London. Ardent spirits talked of preparing
for civil war. The Government resolved that Parliament should meet two months earlier than usual, and
that as soon as it met the Bill should be introduced
again. Should the House of Lords persevere in resisting it, they were resolved to create Peers. A new
session of Parliament opened on the 6th of December.
A third Reform Bill was immediately introduced by
Lord John Russell. Although concessions had been
made to the spirit of opposition, it was in substance
similar to the two previous Bills, and the resolution of
the majority had only been confirmed by resistance.
On the first reading it passed without a struggle. In
the debate on the second reading Macaulay took occasion to twit Peel for his many opportune conversions,
and for his dexterity in obtaining credit for reforms
which had been forced upon him. Often as Peel
had heard such sarcasms, they had lost none of
their sting. Like all highly sensitive persons, he
was self-conscious, and therefore prone to infinite
explanation, justification, and apology. His speech
was rather a reply to Macaulay than an argument upon
the Bill. Yet it was not effective as a reply. The
circumstances attending Catholic Emancipation were
not yet fully known; the passions which it had excited
were still warm; the Tories were little less pleased than

the Whigs by taunts directed to Peel's tergiversation;
and the general impression was that Peel had spoken
feebly. But Demosthenes could not at that hour have
changed the fate of the Reform Bill. On the second
reading it was carried in a large House by a majority of
two to one. The majority on the third reading was
less, but still very large; and the Bill went up once
more to the House of Lords.

So early as the November of 1831 attempts had been
made to avert a second rejection of the Bill in that
House. The wiser Tory Peers had seen that the vast
majority of the nation were bent on passing the Bill,
and that further resistance could lead only to revolution.
The moderate members of the Cabinet did not want
more than the Bill would give; certainly they did not
desire the abolition of that House in which so many of
their own number sat or would hereafter have seats.
Accordingly messages began to pass between Lords
Harrowby and Wharncliffe on the one side, and on the
other side Lords Grey, Melbourne, and Palmerston.
Messages led to meetings, and there appeared to be
a reasonable chance of a majority for the second reading of the Bill without any creation of new Peers.
From these negotiations Peel stood aloof. His great
influence, made greater by his obstinate resistance
to the Bill, would have ensured the success of Lord
Harrowby's party, and their success must have been
desired by a statesman so quick to perceive the signs
of the times. But Peel remembered only too well the
reproaches and insults heaped upon him by his own
followers less than three years before. For himself he
would have preferred destruction sooner than such a
retreat as he had made when he consented to propose
the removal of the Catholic disabilities. Come what

might, no Inglis or Wetherell should be able to taunt
him with having run away.   So he wrote to Lord
Harrowby admitting that much might be said on
behalf of a different course, but urging that it was
of vital consequence to save the consistency of the
Party.   He would not oppose Harrowby's endeavours,
but neither would he assist them.   Greville, who
assisted in the negotiations, charges Peel with doing
what he could do to inflame and divide and repress
any spirit of conciliation.   But Greville always disliked Peel, and put the worst construction on whatever
Peel did.

With infinite labour and anxiety, and at the cost of
much odium to themselves, Harrowby and Wharncliffe
compassed the safety of their House and secured a
majority of nine votes on the second reading.   This was
on the 13th of April.   On the 7th of May the Lords
went into Committee on the Bill, and Lyndhurst carried
by a majority of thirty-five a proposal to put off consideration of the disfranchising clauses until the enfran-
chising clauses had been considered.   The Government accepted this act as the sign of an intention to
re-cast the Bill.   The next day Grey and Brougham
went down to Windsor and proposed to the King that
he should create fifty peers.   The King took a day to
consider the proposal, and then declined it, whereupon
the Ministers gave in their resignation.   The King
next applied to Lyndhurst to make overtures to the
Tory chiefs on the subject of forming a Tory Cabinet
pledged to carry an extensive reform of Parliament.
The Duke of Wellington was first sounded, and replied
that he was ready to serve the King in any office or in
no office.   Then Lyndhurst applied to Peel, who said
that he could not decently take office for the purpose of

carrying a measure which he thought mischievous, and which he had stiffly opposed at every stage in its progress. Lyndhurst next tried Lord Harrowby, but without success. He then turned to Mr. Alexander Baring, afterwards Lord Ashburton, a gentleman of immense wealth and much financial skill, and persuaded him to act as Chancellor of the Exchequer. Manners Sutton, the Speaker, who had presided with credit in six Parliaments, was asked to join. He was not very willing, but was tempted with the post of Prime Minister. He called at Apsley House to seal the bargain, and there harangued Wellington and Lyndhurst for three or four hours consecutively, until Lyndhurst flung out in a passion, saying on his return home that "he could have nothing to do with so d——d tiresome an old ——." After all this eloquence Manners Sutton asked for more time to consider what he should do. Lyndhurst had already told the King that Manners Sutton would not do, and that Wellington must be Prime Minister. Wellington sent Croker to ask Peel for his assistance in forming a Ministry. Peel refused again. Last of all the King sent for Peel and repeated the request, and Peel refused yet a third time. Croker himself, Goulburn, and Herries followed Peel's example. Whilst these negotiations were in progress a petition in favour of the Reform Bill from the City of London gave rise to a debate in which the new Ministers were attacked with a fury which quite overpowered them. Baring himself proposed that the late Ministers should return to office to carry the Bill. After the debate he went to Apsley House and told the Duke that he would face a thousand devils rather than such a House of Commons. Manners Sutton accompanied him, and expressed himself to the same

effect. The new Cabinet was stillborn. On the 16th
of May, exactly a week after his resignation, Earl Grey
was again closeted with the King.

From these transactions Peel emerged with a great
increase of reputation. Alone among the Tory chiefs
he had held utterly aloof from an enterprise which, if
it had been successful would have been immoral, and
as it had failed was ridiculous. Ill-natured persons
who could not blame Peel's conduct comforted themselves by impugning his motives. He had encouraged
the Duke to persevere, partly out of spite, partly out
of desire to injure the only reputation equal to his own.
He had egged on Manners Sutton to take the part of
Addington, whilst he had reserved for himself the part
of Pitt. "Manners Sutton was to be his creature; he
would have dictated every measure of Government; he
would have been their protector in the House of
Commons, and as soon as the fitting moment arrived
he would have dissolved this miserable ministry, and
placed himself at the head of affairs." Such was
Greville's explanation. It is true that Peel had an
absurdly high opinion of Manners Sutton. It is also
true that he showed ungenerous reserve in not warning
his friends of their folly. But as regarded himself, he
could not have done otherwise. His explanations in
the House of Commons were almost word for word the
same as his explanations to Croker. Croker, who hated
Parliamentary Reform almost to insanity, had urged
Peel to take office for the purpose of carrying a Reform
Bill. Peel wrote in reply :—

I foresee that a Bill of Reform including everything that is really
important and really dangerous in the present Bill must pass. For
me individually to take the conduct of such a Bill, to assume the
responsibility of the consequences which I have predicted as the inevi-

table result of such a Bill, would be in my opinion personal degradation to myself. It is not a repetition of the Catholic Question. I was then in office, I had advised the concession as a Minister. I should now assume office for the purpose of carrying the measure to which up to the last moment I have been inveterately opposed as a revolutionary measure.

To those about him, Peel spoke of the salvation of character being everything. But the House of Lords had not saved their character. There the questions so often put still awaited an answer. Will the Lords pass the Bill without waiting for a creation of new peers? The Tories were obstinate, the Ministers were obstinate, the King was in despair. At length he wrote to the Opposition begging them to oppose no more. They obeyed, and the Reform Bill had passed through Committee before the end of May. The last unreformed Parliament was dissolved on the 3rd of December 1832. The elections for the first reformed Parliament went on through December and January. To the Tory Party they proved even more disastrous than the elections of the preceding year. When the new Parliament assembled it seemed as though the Tory Party had vanished. Peel mustered less than one hundred and fifty followers. Everything in his future seemed dark and dreary. It seemed as though it would be his fate to drag out long years of futile and contemptible opposition, growing more embittered as he grew more hopeless, and ending almost forgotten by the nation which he had once aspired to rule. And so it might have proved had Peel been a man like most of his colleagues in the Wellington Cabinet. Being what he was, he had really found his opportunity. The destruction of the old Tory Party opened to him a career far ampler than he had yet known. For him it was a piece of good fortune comparable only to that other good fortune which had

driven him from office. Then he had been released from
incapable colleagues; now he was released from imprac-
ticable followers. New followers and new colleagues
were to gather round Robert Peel; a new Conservatism
was to arise, and he was to be the new Conservative
chief.

Since Conservatism like Liberalism is an imperish-
able instinct of human nature, every society must
contain a Conservative party, and such a party speedily
develops even amid the wildest storm of revolution.
The Reform Act of 1832 had made room for a Conservative party suited to the age. The Tories had been
weak because their strength was confined to the landed
interest. Possessed with a panic dread of change, bred
by the events of the French Revolution, they had
refused to admit any new interests to a share of power.
In their despite the Reform Act had transferred the
control of politics from the aristocracy to the middle
class. But our middle class was naturally Conservative. It was orderly, it was rich, it was sensitive to
social influence, it was devout and serious in a stiff,
unbending way. Some reforms certainly it required;
an effective administration for the great towns where it
lived and traded; the amendment of a poor law which
shocked all its economic maxims; the abolition of
negro slavery which revolted its religion; the abrogation of laws which, pressing harshly upon Nonconformists, revolted its sense of justice. It had not yet
declared for Free Trade, although it might be expected
to do so. The ameliorations which the middle class at
this time desired Peel was ready to approve, and these
ameliorations once granted, the middle class would tend
to be Conservative. But theirs would not be the
Conservatism of squires and rectors. They would

incline to a Conservatism of their own, and they would
want a leader of their own to formulate it and to
organize them.   They would want a statesman who was
bone of their bone and flesh of their flesh; a good
man of business, cautious but open to practicable suggestions, one who would satisfy their ideal of industry
and economy; one who would always be grave and
decorous, never puzzle them with epigrams, or alarm
them with rhetoric; in short, such a great man as
they could conceive. Such Sir Robert Peel was. There
never breathed a politician more truly congenial to them.
He represented their virtues and their failings; he
shared their talents and their prejudices; he was always
growing in their confidence, and when he died lamented
by all his fellow-citizens he was most deeply lamented
by them.

Even in the actual state of affairs Peel's keen perception might find grounds of hope.   The Ministers
had, indeed, a majority larger than any wise Minister
would wish to have. Whilst their majority kept together they were absolute; but such a majority as theirs
could not be kept together long. A crowd flushed with
victory and hoping for great things, but with no bond
of union derived from like thoughts or like feelings; a
motley host of aristocratic Whigs and middle-class
Whigs, of philosophic Radicals and popular Radicals,
of English and of Irish agitators—it could not be
expected long to endure the pressure of discipline, or
the strain of mutual forbearance and concession. Two
things only were needed for its dissolution: tact and
time. If it were not kept together by premature and
unsparing assaults from without, it was certain to break
up from within. If only it were humoured, it would
subserve all the ends of its enemies. The Conservatives

would accomplish most by not trying to do too much. Peel saw this truth, and was able to act upon it, because his followers were so disheartened, and his rivals so discredited. The vanquished party were obliged to cling to the only chief who could—not restore them to power, for that appeared an idle fancy—but give them any weight in the councils of the kingdom.

The faults of a majority may be made good by the capacity of its leaders; but the Cabinet too faithfully reflected the divided councils and jarring tempers of its friends. Talent indeed was not wanting to the Cabinet, nor yet virtue and public spirit. Seldom had England seen a Cabinet so rich in men of fine gifts and high qualities. But in almost every instance these gifts and qualities were neutralized by lack of the power of working harmoniously with others. In person, in bearing, in eloquence, in high consistency and rectitude, Earl Grey was well-nigh an ideal Premier. He was old, however, and too proud to place himself in the hands of younger men; too gentle to keep them in subordination. Brougham had energy, versatility, quickness of perception, and fulness of utterance enough to make the reputation of a dozen ordinary statesmen. He had fought hard in many a good cause: for the improvement of the law, for the advancement of education, for the reform of Parliament, and for the abolition of slavery. Yet there were blended in Brougham's composition faults which spoiled his career, annulled his usefulness, made him a weariness to his best friends, and left him a laughing-stock to the ungrateful public, a joy to stupid mediocrity which might exult that it had never compromised itself like Brougham. John Russell's name must always be mentioned with respect; but he never could be reckoned an adroit or successful

politician. Lord Althorp joined uncommon beauty of
character to very common abilities. A fairly good
leader of the House of Commons and an indifferent
Chancellor of the Exchequer, he was more desirous to
be rid of office that ever was wire-puller to secure it. Palmerston had seen quite as much innovation as he wanted,
and from this time forward gave himself up to foreign
policy. Melbourne's fine talent and large acquisitions
were made almost useless by indolence and melancholy.
To Stanley no gift of fortune or of nature was wanting
except that mysterious something which distinguishes
a man of brilliant ability from a great statesman. He
and Graham were to find that in the new age the limits
of aristocratic Whiggism are soon reached. At present
they were among the most efficient ministers. But such
a Cabinet, although it might leave its mark on history,
could not retain power for long. Such a Cabinet,
leaning upon such a majority, must afford frequent
opportunities to an adversary of so much talent, so
much knowledge, address, and industry as Sir Robert
Peel.

Peel and Wellington had been led to similar conclusions: the one by his shrewdness, the other by his
simplicity. "I mean," said Wellington to Greville,
"to support the Government—support them in every
way. The first thing I have to look to is to keep my
house over my head, and the alternative is between this
Government and none at all." Peel was not quite so
frank; but his action was in harmony with these words.
On the 5th of February 1833 the King opened the
Session with a Speech recommending reforms in the
Church and measures to restore order in Ireland.
Peel's speech on the debate on the Address was a model
of dexterity. He announced that he would be no party

to any measure for transferring to other uses any part
of the revenues of the Established Church in Ireland;
but he admitted that there might be good ground for
reforms which did not violate this principle.   Upon the
subject of repressive enactments he professed that his
mind was open, but he took care to pay a handsome
compliment to Stanley, who, as Chief Secretary, was
the principal object of attack to O'Connell and all
his followers.   Stanley was the more likely to feel this
compliment, inasmuch as he got little sympathy from
his own colleagues.

A stringent Coercion Bill having passed the House of
Lords, was introduced into the House of Commons by
Althorp.   The gentle Althorp may have doubted the necessity for so severe a measure.   Certainly he made a statement even less effective than usual to a House which was
not very willing to be convinced.   Mortified at the coolness
of his colleagues, and at the imminent failure of a Bill
on which he had staked his credit, Stanley took back
his papers from Althorp and, after rapidly refreshing
his memory, got up, drew a terrible picture of the state
of Ireland, and assailed O'Connell with extraordinary
impetuosity.   Peel spoke on the same side, with less
eloquence and with less bitterness than Stanley, but
with more warmth than was usual to him.   Their combined efforts probably saved the Bill.   Men noticed that
Stanley began to hold Tory language.   The Tories
and the dissatisfied Whigs were drawing together.   "It
must end in Peel and Stanley unless everything ends,"
wrote Charles Greville.

When Althorp introduced the Bill dealing with the
Established Church of Ireland, Peel was equally
prudent.   The Bill proposed to reduce by ten the
twenty-two Irish bishoprics, to impose a graduated

tax on the larger clerical incomes, and out of the revenue thus obtained to make good the Church cess, which was no longer to be levied. Goulburn and Inglis and the Protestant fanatics generally were furious at the announcement of such a measure. Peel took it with the utmost calmness. He requested, indeed, that as the Bill was not yet in print, the second reading should not be taken so soon as the 14th of March, and this request Althorp declined to grant. On the 14th, Charles Wynn objected to the second reading as irregular, because the Bill taxed all Irish benefices of more than a certain value, and all Bills which impose taxes must originate in a committee of the whole House. Peel and O'Connell for once joined in supporting Wynn. Accordingly the second reading was deferred; a committee was appointed to search for precedents; the committee affirmed Wynn's view and the Ministers found themselves obliged to act upon it. The second reading did not take place until the 6th of May. In committee the Ministers conceded the principle that Church funds should be applied only to Church uses. With this concession Peel was satisfied. The Peers were more troublesome; but by a mixture of threats and concessions, together with Wellington's abstention from debate, their opposition was overcome and the Bill passed its third reading by a large majority.

The abolition of slavery in the colonies was the most momentous of the other topics agitated in this session. Peel had always professed his goodwill to negro emancipation, in that cool temporizing way in which persons of an official mind express themselves about measures which they believe are right, and will be carried some day or other, but know to be hard of execution

and hateful to strong interests. He had voted in 1823
for Canning's resolutions which affirmed the necessity
of improving the condition of the slaves, and qualifying
them for eventual freedom.   He now criticised the
ministerial plan in a dull, diffuse, and rather obscure
speech, which was the more striking by contrast with the
magnificent oration in which that plan had been set out
by Stanley. For Stanley, tired of Irish business and
hated by the Irish members, had been transferred from
the Irish Secretaryship to the Secretaryship for the
Colonies.   Lord Althorp considered that Peel agreed
with the Government upon every point except the time
for emancipation.   Had Peel been more outspoken upon
subjects of this class, he would have ranked lower as a
party chief, but he would have been a more attractive
personage in history.

As distress was very general at this time, the policy
of the resumption of cash payments was repeatedly
assailed. In this very session Peel had made one of his
most elaborate speeches in reply to a motion by Mr.
Attwood for a committee to inquire into our monetary
system.   Cobbett, now member for Oldham, diverted the
attack from the measures to the man. About the
currency he probably knew no more than he knew about
the fixed stars; but he shared the belief that Peel was
the author of the suffering which was only too evident.
He now brought forward a series of resolutions of prodigious length, containing a general censure of Peel's
political conduct, and a particular censure of the
currency Acts, and moved a dutiful address praying for
Peel's expulsion from the Privy Council. He charged
Peel, not with wicked intentions, but with gross
ignorance; a ground of dismissal which, if admitted,
would sadly reduce the size of councils and of cabinets.

Cobbett no longer spoke with his former homely force, nor had he any following in the House. But Peel chose to answer him seriously, or at all events with solemn humour. The House would not listen to Cobbett's reply, rejected his motion, and voted that it should not be entered on the journals. Somehow or other, Peel seemed to gain by every attack upon him.

At the close of the session of 1833, the timid persons, who were ever apprehensive of a revolution, confessed that things had not turned out according to their fears. Yet the Government remained weak, and the honours of the day seemed to have fallen to the leader of the Opposition. Lord Tavistock, heir of the great Whig house of Russell, told Charles Greville that he did not think the bulk of the Liberal party would be unwilling to serve under Peel, an opinion disproved by subsequent facts, yet showing how highly Peel was considered by men of all parties. The recess was empty of events, and Parliament re-assembled in February of 1834 amid general indifference. The Speech from the Throne was singularly colourless. But the caution of the Ministry procured it no rest. As the Chancellor of the Exchequer seemed at a loss what to do with his surplus, the Marquess of Chandos moved that in the reduction of taxes the agricultural interest should be considered. He was defeated only by four votes. Emboldened by this division, Sir William Ingilby proposed the repeal of the malt tax. He was defeated by a great majority, but his defeat was largely due to Peel, who opposed him in a statesman-like speech. Then the Government lost its way in the maze of Irish business. First, Althorp had a personal quarrel with Sheil. Next Althorp and Littleton consented to give a select committee to inquire into the conduct of Baron Smith, an Irish judge

7

who had made himself obnoxious to the Repealers.
Graham and Spring Rice voted against Althorp and
Littleton, and a few days afterwards Sir Edward Knatchbull carried against the Government a motion to reverse
the vote for a committee. Then came the question of
Irish tithe. An Act for voluntary composition had been
passed in 1823, and another Act for compulsory composition had been passed in 1832 ; and now Littleton
brought in a Bill having three principal objects, a reduction in the amount of the tithe, its conversion into a land
tax payable by landowners, and the giving of facilities
for total redemption. Unpleasing alike to the followers
of O'Connell and to the High Churchmen, this scheme
had only the lukewarm approval of Stanley. In the
debate on the second reading, Russell asserted that the
State had a right to dispose of the surplus revenues of
the Irish Church. His declaration was noted by the
radical members, who were weary of a divided ministry.
Mr. Henry Ward gave notice of a resolution that
the surplus revenues of the Irish Church should be
applied to public purposes. The Cabinet met, and
wishing to avoid a division in which some of its members would have to vote against others, resolved to
move the previous question. But the Ministers were
so doubtful whether they could carry it, that in order to
remove anxiety, Stanley resigned together with Sir
James Graham, the Duke of Richmond, and the Earl of
Ripon. By the loss of these four members, who represented a small but powerful party of trimmers, the
Cabinet was brought into a state of utter weakness.
After all, the previous question was carried by an
immense majority, the Ministers having promised a commission to inquire into the whole subject.

 Only one Act of the first consequence was passed in

this session. The reform of the Poor Law was the wisest measure of a Cabinet which had done many great things. England had been gradually sinking deeper and deeper into a morass of pauperism, whence she could never emerge until the system of relieving the poor was altered. Wise men saw the fatal character of the disease, but shrank from the painful and unpopular remedy. For even under an aristocratic system, the rulers of the State are loth to encounter the fury of the multitude. Earl Grey's administration undertook the odious task of saving society, and was strenuously supported by the Duke of Wellington, who always aimed at the general good so far as it was discernible to him. Peel took a less magnanimous course. He approved of the Bill and he helped it loyally but as quietly as possible. He voted in its favour but made no speeches. Some years later he described the Act for the amendment of the Poor Law as tending to rescue the country from a progressive evil, fraught with the most awful consequences, not only to property, but also to the independence and morals of the poor. Some such emphatic declaration would not have been amiss when this vital reform was struggling against the powers of short-sighted interest and of short-sighted benevolence combined. Yet it may be that a reform, in appearance so unpopular, would have lost almost as much as it would have gained by ardent advocacy from the Conservative leader.

The places left vacant by the secession of Stanley and his friends had been filled by men who gave no offence and did their duty well. But the trickery of Brougham and folly of Littleton brought about another and a fatal crisis on the question of renewing the Coercion Act for Ireland. Althorp felt bound in

7 *

honour to resign, and Grey felt unable to go on without Althorp. He tendered his resignation to the King. The King accepted it willingly, for by this time he was utterly weary of Whigs and Whiggism. But the Whigs, although their power was paralysed by dissension, still formed the overwhelming majority of the House of Commons. The King, therefore, pitched upon Melbourne, who was well known for a lukewarm politician, and enjoined him to negotiate with Wellington, Peel, and Stanley, for the construction of a Cabinet which should include the chiefs of all the important parties. Melbourne replied that he had no hope of any result from such negotiations, and, by the King's order, communicated this reply to Peel, who wrote to the King expressing himself entirely of Melbourne's opinion. Melbourne was thus obliged to new-model the old Whig Cabinet. Althorp had hoped to escape from power, but he yielded to Melbourne's entreaty and the unanimous wish of all the Liberals, from Grote to O'Connell. The remaining appointments were easily made. The Cabinet thus refitted contrived to pass a qualified Coercion Bill, failed to pass the Tithes Bill, and wound up the Session without any more agitation.

By this time Peel had fully justified the confidence reposed in him. When the Reform Bill was passed, men of all parties thought that the Ministers who had carried it were secure of power for the next twenty years. Two years had scarcely passed when power all but slipped from their hands. They had exhausted the spell of success, the influence of talent, the gratitude of the people, and the power of numbers. All this while their adversary had been waiting and watching, had aroused his desponding and controlled his violent

followers, had taken advantage of every turn of
chance, had profited by every dissension in the
Cabinet, had gained weight in the House by acting
when he could with that portion of the majority
which differed least from himself, had gained the good
opinion of the country by proving his temper, knowledge and capacity for great affairs, and had crowned all
his other achievements by a dignified refusal of high
office, which he could not have held with entire freedom
and independence. Such capacity and such self-command are sure of success in almost every situation, and
not least sure of it in the rivalry for the confidence
of the people of England. It was now certain that
Peel would return to power; only the time of his return
was still doubtful.

For the present Peel was free to enjoy the leisure
afforded by the recess. He left this country on the
14th of October, intending to pass the winter in Italy.
He was accompanied by Lady Peel and their daughter
Julia.

CHAPTER VI.

WHEN Sir Robert Peel left England, the Melbourne
Ministry seemed for the time secure in the enjoyment
of power. Unfriendly or desponding observers shook
their heads over an unruly majority and an indolent
Premier; but these were causes of future weakness, not
of immediate overthrow. When the catastrophe came
it was occasioned by the death of one old gentleman
and the prejudice of another. Lord Spencer died in
the November of 1834, and his son, Lord Althorp,
succeeding to the peerage, was withdrawn from the
House of Commons. Lord Melbourne went down to
Brighton to consult the King upon the choice of a new
leader of the House and Chancellor of the Exchequer.
He suggested Russell for leader, and in his default,
Spring Rice or Abercromby. He also told the King

that since the Cabinet was to be re-arranged, the re-arrangement ought to strengthen its Liberal element. The King did not relish any of the names proposed for the leadership of the House of Commons, and he relished still less any general change in the interest of Liberalism. He particularly disliked the project of appropriating to new uses the surplus revenues of the Irish Church. After taking a day to consider, he refused Melbourne's proposals and accepted his resignation. Brougham happened to see Melbourne the same evening, heard the news, and sent it on to the *Times*, and in the *Times* of next morning his colleagues, with much surprise and more anger, read that they had ceased to be ministers. The Duke of Wellington became First Lord of the Treasury, and undertook the charge of the Home, the Colonial, and the Foreign Offices, until such time as the ministry should be completed. The Great Seal was put into commission and Lyndhurst was named the first commissioner. Mr. Hudson, gentleman usher to the Queen, was at once despatched in quest of Peel. He carried a letter from the King announcing the appointment of Wellington and Lyndhurst, and summoning Peel back to England, together with a letter from Wellington explaining the circumstances which had led to a change of Government.

These letters were delivered to Peel at his hotel in Rome, just as he had returned from a ball at the Duchess of Torlonia's. He had made his arrangements for a visit to Naples, and had actually taken a passage for the return voyage from Naples to Civita Vecchia. All plans of pleasure were now broken off. By dint of energy everything was made ready in a few hours, and the Peels left Rome next day. Peel had taken a separate passport for his wife, lest she should prove unequal to the fatigue of a forced journey. Lady Peel, however, accompanied him all the way to Dover, which they reached on the 8th of December, having spent only twelve days on the road. Before quitting Rome, Peel had written to the King and the Duke. In his *Memoirs* he has assured posterity that he had not the remotest concern in the dissolution of the Melbourne Ministry. He had received only a meagre account of what had happened ; he would not pledge himself to take office, and so become responsible for the dismissal of his predecessor. He doubted the wisdom of dis- placing the Whig Cabinet. He had little hope that any other Cabinet could be stable, or could command a sufficiently powerful majority in the House of Commons. Reflection, however, showed him that as soon as he arrived he would have to be Prime Minister whether or no he desired it. He then resolved freely to under- take that which would be forced upon him. Travelling by night from Dover, he waited upon the King early in the morning of the 9th of December, and declared himself ready to become Prime Minister and Chancellor of the Exchequer.

Peel had been too successful. He had restored the credit of his party before it had recovered its strength. To reinforce the party was his first and most pressing necessity. He therefore wrote to Stanley and Graham, the leaders of those Whigs whom Liberalism had left behind, and invited them to join his Ministry. With many expressions of esteem and goodwill, Stanley de- clined the invitation. It was easy to see that some other time he would probably accept it. For he laid stress, not so much on any differences of opinion separating him from Peel, as upon the censure which Wellington,

Peel's colleague, had bestowed upon the acts of Lord Grey's Administration. Still, no present aid was to be had from Stanley. Graham replied to Peel's invitation much as Stanley had done, and Richmond and Ripon approved of their abstinence. These politicians continued to lead a small party which sided sometimes with Peel and sometimes with Russell. Peel wrote to Lady Canning offering her eldest son a place in his Government. She replied in a friendly strain, but said that she agreed with her son in thinking that he ought to wait. So Peel found himself obliged to fall back on the Conservatives. Lyndhurst became Chancellor, Wellington took the Foreign Office, Aberdeen the Colonies, and Goulburn the Home Department. Earl de Grey was First Lord of the Admiralty, and Herries Secretary-at-War. Wharncliffe received the Privy Seal, Rosslyn was made Lord President, and Sir Henry Hardinge took the Secretaryship for Ireland. Whigs styled this selection unmitigated Toryism; yet the high Tories were not content. "No consideration under heaven shall force me to serve under Peel," was the saying of Croker, who now and long afterwards remained Peel's intimate friend.

The Conservative party in the House of Commons did not muster more than 150 members. With such a slender support it was impossible to govern for any length of time. A dissolution was inevitable, but would it be better to dissolve at once, or to struggle on with the existing Parliament until defeated on some vital question? For a moment Peel doubted whether he should not follow the example set by Pitt in 1784, and give time for the spread in the country of a reaction against the party dominant in the House; but upon consideration, he resolved to have a general election immediately. By the 17th of September he had prepared and submitted to his colleagues the manifesto which he had drawn up for the constituencies. It was couched in the form of an address to the electors of the borough of Tamworth. In this famous manifesto, the first authoritative utterance of the new Conservatism, he addressed the burgesses of Tamworth as members "of that great and intelligent class of society—that class which is much less interested in the contentions of party than in the maintenance of order and the cause of good government." Peel continues, "I will never admit that I have been, either before or after the Reform Bill, the defender of abuses or the enemy of judicious reforms." Enumerating the improvements which he had effected before 1832 in the currency, in the criminal law and in other departments, he declared that he considered the Reform Bill to be the "final and irrevocable settlement of a great question." He advocated "a careful review of institutions, civil and ecclesiastical, undertaken in a friendly spirit." He then showed that he had offered no unqualified opposition to the measures of the Whig Cabinet, promised that he would continue their inquiries into ecclesiastical and municipal affairs, and announced that he was favourable to a commutation of tithe, an improved distribution of Church revenues, relief to Nonconformist marriages, and the limitation of the Pension List. Peel still refused to divert from ecclesiastical use any part of the revenues of the Irish Church, and he would not pledge himself to place Nonconformists on a level with Churchmen at the Universities. Yet any reader who compares the doctrines of the manifesto with the doctrines of the school in which Peel had been trained will be forcibly struck with the expansion of his mind, and will ratify

Russell's opinion that Peel was a great lover of change and innovation.

The Tamworth Manifesto made a good impression; but it could not turn the balance of parties. In the general election the Conservatives were at least as much disappointed as were the Whigs. They carried many of the counties, and were stronger by nearly a hundred members in the new Parliament than in the old one. But the Whigs had kept their hold on the boroughs. In the city of London every Conservative candidate was defeated.

When Parliament reassembled on the 19th of February 1835, the Whigs still formed an overwhelming majority of the House of Commons. Peel as Prime Minister found himself in a false position. In its latest form the English constitution requires the Sovereign to keep his Ministers so long as they command an undoubted majority in the lower House. To replace them with the leaders of the minority is to put the most serious of all obstacles in the way of public business. William IV. had dismissed Melbourne, not because Melbourne's Government had ceased to have a majority, but because William IV. had ceased to believe in the Whigs. The late Ministry had been turned out, the actual Ministry had been called in by the direct act of the King. The Whigs believed that the King had been the puppet of an intrigue managed by Peel and Wellington, and were resolved that the intriguers should not gain by their unconstitutional conduct. The election of a Speaker gave the first opportunity for a trial of strength. Manners Sutton had been Speaker for eighteen years in unreformed and in reformed Parliaments, under Tories and under Whigs; nor had he ever incurred censure in his discharge of that high office. But he was a Tory—had been talked of as a Tory Minister, and was intimate with members of the Cabinet. The Whigs chose for their candidate Mr. Abercromby. He was elected Speaker by 316 votes, against 306 given for Sutton. Peel, who had spoken warmly for his friend, made him a peer by the title of Lord Canterbury.

The Government was again defeated on the Address. The speech from the Throne, repeating the Liberal professions of the Tamworth Manifesto, did not soothe the indignation of the Whigs. On their behalf Lord Morpeth moved an amendment, lamenting that the progress of reform had been interrupted and endangered by the unnecessary dissolution of a Parliament earnestly intent upon the vigorous prosecution of measures to which the wishes of the people were most anxiously and justly directed. Peel spoke against the amendment with all his accustomed skill, and more than his accustomed spirit. He defended himself against the charge of having seized power unfairly, as well as against the charge of inveterate resistance to reform. He showed that he was prepared to give effect to the professions made in the Speech from the Throne, and he concluded with a peroration expressive of the new spirit which he had infused into Conservative politics.

With such prospects I feel it to be my duty, my first and paramount duty, to maintain the post which has been confided to me and to stand by the trust which I did not seek but could not decline. I call upon you not to condemn before you have heard, to receive at least the measures I shall propose, to amend them if they are defective, to extend them if they fall short of your expectations, but at least to give me the opportunity of presenting them, that you yourselves may consider and dispose of them. I make great offers which should not lightly be rejected. I offer you the prospect of continued peace, the restored confidence of powerful states that are willing to seize the opportunity of reducing great armies and thus diminishing the chances of hostile

collision. I offer you reduced estimates, improvements in civil juris-
prudence, reform of ecclesiastical law, the settlement of the tithe
question in Ireland, the commutation of tithe in England, the removal
of any real abuse in the Church, the redress of those grievances of
which the Dissenters have any just ground to complain. I offer you
these specific measures and I offer also to advance, soberly and
cautiously it is true, in the path of progressive improvement. I offer
also the best chance that these things can be effected in willing concert with the other authorities of the state, thus restoring harmony,
ensuring the maintenance, but not excluding the reform (where reform
is really requisite) of ancient institutions. You may reject my offers,
you may refuse to entertain them, you may prefer to do the same
thing by more violent means; but if you do, the time is not far distant
when you will find that the popular feeling on which you rely has
deserted you, and that you will have no alternative but either again
to invoke our aid, to replace the government in the hands from which
you would now forcibly withdraw it, or to resort to that pressure from
without, to those measures of compulsion and violence, which at the
same time that they render your reforms useless and inoperative, will
seal the fate of the British Constitution.

On the next night Stanley spoke. His tone was that
of an independent critic, but he declared his intention
of voting with the Government. On a division there
were 309 votes for and 302 votes against the amendment. The Opposition had not been able to secure a
majority of more than seven.

The result of this division, which took place late in
the night of the 26th of February, gave a brief check
to the Opposition and fresh strength to the Ministry.
Peel used the respite to push forward the reforms
which he had promised. The Bill for the Establishment of a new Ecclesiastical Court was introduced
by the Attorney-General on the 12th of March. The
Bill dealing with Dissenters' marriages was introduced on the 17th of March by Peel himself. Conservative Ministers have often borrowed a reform
from their Liberal adversaries; but they rarely render
it more complete and logical. Peel, however, could boast

that he had made exceptions to this rule. If he were
slow to adopt a new principle, he gave it full scope when
once adopted. Lord John Russell had already brought
in a Bill to relieve Nonconformists from the necessity
of having their marriages celebrated according to the
rites of the Established Church. He had proposed
that the banns should continue, as formerly, to be
published in church by the clergyman, who should
certify to the fact of publication, and that the marriage
should afterwards be celebrated in a Dissenting chapel,
duly licensed for the purpose. The license was to be
exhibited conspicuously within the chapel. This Bill
did not satisfy the Nonconformists, who objected to the
publication of banns in the parish church, to the re-
quirement of a license, and to the exhibition of the license
in chapel. Peel's Bill was not open to these objections. It was based on the principle that marriage,
although it may be something more, is at all events a
civil contract. It substituted a civil contract entered
into before a magistrate for the compulsory religious
rite. It replaced the publication of the banns by notice
to a magistrate. The register of marriages was to be
kept by the clergyman, who was entitled to a petty fee
for each entry, but no further necessity to call in his
service was imposed on any person. Even a hostile
House of Commons received the Bill with almost unanimous approval. A few days later Peel explained his
scheme for the commutation of tithes in England.

The Opposition had been unskilful in its tactics. It
wanted courage to propose a direct vote of want of
confidence, and patience to wait for the occurrence of
some question of principle on which parties might fairly
try their strength. It stooped to harass, to annoy, to
waste time, and to throw the business of the country

into confusion. Moved by the rumour that the Government would take the earliest opportunity of dissolving again, Russell questioned Peel on the subject. Peel replied that he had not authorized any such rumour, but could not pledge himself to hold in abeyance any prerogative of the Crown. He thus kept the fear of dissolution alive in the hearts of those who would otherwise have been eager to get rid of the Government. Baffled in this enquiry, the Opposition next thought of limiting the grant of supply to three months. But when Hume undertook to move, and Russell promised to support, a motion to this effect, it had to be dropped because of the disapproval expressed by many Whig members, who liked Peel's courage, admired his talent, and appreciated his Liberalism. Whilst the Opposition hesitated thus, the Ministers steadily rose in the public regard, and gossips began to prophesy that they would yet come off victorious.

In this critical posture of his affairs Peel rashly appointed Lord Londonderry to the embassy at St. Petersburg. Lord Londonderry was the brother of the late Marquis, so famous as Viscount Castlereagh, and shared those illiberal opinions which had made him so unpopular. His appointment provoked an angry debate in the House of Commons. Stanley forsook his neutrality to take part with his old friends. For once the Opposition was unanimous, enthusiastic, and sure of popular support. Londonderry thought that his only possible course was to resign. The Government gladly accepted his resignation, but got no rest. On the 26th of March, Mr. Tooke moved an address to the Crown praying that a charter of incorporation should be granted to the University of London. He had made a similar motion in each of the last two years.

The subject had been referred to the Privy Council,
which had settled nothing. Had the House of Commons
merely desired to quicken the Privy Council, it might
have addressed the King to order an account of the proceedings in the Privy Council to be laid before the
House of Commons.   On behalf of the Government,
Mr. Goulburn moved an amendment to this effect.
Whatever might be the actual bias of the Government,
it could scarcely be expected to put an affront on the
Council by accepting a motion which altogether ignored
the inquiry held by that body.   But a motion which the
Government could not accept was the motion which best
suited the Opposition.   Mr. Tooke had a majority of 110
votes.

Peel could not be turned out, however, by a defeat
upon an academic question. For this purpose an Irish
question was more useful than any other. The Protestant
Church of Ireland had for a long time compelled the
public attention.   Two circumstances in its condition
were notorious.   On the one hand, the tithe could not
be collected except by the harshest measures; on the
other hand, the gross revenue of the Church was far in
excess of the work which it had to do.   Two reforms,
therefore, were urgent.   It was necessary to end the
difficulties arising out of the collection of tithe, and it
was most desirable to ascertain and to apply to public
purposes such revenues as the Church could not usefully
employ.

Upon the first of these reforms all parties were agreed.
On behalf of Peel's Government, Sir Henry Hardinge
had moved a series of resolutions intended to form
the basis of a Bill dealing with Irish tithe.   These
resolutions followed the outlines of the Bill which
Littleton had introduced on behalf of the Whig

Ministry. They provided that the tithe composition should be replaced by an annual rent-charge, at the rate of £75 of rent-charge for every £100 of composition, and gave facilities for the redemption of the new payment, besides providing that the arrears for the year 1834 should be made up out of the balance of the sum of £1,000,000, which Parliament had already voted for the relief of the Irish tithe-owners. In so far as Hardinge's Bill differed from Littleton's Bill, it was less favourable to the tithe-owners, since Littleton had provided for a tithe rent-charge amounting to 77½ per cent. of the composition. The Whigs were bound in duty to assist in passing what was practically their own measure somewhat enlarged ; a measure urgently needed for the relief of the tithe-owner, the quieting of the tithe-payer and the general peace of Ireland. But the Whigs regarded Peel's Bill merely as a circumstance affecting their schemes for turning out the Ministry.

Upon the second of these reforms, not only had the Whigs to encounter the obstinate resistance of the Tories, but the Whigs themselves were not united. It was upon the question of appropriation Stanley and his followers had seceded from the Government of Lord Grey. Lord Melbourne's second Government found itself unable to deal with the question of appropriation. Yet the Whigs insisted on coupling with a reform which was approved by all parties, a reform which could barely be carried through the House of Commons, and had no chance of passing the House of Lords. Sacrificing the welfare of Ireland and the peace of the United Kingdom to a factious consistency, they resolved to assert in opposition a maxim which they knew themselves unable to enforce in office and forget their own disgrace in the exultation of turning out Sir Robert Peel.

8

On Monday, the 30th of March, Russell moved that
the House resolve itself into a Committee of the whole
House to consider the temporalities of the Irish Church.
After a protracted debate, in which Peel highly distinguished himself, the Government was defeated by 322
votes to 289. But a resolution which pledged the
House merely to consider the state of Church property
in Ireland, was not enough to force the Ministers to
resign. Russell, therefore, moved in a Committee of the
whole House, a further resolution that any surplus
which might remain after providing for the spiritual instruction of members of the Irish Church, ought to be
applied locally to the general education of all classes of
Christians. A long and stormy debate followed, and
the resolution was carried by 262 votes to 237. But
neither did this resolution necessarily bind the Government to do violence to its convictions. It laid down no
principles whereby the surplus could be ascertained; it
left undecided the question whether there were actually
any surplus or not, and if there should prove to be none,
the resolution would be destitute of effect. Peel, therefore,
did not resign, and Russell resolved to press him to the
utmost. On the 7th of April, he moved a resolution to
the effect that no measure dealing with tithes in Ireland
could lead to a final adjustment, unless it embodied the
principle of the foregoing resolutions. Peel again spoke
with much energy and eloquence, but mustered only 258
votes against 285 votes given for Russell. This defeat
was followed by Peel's resignation.

Never was victory more useless to the victors or less
hurtful to the vanquished. The Whigs had prevailed
only by binding themselves to a principle which, however right in itself, was to delay for three years the adjustment of the tithe question, and then to be dropped by

those whom it had restored to power. Peel, although worsted, had all the honours of the campaign. Placed in office by means which gave no hope of his continuing there; followed only by a party as weak in debate as on division; attacked with every weapon which a majority can wield, Peel had signally shown how much the force of one brave man can do. He had made every disadvantage subserve his glory. He had not set, and under the circumstances it was impossible that he should set, a lasting stamp on policy or legislation; but he had impressed all his contemporaries with an extraordinary idea of his personal qualities. That no minister ever returned to power more triumphantly than Peel left it, was the saying of a Whig as distinguished in literature as in politics. Charles Greville long afterwards pronounced the administration of a hundred days the most brilliant period of Peel's career. After these tributes from unfriendly or indifferent critics, the applause of friends and followers would seem a matter of course. Yet among friends and followers, if anywhere, had Peel's administration raised a misgiving which could be neither uttered nor suppressed. Whither will he lead us? asked the stern and unbending Tories. Whither, indeed?

CHAPTER VII.

IN OPPOSITION AGAIN.

1835-1841.

The Whigs resume Office—Their Weakness—Peel joined by Stanley and Graham—Accession of Queen Victoria—Growing strength of the Conservative Party—Session of 1839—Defeat of the Ministry on the Jamaica Bill—The Bedchamber Question—Continued decline of the Whig Party—Session of 1840—Vote of Want of Confidence in the Ministry defeated—Session of 1841—Financial Schemes of the Ministry—Peel carries a Vote of Want of Confidence—General Election—Large Conservative Majority—Resignation of the Ministry.

WILLIAM IV. submitted with a tolerable grace to the return of the advisers whom he detested, and Lord Melbourne had no trouble in forming a new Cabinet similar to that which had been dismissed in the year before. A general apathy pervaded even the victorious Whigs and seemed personified in their easy indolent Premier. Charles Greville wrote in his diary: "I certainly never remember a great victory for which *Te Deum* was chanted with so faint and joyless a voice. Peel looks gayer and easier than all Brookes' put together, and Lady Holland said, 'Now that we have gained our object I am not so glad as I thought I should be,' and that I take to be the sentiment of them all." The Whigs had recovered power, but they had no distinct ideas as to how they should use it.

Lord Melbourne remained in office for six years. During those years the tide of change continued to flow in England as in other countries of Europe. Many excellent measures were passed, but almost always under circumstances which abated the merit, or at least the credit of the Ministry. Thus the Acts dealing with Nonconformist marriages, the composition of tithe in England, and the composition of tithe in Ireland, closely resembled the three Bills dealing with these subjects which Sir Robert Peel had introduced in 1835, and might have carried then with a little forbearance on the part of his adversaries. The Act which laid the foundation of our system of elementary education, good so far as it went, was pitiably meagre. The Act which reformed municipal corporations in England was a great measure, but, if it was saved from mutilation the praise lay less with the Ministers than with Peel, who listened to reason and checked the wilfulness of his party. Peel lent himself to the business of attenuating a similar Bill for Ireland, and had his way in spite of the Ministers. We may say that during those years Peel was almost as powerful as all the Ministers united. The Leader of the Opposition was the first public man in England.

In his second period of opposition Peel exhibited the same skill and temper which he had displayed in the first. He became, it is true, more aggressive. Not to be obliged to carry out any policy of your own, yet to be able to thwart the policy of others, is a situation too trying for human virtue. The temptations of being in office are nothing to the temptations of being out of office. Yet Peel exercised his anomalous

influence with as much public spirit as we can hope
from a party leader. Probably we shall never know
how much he did to calm the fears and sooth the pug-
nacity of his followers. We seldom realise how much
of the time of those who are fit to rule is taken up with
persuading others to let themselves be ruled. We
blame a party leader for the mischief which he does
and forget the mischief which he prevents. If we consider Peel simply in relation to his Party, his conduct
at this time deserves all possible praise. Under his
fostering care the new Conservative Party improved
daily in numbers, in spirit, and in discipline, whilst it
kept pace with the general movement of the time and
opened its arms to all who were not of a decidedly
Liberal way of thinking.

In the beginning of the July of 1835 Stanley and
Graham quitted the Ministerial benches and took their
seats among the Opposition. Half-a-dozen faithful
followers accompanied them, but the rest of their little
party melted away, and they no longer pretended to
hold the balance of the House of Commons. Sir
Robert might rejoice that he was rid of two dangerous
rivals, and had gained two admirable lieutenants, a
brilliant orator and an excellent man of business.
Various petty personal reasons for this conversion were
suggested by the gossips of the day, but the truth is
that Stanley and Graham had long been made uneasy
by the incessant inroads of change. They were really
less liberal than Peel, who was always ready to compromise with any new power when it had once asserted
itself. At first Stanley's old colleagues imagined that
he was in accord with them on every question not connected with the Church. They were not undeceived
until he assailed them in the debate on the Address of

the session of 1836.   Even then they might have been
surprised if anyone had foretold that in a few years
Stanley would abandon Sir Robert Peel as being too
radical an innovator.

The death of William IV. and the accession of Queen
Victoria gave to the Whigs the support of a young
and popular Sovereign, who cherished their principles
and felt a warm personal regard for Lord Melbourne;
but it involved a general election, which proved extremely unfortunate.   Many of the boroughs returned
Conservatives.   Even in the City of London, Grote, the
most eminent man among the philosophic Radicals,
was elected only by a very small majority.   Roebuck and
Palmer at Bath, Ewart at Liverpool, Wigney at Brighton, Thomson at Hull, were all defeated.   Leeds was
the only important capture made by the Liberals from
the Conservatives.   The counties were even more faith-
less than the boroughs.   It was said that the Conservatives could have done much more had they but known
their own strength.   When Parliament met, the Ministers suffered almost as much from the Radicals as from
the Conservatives.   The Radicals wanted another reform
of Parliament, and the introduction of vote by ballot,
which were opposed by Lord John Russell.   Although
these differences were patched up, they left a fatal weakness behind.   In debate the Government was always
getting the worst of it.   Peel took a tone of superiority
in the House of Commons ; in the House of Lords
Brougham thundered against his old friends ; the *Times*
lent its weight to the Conservatives, who became more
and more impatient for decisive action.   Unwillingly
Peel agreed to let them try their power.   The Radicals
had resolved to challenge the Canadian policy of
the Ministers.   Sir William Molesworth, a distin-

guished member of a distinguished group of philosophic
reformers, proposed a direct vote of want of confidence in the Secretary for the Colonies. On behalf
of the Conservatives, Lord Sandon moved, by way of
amendment, a vote of censure upon the Government.
Peel spoke in favour of the amendment without caring for
its success. The Radicals could not vote for it; and
the Conservatives alone were unable to carry it. The
division strengthened the influence of moderate men on
both sides. The Ministry had a majority of twenty-
nine, a majority unusual for them and enough to damp
the fighting Conservatives. The Conservatives, including those who had paired or stayed away, mustered a
force of 317 members of the House of Commons, infinitely more compact than any force which could be
brought against it. The Radicals were thus convinced
that they must uphold Russell if they did not want to be
governed by Peel. Things accordingly became quieter
for a little while.

The strength of the Conservatives was ostentatiously
displayed at the banquet given to Sir Robert Peel in
Merchant Taylors Hall on the 12th of May 1838.
The invitation was signed by 313 members of the House
of Commons. The Marquess of Chandos, the champion of the landed interest, took the chair, and among
those who supported him on that occasion Sir
Francis Burdett appeared beside Sir Robert Inglis.
The health of their chief was drunk with nine rounds of
cheering. In returning thanks, Sir Robert Peel reminded the company that less than six years before the
number of their party in the House of Commons had
been reduced to little more than a hundred; that he had
then hoped and foretold the resurrection of that defeated
party; that the next dissolution had nearly doubled

their numbers; that a second dissolution had brought
them an increase of strength; that on such questions
as the exclusion of bishops from the House of Lords, the
repeal of the Corn Laws, and the introduction of vote by
ballot, the Ministers had been saved from overthrow only
by the votes of the Opposition; and then, with all the
authority which this veiled reminder of his own services
could bestow, he urged the necessity of temper and
moderation.

I hope [he said] we shall never be betrayed, for the sake of any
temporary advantage, into a union with those from whose principles
we dissent. I also hope that we shall never adopt the advice which I
have sometimes received from ardent friends and professed admirers,
to abandon our duty in Parliament and, for the purpose of creating
embarrassment to the Government, to leave it to fight the battle alone.
My object is that by steadily attending to our duty, by censuring the
Government on all occasions when they deserve it, enforcing our
principles by aiding them to carry those measures which we think
right, even though by so doing we may be rescuing the Government,
we may establish new claims upon the approbation of the country.

Having heightened by an unfriendly criticism of the
Ministry the merit of that self-command which refrained
from taking advantage of its errors, and even saved it
from the violence of its friends, he resumed his seat amid
tumultuous applause. Catholic Emancipation was forgotten; and who could foresee the repeal of the Corn
Laws? Stanley's eloquent voice swelled the chorus of
praise and congratulation, and Graham in tones less
resonant professed the allegiance which outlasted the
desertion of Stanley. It was one of the most joyous
moments in Peel's life.

In this session Peel enjoyed the personal satisfaction
of making the Whigs forego the principle which they
had made the ground for turning him out of office.
In each of the preceding sessions they had brought in a

Bill dealing with Irish tithe, and had failed to carry it, because they had insisted upon the principle of appropriation.
They now agreed to say nothing about that principle, and
were suffered to carry a Bill which gave the tithe-owners
terms slightly more favourable than Peel had offered
three years before. No defeat could be more damaging
than this success on sufferance.

Another tedious session opened in February 1839.
Vexed by a vote of the House of Lords which they
construed as a censure of their policy in Ireland, the
Ministry resolved to make the House of Commons declare
its approval of that policy. This led to a curious
negotiation. Lord John Russell was of opinion that the
Government could not in any case last long. He did
not desire office for himself. He was tired of his
humiliating position, mortified by the way in which the
Radicals had treated him, and heart-broken on account of
the recent loss of his wife. But he was anxious, if
defeated, to avoid a dissolution, and to give Peel his
independent support, and he feared that this would be
impossible unless the Conservatives put a curb on their
temper in the approaching debate. All this he said to a
friend, who told it to Charles Greville, who made it known
to Graham, through whom it reached Peel. Peel was
somewhat annoyed, for he thought that he had the Government at a disadvantage and counted upon a signal
triumph, which he must resign if he were to go into
battle with the preliminaries of a treaty of peace already
settled. Still he would not sacrifice to vanity or ill-
humour a prospect so congenial to his deeper instincts, and
he resolved that if Russell spoke calmly he would do so
likewise. He told Stanley that he must go down to the
House with two speeches in his pocket. As Russell was
very guarded, Peel made the tamer speech of the two,

displeased his own friends, and did not turn out the Government. But the Government had enough to endure. In the course of the debate Lord Morpeth, the Chief Secretary, took heart to declare that the Ministry would no longer exist on sufferance. He only drew down the taunts of his Radical friends. Mr. Leader, the member for Westminster, replied that for the last two years the Ministers had held power on that tenure. " In what position, then, is the Government placed ? Why, the right honourable member for Tamworth governs England. The honourable and learned member for Dublin governs Ireland. The Whigs govern nothing but Downing Street. The right honourable member for Tamworth is contented with power without place or patronage, and the Whigs are contented with place and patronage without power. Let any honourable man say which is the more honourable position ? "

The Bill which was to end the struggles of the Government had already been introduced. An Act for the better regulation of prisons in Jamaica was received as an outrage by the House of Assembly, which consisted chiefly of planters and was embittered against the mother country by the long struggle over the emancipation of the negroes. The Assembly resolved to record its displeasure by refusing to transact business. It was not subdued by prorogation ; and after a dissolution the new Assembly showed itself to be as stubborn as its predecessor. Finding all the public business of the island arrested, Lord Melbourne's Government introduced into the House of Commons a Bill suspending for five years the constitution of Jamaica. Whether or no the circumstances of Jamaica required this severe proceeding, the Opposition naturally took the view contrary to that taken by the Government. Although the Bill was read

twice, the motion for the House to resolve itself into a
Committee on the Bill provoked a lively debate, followed
by a division in which the defection of certain Radical
members left the Ministry a majority of no more than
five.

The division took place on the night of Monday the
6th of May. Next day the Cabinet met and resolved
to resign. Lord Melbourne advised the Queen to send
for the Duke of Wellington, who in turn advised her
to send for Sir Robert Peel. Peel accordingly went to
the Palace and received the Queen's commission to form
a Government. This time Peel had no difficulty in
securing the assistance of Graham or Stanley, and the
Cabinet was virtually formed, when it was dissolved by a
trivial incident remembered now only because of the illustrious persons whom it concerned. The ladies of the
Queen's household, to whom Her Majesty was warmly
attached, were all Whigs. Sir Robert Peel thought that
he would be prejudiced in his place of Prime Minister if
the Queen's familiar associates were all of the adverse party.
He therefore asked that some at least might retire and
be replaced by ladies of his own persuasion. To this
request the Queen gave an indignant refusal. Peel
thereupon informed her that he must consult his friends,
which he did at a meeting held on the afternoon of the
same day, the 9th of May. As the late Ministers were
aware of what had happened, Russell requested Melbourne, if the negotiations with Peel were broken off,
not to give the Queen any advice without consulting his
colleagues. A few hours after the Conservative chiefs
had met at Peel's house, the Liberal chiefs repaired to
Melbourne's and listened to a letter in which Her
Majesty complained warmly of Peel's suggestion. After
some debate, Melbourne and his friends composed a

letter by which the Queen declined to leave the places in her household to Peel's discretion. Upon receiving this letter Peel sent a reply resigning his commission into Her Majesty's hands. The news soon spread all over the town, giving occasion to infinite chatter and excitement.

Lord Melbourne and Lord Russell went to wait upon the Queen, who told them all that had happened and ended by saying, " I have stood by you, you must now stand by me." Moved by the distress of their Sovereign they resolved to stand by her, and their example decided their colleagues, who agreed to resume that most ungrateful duty from which they had just escaped. In this curious transaction the Queen had been in correspondence with two Prime Ministers and two Cabinets at once ; she had received the unanimous resolutions of the one, and by the other she had been advised how to reply to those resolutions. It was irregular, but the blame of the irregularity rests chiefly with the veteran leaders of the Whigs, who must have known that so long as Sir Robert Peel held the commission to form a Cabinet, they had no status as advisers of the Crown. Sir Robert Peel showed himself somewhat formal and pedantic by insisting on his strict rights on a point which concerned the feelings of the Sovereign much and the public business little. Her Majesty, however, who was then very young, might be more under the influence of personal friends than a sovereign of longer experience. She displayed a strong preference for Lord Melbourne and the Whigs, and her disfavour might have prejudiced a ministry which did not command a majority in the House of Commons.

The Whigs returned to place and patronage without power. They lingered on for two years, sinking by degrees into nullity, and at last doing almost nothing without Peel's consent.   They were able to assert their views respecting the publication of Parliamentary papers because those views were espoused by Peel, who sided with the Government against many of his own followers, They were able at length to reform municipal corporations in Ireland because Peel discouraged resistance.   They accepted Peel's scheme for the reform of election committees, and they feebly resisted Stanley's Irish Registration Bill.   All heart and strength went out of the Whig party.   All the bold uncompromising spirits fell away from them.   The philosophic Radicals mostly withdrew from political life altogether.   The middle-class Liberals, who believed in free trade, found scope in organizing the Anti-Corn Law League. The discontented populace ceased to hope anything from any Minister and became Chartist.   Then came national petitions and monster meetings and riots, and all the other symptoms of suffering which does not understand itself.   For suffering was general and severe at this time, Commerce hardly expanded at all ; manufactures were dull, agriculture was not much better, and the labouring poor were in a deplorable condition.   The same vast dissatisfaction which had carried the first Reform Act was again swelling round the Whig leaders, but this time they had no great measure ready to appease it.

The session of 1840 began with an incident which might have further prejudiced the Queen against Sir Robert Peel.   When opening Parliament Her Majesty had announced her approaching marriage, and expressed her confidence that a suitable provision would be made for Prince Albert.   The Ministers proposed to settle £50,000 a year upon the prince.   Mr. Hume proposed £21,000 and Colonel Sibthorp £30,000 a year as the

proper sum. Peel spoke as well as voted for Sibthorp's
amendment, which was carried by a large majority.
About the same time the Conservatives made another
push to displace the Ministry. A leading county member, Sir John Yarde Buller, was chosen to propose a vote
of want of confidence. Peel put forth all his strength
in a speech which fatigued the House by its length and
elaboration, although the reader finds it one of his
happiest efforts. The Ministry had the unusual majority
of twenty-one votes; but the division only served to
prolong their agony. We were at this time engaged in
three Asiatic wars; a war with Persia, a war with Afghanistan, and a war with China, the ill-famed opium war.
Sir James Graham moved a resolution throwing the
blame of the war with China upon the Ministers. Peel
was able to support it with consistency, for he had
always shown a pacific disposition. Whilst he allowed
that war might have been made inevitable by our mistakes, he implored the House not to wage the war in a
vindictive spirit, and to seize the first opportunity of
coming to terms. On a division Graham was beaten
only by 271 Noes to 262 Ayes. A little later the contest
between the Pacha of Egypt and the Sultan of Turkey
set France in opposition to the other Great Powers and
threatened a European war. In January of 1841
Peel took advantage of the debate on the Address to
soothe the irritation of the French by a speech full of
courtesy and kindliness, which was long and gratefully
remembered by our neighbours.

It was not, however, upon any question of foreign policy
that Peel finally prevailed against the Government.
Their financial policy gave him the desired occasion.
It had been unfortunate or unskilful. During their term
of office the revenue was steadily declining; the expen-

diture was steadly growing.   In every one of the five
years from 1837 to 1841 inclusive there was a deficit;
and the sum total of the five deficits was roughly
£8,000,000, which had been made good by borrowing.
Baring, who had succeeded Spring Rice in 1840, had
tried to make the revenue balance the expenditure by
making small additions to sundry small imposts.   But
in the distressful condition of the country a tax did not
necessarily prove more productive because it had been
made more severe.   In the commencement of 1841 Baring
found that he had to meet a deficit of £2,421,000.   The
result of this experiment convinced the Cabinet that only
a radical change of system could restore elasticity to
the revenue, and at the same time their weakness made it
imperative to propose some reform which should rally
the people around them.   They determined, therefore, to
do something for freedom of trade. Among the innumer-
able items of the tariff, corn, sugar, and timber were the
most important.   Colonial timber and sugar were
charged with a duty lighter than was imposed on foreign
timber and sugar; and foreign sugar paid a lighter or a
heavier duty according as it was imported from
countries of slave labour or countries of free labour.
It was resolved to raise the duty on colonial timber, but
to lower the duty on foreign timber and foreign sugar,
and at the same time to replace the sliding scale of the
Corn Laws then in force with a fixed duty of 8s. per
quarter.   The changes relating to sugar and timber
were announced in Baring's budget for 1841.   Lord
John Russell gave notice of a resolution in favour of a
fixed duty on corn.   But it was now too late.   After
Melbourne's former declarations in favour of the Corn
Law, nobody gave him or his colleagues credit for anything more than a desire to purchase support at all costs.

The concessions offered by the Ministry, too small to excite the enthusiasm of the free traders, were enough to rally all the threatened interests around Peel. Baring's revision of the sugar duties was rejected by a majority of thirty-six. Everybody expected the Ministers to resign upon this defeat; but they merely announced the continuance of the former duties. Then Peel gave notice of a vote of want of confidence, and carried it on the 4th of June by a single vote in a House of 623 members. Instead of resigning, the Ministers appealed to the country. The elections went on through the last days of June and the whole of July. When the new Parliament was complete, it appeared that the Conservatives could count upon 367 votes in the House of Commons.

The Ministry met Parliament on the 24th of August. Peel in the House of Commons and Ripon in the House of Lords moved amendments to the Address, which were carried by majorities of ninety-one and seventy-two respectively. There could no longer be the pretence of a doubt as to the feeling of the country. Lord Melbourne and his colleagues could no longer doubt that it was their duty to resign office. It was assumed by the ablest statesman of the day, supported by numerous majorities in both Houses, strong in the confidence of all the great interests, esteemed even by men of the opposite party, and a favourite with the other Cabinets of Europe. A powerful hand grasped the tiller and laid the ship before the wind, the flapping sails suddenly filled, and the sea was cleft before the rushing prow.

CHAPTER VIII.

PEEL'S SECOND ADMINISTRATION.

1841–1846.

Composition of the Cabinet—Peel's Policy—Session of 1842—The new
Corn Law—The Budget—The Tariff—Peel's Views regarding
Protection—Foreign Affairs—France, the United States—The
East—Session of 1843—Altercation between Peel and Cobden—
The Budget—The Factory Bill—Irish Affairs—Return of Pros-
perity—Session of 1844—Budget—Bank Charter Act—Factory
Act—Measures of Religious Toleration—Foreign Affairs—Difficul-
ties of the Ministry—Session of 1845—Budget—Disraeli's attacks
on Peel—Acts for increasing the Maynooth Grant and founding the
Queen's Colleges—Peel's position at the close of the Session—
Failure of the potato crop—Deliberations of the Cabinet—Peel
resigns—Russell commissioned to form a Ministry—His ill
success—Peel returns to Office—Session of 1846—The Proposals
of the Ministry—Schism in the Conservative Party—Disraeli and
Bentinck—Tactics of the Whigs and Protectionists—Defeat of
the Ministry—Peel resigns—Reflections on Peel's Fiscal Policy—
On his Conduct towards the Conservative Party.

SIR ROBERT PEEL now became First Lord of the Treasury. Wellington entered the Cabinet without office,
and Lyndhurst assumed for the third time the honours
of Lord Chancellor. Goulburn was made Chancellor of
the Exchequer. The country gentlemen were pleased
to see their champion the Duke of Buckingham entrusted
with the Privy Seal. Wharncliffe's services to his party

were rewarded with the rank of Lord President, Hardinge took the War office, Haddington the Admiralty, Ellenborough the Board of Control, and Aberdeen Foreign Affairs. Sir Edward Knatchbull was Paymaster of the Forces. Lord Eliot became Chief Secretary for Ireland.

These were purely Conservative appointments, but the adhesion of the malcontent Whigs was rewarded by giving the Colonial Office to Stanley, the Home Department to Graham, and the Presidency of the Board of Trade to Ripon. The Cabinet consisted of fifteen persons, eight peers and seven commoners. It contained three or four admirable officials, and it was strong in the authority and energy of its chief. The sauntering Melbourne had made room for a Premier of heroic industry. Without Melbourne the Liberals might have done more ; without Peel the Conservatives could do nothing. Except by a few, Peel was little loved and scarcely understood ; but by all he was honoured and felt to be necessary. He was therefore punctually obeyed, and had his colleagues and his followers as well disciplined as the crew of a man-of-war.

This time Peel experienced no difficulty with regard to the Queen's Household. It had been previously arranged that in the case of Lord Melbourne's resignation three Whig Ladies, the Duchess of Bedford, the Duchess of Sutherland, and Lady Normanby should resign of their own accord. One or two other changes in the Household contented Peel, and these the Queen accorded with a frankness which placed him entirely at his ease. He explained to the Queen that his assured position in the House of Commons enabled him to consult her feelings more fully than he was able to do when he had only a minority there ; that he could not avoid taking office, but that he was most anxious to provide for her happi-

ness. It may be said here that time and frequent intercourse soon obliterated any prejudice which Her Majesty
entertained towards Sir Robert Peel. The vote which
the Minister had given on the subject of the Prince
Consort's annuity did not blind the Prince to Peel's
real worth. Drawn together by the sympathy natural
between serious and cultivated men, as well as by
loyalty to the Crown and an intelligent appreciation of
the wants of the country, Prince Albert and Sir Robert
Peel formed a close friendship, which confirmed the
good relations between Sir Robert Peel and the Queen.
In the year 1843 the Queen and her husband honoured
Sir Robert Peel with a visit at Drayton Manor. Prince
Albert's confidential friend, Stockmar, has drawn his
portrait in favourable although discriminating colours.

By the time that the Ministry was complete the
autumn was so far spent that little business could be
done. Goulburn obtained authority to borrow a sum of
£5,000,000, to be applied, half in meeting the deficit,
and half in funding Exchequer bills. Having sanctioned this loan, and continued the Poor Law until next
July, Parliament was prorogued on the 7th of October,
only three weeks after Peel had taken his seat on re-
election as a Minister. The Opposition had been very
pressing to know by what expedients Peel meant to
restore order in the affairs of the country. Peel
answered every such demand by saying that he must
have time to gather information and to mature his
plans; with which reply, backed by reason and a
majority, the Opposition had to rest content.

The time thus gained was well employed. During
the recess Peel took a wide survey of the ills affecting
the commonwealth, and of the possible remedies. To
supply the deficiency in the revenue without laying new

burthens upon the humbler class; to revive our fainting manufactures by encouraging the importation of raw material; to assuage distress by making the price of provisions lower and more regular, without taking away that protection which he still believed essential to British agriculture: these were the tasks which Peel now bent his mind to compass. They were all problems of finance, but such problems as touch upon the interests and the passions of every class of the community. Having solved them to his own satisfaction, he had to persuade his colleagues that they were right. Only one proved obstinate. The Duke of Buckingham would hear of no change in the degree of protection afforded to agriculture. He surrendered the Privy Seal, which was given to the Duke of Buccleugh. His resignation was noticed with impatient curiosity, but its precise cause remained unknown.

The Queen's Speech recommended Parliament to consider the state of the laws affecting the importation of corn and other commodities. It announced the beginning of a revolution which few persons in England thought possible, although it was to be completed in little more than ten years. On the 9th of February Peel moved that the House should resolve itself into a Committee to consider the Corn Laws. His speech, which lasted nearly three hours, was necessarily dull, and his proposal was equally offensive to the country gentlemen and to the Anti-Corn Law League. It amounted merely to an improvement of the sliding scale which had been devised by the Duke of Wellington's Cabinet, and was based on the axiom that the British farmer, taking one year with another, could not make a profit by growing corn if foreign corn were admitted at a price of less than 70s. a quarter. By a calculation of

prices extending over a long term of years, Peel had
satisfied himself that a price of 56s. a quarter would
remunerate the British farmer.   He proposed to modify
the sliding scale accordingly.   Under the sliding scale
of 1828, when wheat fetched 60s. a quarter, foreign
wheat was admitted subject to a duty of 27s. a quarter,
and as the price rose the duty fell, until, when the price
was 69s., the duty was 16s. 8d.; but when the price
rose above 70s. the duty fell by 4s. for every rise of 1s.
in the price, and when the price rose to 73s. the duty
sank to 1s.   This arrangement involved the peculiar
inconvenience that when corn rose to 69s. the quarter,
the importer was interested in holding it back until it
had risen further to 73s., for this slight increase in price
brought about a fourfold diminution in duty.   Peel
retained the minimum duty of 1s. when corn was selling
at 73s. the quarter; he fixed a maximum duty of 20s.
when corn was selling at from 50s. to 51s. the quarter;
and he so altered the graduation in the increase of duty
as to diminish the inducement to hold grain back when
it became dear.   By reducing the amount of the duty,
and by so adjusting it as to encourage importation, he
took away some part of that protection which the
farmer had hitherto enjoyed, and gave some relief to
consumers.   To us the details of his scheme are less
interesting than the arguments in favour of a Corn Law
put forward in his speech on this occasion :—

The protection which I propose to retain, I do not retain for the
especial protection of any particular class.   Protection cannot be
vindicated on that principle.   The only protection which can be
vindicated is that protection which is consistent with the general
welfare of all classes in the country.   I should not consider myself a
friend to the agriculturist if I asked for a protection with a view of
propping up rents, or for the purpose of defending his interest or the
interests of any particular class, and in the proposition I now submit

to the House I totally disclaim any such intention. My belief and the belief of my colleagues is that it is important to this country, that it is of the highest importance to the welfare of all classes in this country, that you should take care that the main sources of your supply of corn should be derived from domestic agriculture, while we also feel that any additional price which you may pay in effecting that object is an additional price which cannot be vindicated as a bonus or premium to agriculture, but only on the ground of its being advantageous to the country at large. You are entitled to place such a price on foreign corn as is equivalent to the special burdens borne by the agriculturist, and any additional protection you give to them, I am willing to admit, can only be vindicated on the ground that it is for the interest of the country generally. I, however, certainly do consider that it is for the interest of all classes that we should be paying occasionally a small additional sum upon our own domestic produce in order that we might thereby establish a security and insurance against these calamities that would ensue if we became altogether or in a great part dependent upon foreign countries for our supply. My belief is that those alternations of seasons will continue to take place, that whatever laws you may pass, you will still occasionally have to encounter deficient crops, that the harvests of other countries will also at times be deficient, and that if you found yourselves dependent upon foreign countries for so important an amount of corn as 4,000,000 or 5,000,000 of quarters, under these circumstances and at a time when the calamity of a deficient harvest happened to be general. my belief is that the principle of self-preservation would prevail in each country, that an impediment would be placed upon the exportation of their corn, and that it would be applied to their own sustenance. While, therefore, I am opposed to a system of protection on the ground merely of defending the interests of a particular class, I on the other hand would certainly not be a party to any measure the effect of which would be to make this country permanently dependent upon foreign countries for any very considerable portion of its supply of corn. That it might be for a series of years dependent on foreign countries for a portion of its supply, that in many years of scarcity a considerable portion of its supply must be derived from foreign countries, I do not deny; but I nevertheless do not abandon the hope that this country, in the average of years, may produce a sufficiency for its own necessities. If that hope be disappointed, if you must resort to other countries in ordinary seasons for periodical additions to your own supplies, then do I draw a material distinction between the supply which is limited, the supply which is brought in for the purpose of repairing our accidental and comparatively slight deficiency, and the supply which is of a more permanent and extensive character.

So general was the dissatisfaction with Peel's Corn Law, that Russell ventured once more to place before the House his alternative of a fixed 8s. duty. He was defeated by a majority of upwards of one hundred and twenty votes. Two days later Mr. Villiers made his annual motion for the total repeal of the Corn Laws, and was beaten by more than four votes to one. The murmurs of Peel's own supporters were easily overborne, and the Bill was carried through the House of Commons after a month spent in debates. As soon as it had passed, and the estimates for the army and navy had been voted, Peel produced what was really his Budget, nominally Mr. Goulburn's.

We have seen what was the condition of the finances. In every one of the last five years there had been a deficit, and the sum total of these deficits was little less than £8,000,000. It was known that, unless a remedy were applied the current year would add to this sum total a fresh deficit of £2,469,000. The ordinary revenue of the State had become, and seemed likely to remain, unequal to its ordinary expenditure. How was this evil to be remedied? The old familiar remedy was to add a little to each of many indirect taxes; but this remedy had been lately tried in vain. Every increase of the tax upon a commodity diminishes the consumption, and thus in a time of distress the anticipated gain is often entirely lost. So general and so severe was the public distress in the year 1842 that to augment the taxation of the poor might prove not only cruel and useless but dangerous too. Peel therefore resolved to impose an income-tax. He calculated that an income-tax of 7d. in the pound, imposed only on Great Britain and on incomes of £150 a year and upwards, would bring in a sum of £3,770,000, sufficient to cover the deficit and leave a balance to be employed in fiscal reform. He added 1s. a gallon to the duty on Irish spirits, equalized the duty on coal exported in British and in foreign bottoms, and made some changes in the stamp duties. These innovations were estimated to add £1,000,000 to the revenue. With these and with the income-tax he calculated that he would have a surplus of £1,900,000, Peel was thus able to propose a reduction of the tariff upon uniform and comprehensive principles. He proposed to limit import duties to a maximum of 5 per. cent. upon the value of raw materials, of 12 per cent. upon the value of goods partly manufactured, and of 20 per cent. upon the value of goods wholly manufactured. Out of the twelve hundred articles then comprised in the tariff seven hundred and fifty were more or less affected by the application of these rules, yet so trivial was the revenue raised from most of them that the total loss was computed at only £270,000 a year. Peel reduced the duty on coffee; he reduced the duty on foreign and almost entirely abolished the duty on Canadian timber. Cattle and pigs, meat of all descriptions, cheese and butter, which had hitherto been subject to a prohibitory duty, he proposed to admit at a comparatively low rate. He also diminished the duty upon stage coaches.

So extensive a change in our system of national finance had never before been effected at one stroke. The principle of free trade had been accepted by many of Peel's predecessors who had been slow to apply it. The cost of the concessions now made by Peel to that principle was not heavy. The really bold and striking feature in his Budget was the imposition of the property tax. Such a tax had hitherto been imposed only in time of war. In time of peace it was again imposed by Peel in order to restore the balance of our revenue and expenditure, and to relieve commerce from some of its many burthens. He imposed it upon those classes from which his own party was for the most part recruited. It is true that he originally intended to levy it for three years and no more. Yet, when we remember that its imposition was conjoined with an extension of free trade which was widely believed to be noxious to great interests, we must admire the courage and self-confidence of the Minister, nor can we refuse due praise to the subordination and public spirit of his followers. The Conservative Cabinet proposed and the Conservative party sanctioned the most important of all the changes which have thrown the heaviest share of taxation upon the richest part of the community.

Immense was the excitement caused by the statement of the Budget. All people discussed, and most people praised it. Even Greville broke into enthusiasm. "This just measure, so lofty in conception, right in direction, and able in execution, places him (Peel) at once on a pinnacle of power, and establishes his Government on such a foundation as accident alone can shake." The Opposition criticised indeed, as is the duty of an Opposition. The income-tax was stiffly opposed by both Whigs and Radicals, in fact by the whole Liberal Party. Every part of Peel's scheme was debated with the utmost energy. The whole of our financial policy was reviewed again and again as each of the principal innovations of the Budget came before the House embodied in a separate Bill. The tariff called forth all the energies of those who favoured free trade and those who favoured protection; of those who thought it miserably inadequate, and of those who thought it revolutionary. But Peel disposed of an obedient majority and a favourable public opinion. No man was more prompt to yield to overwhelming power, but with power on his side no man was more obstinate. He procured the ratification of all his measures subject to some slight amendments, and at the cost of a whole session spent in discussing them. Little or nothing else was accomplished by Parliament in this year.

Peel had returned to power as the champion of protection. His first great achievement was the extension of the freedom of trade. Through what process of thought did this remarkable man arrive at conclusions which seem at variance with his declared opinions? Did he yet see all the consequences which followed from these novel conclusions? His later policy led some to charge him with lightly changing his beliefs, and others to charge him with disingenuous concealment of beliefs long since matured. An authentic expression of his real frame of mind at this time is afforded by his correspondence with his old friend Croker. It is clear, from the tone of Peel's letters, that Croker was one of those Conservatives who began to doubt at least the firmness and consistency, if not the good faith, of Sir Robert Peel. Sir Robert writes to him in July of this year :—

I can assure you that the difficulty will be to prove that we have gone far enough in concession—that is, relaxation of prohibitions and protections—not that we have gone too far. Something effectual must be done to revive, and revive permanently, the languishing commerce and languishing manufacturing industry of this country.

France, Belgium, and Germany are closing their doors upon us.

Look at the state of society in this country; the congregation of manufacturing masses; the amount of our debt, the rapid increase of poor-rates within the last four years, which will soon, by means of rates in aid, extend from the mixed manufacturing districts to the rural ones; and then judge whether we can with safety retrograde in manufactures.

The declared value of the exports of cotton manufacture fell off above a million last year compared with the former. Seventeen millions in 1840; sixteen millions in 1841. If you had to constitute new societies you might on moral and social grounds prefer corn fields to cotton factories, and agricultural to a manufacturing population. But our lot is cast; we cannot change it, and we cannot recede. The tariff does not go half far enough in the direction in which it does go. If we could afford it, we ought to take off the duty on cotton wool and the duty on foreign sheep's wool.

I repeat that the man who pays £2 18s. per cent. on his income, may make that saving in consequence of the tariff.

I am confident of it, and yet in the same breath I say to the agriculturist: Your apprehensions about fat pigs and fat cattle from Hamburg are absurd. There will be no reduction in the price of meat or cattle which need terrify you.

I have made no abatement in the Tariff or in the Corn Law in deference to repealers of the Corn Laws. There is nothing I have proposed which is not in conformity with my own convictions I should rather say, I have not gone in any one case beyond my own convictions on the side of relaxation.

Experience will show that nothing but good will result from the extent of relaxation.

The following passage from a letter addressed to Croker a few days later puts still more forcibly the case for free trade :—

We must make this country a *cheap* country for living, and thus induce parties to remain and settle here.

Enable them to consume more by having more to spend.

The argument that people must pay more for the articles they consume, because they are heavily taxed, is absurd.

If you have to pay annually sixty-four shillings a quarter for 24,000,000 quarters of wheat, there is a dead loss of £12,000,000 sterling annually.

Comparing the expenditure on one article with that which would be requisite were wheat at fifty-four shillings, how will that £12,000,000 be employed ? In consuming more barley, more wheat, more articles of agricultural produce. It is a fallacy to urge that the loss falls on agriculturists. They too are consumers ; they lose almost as much in increased poor-rates alone, the burden of which, as they contend, falls almost exclusively on them, as they gain by increased price.

Lower the price of wheat, not only poor-rates, but the cost of everything else is lowered.

We do not push this argument to its logical consequences, namely, that wheat should be at thirty-five shillings instead of fifty or fifty-four.

We take into account vested interests, engaged capital, the importance of independent supply, the social benefits of flourishing agriculture, &c.

We find that the general welfare will be best promoted by a fair adjustment, by allowing the legitimate logical deductions to be controlled by the thousand considerations which enter into moral and political questions, and which, as friction and the weight of the atmosphere disturb your mathematical conclusions, put a limit to the practical application of abstract reasoning.

In the same spirit he justified his property tax as a special contribution from the wealth of the country to its extreme need, which would at length benefit the owners of that wealth even more than any other class of men.

But the finances could not recover, nor could trade revive unless economy and industry were assisted by continued peace. Peace was always dear to Sir Robert Peel. Although guarded by strong common sense against the fancies of the Peace Society, and the unqualified dogma of non-intervention, although convinced of the power of England and zealous for her honour, he was always anxious to shun occasions of war, which shocked his humane and thrifty disposition. From the first moment of his return to office he laboured to confirm peace. He was well seconded by his Foreign Secretary, and by the chances of the time. France no longer remained in opposition to the other Great Powers on the Eastern Question. Louis Philippe regarded Peel with an esteem and friendship which Peel cordially returned, and which were most useful in restoring the harmony of the two nations. Guizot co-operated zealously with Aberdeen in this good work. In the December of 1841 the French Government had proved its amiable sentiments by admitting into a treaty for the suppression of the slave trade a clause which provided for a mutual right of search, a right most distasteful to all the nations which envied the maritime supremacy of England. The other Cabinets of Europe were well disposed to Peel's Government, partly because they understood it to be the Conservative Government, partly because they found it pleasanter to transact business with Aberdeen than with Palmerston.

But our relations with countries outside Europe were less agreeable. In the west there was ill-feeling, and in the east there was war.

For many years previous to Peel's return to office grievances had been gathering between the United Kingdom and the United States. The frontier dividing the United States from Canada was disputed both in its eastern and in its western portions. The need of determining a frontier in the west had arisen but lately and was not met till just before Peel's resignation. But the debate respecting the frontier in the east was as old as the recognition of the United States by the British Government. The Treaty of Paris had determined that frontier by reference to supposed natural features which did not exist. In the year 1827 the King of the Netherlands had been invited to arbitrate upon the differences arising from this inaccuracy. Finding that it was impossible to obtain the data which would have enabled him to put a true construction on the terms of the treaty he thought himself entitled to go beyond the letter of his trust, and suggested a compromise which would have given to the United States three-fifths of the disputed territory. This compromise was accepted by England but refused by the United States, and after much fruitless controversy England withdrew her acceptance. The frontier was thus left as unsettled as before. The ill-humour arising from this unsettlement was inflamed by a series of incidents highly disagreeable to the pride of the United States. An angry correspondence between the two Foreign Offices was in progress when Lord Melbourne resigned, and Lord Palmerston, who had hitherto been responsible for the negotiations, returned to the Opposition benches.

Peel and Aberdeen resolved to compose all questions at issue between this country and the United States. For this purpose they sent on a special embassy Lord Ashburton, who had married an American lady, and was a warm friend to America. Ashburton left England in the February of 1842 and spent the whole summer in negotiation. By the Treaty of Washington, signed in the August of the same year, he procured a settlement of the frontier which gave us rather a larger share of the debateable ground than we had accepted from the King of the Netherlands. The same treaty determined other disputes of less consequence, and Ashburton's tact subdued the irritation of the Americans. In England and in the United States public men were found to denounce the treaty as a humiliating surrender. But even if it did not do justice to our claims, it obtained as much as could have been obtained without entering on a war, in which success must have been barren and defeat ruinous.

Following on the news of the Treaty of Washington there came the news of the happy termination of two Eastern wars. Soon after the formation of the Ministry it was resolved to recall Lord Auckland and to make Lord Ellenborough Governor-General of India. Lord Ellenborough arrived in Calcutta on the 28th of February

1842, and immediately applied himself to finishing the
war with Afghanistan begun by Lord Auckland. He
breathed fresh vigour into the administration and the
army. Ghuznee was stormed, Cabul was once more
occupied, the prisoners taken by the Afghans in the
year before were recovered, and the British armies re-
treated with honour if without profit from an invasion
which should never have been undertaken. At the
same time our first war with China was ended by a
peace which was profitable if not honourable. These
wars the Government of Sir Robert Peel had inherited
from their predecessors. By their termination, and
by the adjustment of our differences with America,
peace was confirmed at once in the East and in the
West.

Peel and his colleagues had done what they could for
the prosperity of the United Kingdom. But a healing
policy cannot produce its effect all at once. The
commencement of the year 1843 found the people
still suffering, and Peel more unpopular than ever.
Between the discontent of his followers, and the furious
attack of the Anti-Corn Law League, he was severely
tried in strength and temper. An incident which
happened about this time gave a violent shock to his
nerves. On the 21st of January his private secretary,
Mr. Edward Drummond, was shot in Parliament Street
by a man named Daniel Macnaghten. Mr. Drummond
was not in any way conspicuous, nor had he given
offence to any person. People hastily assumed that
Macnaghten had intended to kill Sir Robert Peel.
This is doubtful; for Macnaghten was so infirm in
mind that he might well have had no purpose in his
crime. But Peel seems to have believed that he had
been the assassin's mark, and that the act was sug-

gested by the violent language so freely employed in the Free Trade agitation.

Parliament began its labours on the 2nd of February. In the debate on Lord Howick's motion for a Committee of the whole House to consider the depression of the manufacturing interests, Sir Robert took occasion to refer to Mr. Cobden's statement, made both in the House and elsewhere, that he held Sir Robert individually responsible for the distress of the country. Sir Robert went on to say that he would never let himself be moved by menaces, wherever uttered, to adopt a course—— The rest of the sentence was drowned in the tumult which followed these words. Cobden immediately rose to explain that he had said, not that the right honourable gentleman was personally responsible, but that the right honourable gentleman was responsible by virtue of his office—a distinction somewhat too fine to make much impression on an excited House of Commons. The disorder which continued hindered Cobden from explaining himself further, and Peel, after repeating what he had said, went on to make one of his characteristic speeches, about the time and caution necessary for applying even the soundest general principles to the complex affairs of a vast community. Nothing could be more temperate or business-like. In the course of the debate, Lord John Russell took occasion to disclaim for himself and his friends the construction which Peel and his friends had placed upon Cobden's language. At the close of the debate Cobden again rose to explain, and Peel received his explanation in the tone in which such explanations are commonly received. Cobden would, of course, have shrunk with horror from the idea of recommending assassination ; but Peel was probably sincere in his unusual

10

outburst of passion. Gentlemen whose friends have been shot, apparently by somebody who wanted to shoot them, are apt to be excessively peevish, and a peevish man will readily believe anything that can feed his ill-humour.

The Budget of 1843 was in no way remarkable. The Budget of the previous year, so masterly in design, had not been perfectly accurate in calculation. Peel had overrated the elasticity of the revenue derived from indirect taxation, and he had assumed that the whole of the income tax due would be collected within the current year. In the spring of 1843 he learned that the Customs and Excise had produced £2,000,000 less than he had expected, whilst of the income tax only one half had been received. It was some set-off to this disappointment that the income tax had produced one-third more than the sum estimated by Peel. Nevertheless, Peel found that instead of the surplus on which he had reckoned, he had to meet a deficit of £2,500,000. As he could not offer any reforms comparable to those of the year before, he left Goulburn to make the customary statement. It announced a slight further reduction on the duties on timber, and promised a lessening of expenditure, which had been made possible by the conclusion of peace with China, and the settlement of disputes with the United States.

In this year the prohibition on the export of tools and machinery was repealed, and the import of Canadian flour was allowed, subject to a nominal duty.

The debates on the condition of the mass of the people now became more frequent than ever. The generous labours of Lord Ashley were bearing fruit. In the Session of 1842, Lord Ashley had carried an Act forbidding the employment of women, and limiting the employment of children, in mines and collieries. In the next Session he proposed an Address to the Crown praying for measures to further the education of the working classes. This Address was carried with such general enthusiasm that the Government undertook to act upon it. In pursuance of their promise, the Home Secretary brought in a Bill at once to lessen the labour and to provide for the education of young persons employed in factories. He proposed that children under eight years should not be employed at all; that children under thirteen years should not work more than six and a half hours in the day; and that males under eighteen and females under twenty-one years should not work more than twelve hours, and should have a half-holiday on Saturday. Children between eight and thirteen years were required to attend school, and schools sufficient for their use were to be provided by the district, assisted by the State. The schools were to be vested in two trustees, of whom the clergyman of the parish was to be one. The appointment of masters and inspectors, as well as the choice of school books, was to be given to the Bishop of the Diocese.

Instantly a clamour arose like that which filled Satan's ears when he stood on the verge of chaos. With much reason the Catholics and the Dissenters complained of the predominance in the new schools which the Home Secretary had reserved to the Church of England. With no reason at all fanatical churchmen complained that the Church had not been made more predominant. With characteristic blindness the politicians of the Manchester school denounced interference with the labour of young persons. Graham had only a general sentiment of benevolence behind

10 *

him, and in front he had to encounter the fiercest of human passions. First he tried to appease by concessions the fury of the churches; but whilst he did hardly anything to conciliate one party, he gave the deepest offence to another. Then he threw away the clauses dealing with education; and then he gave up the remaining clauses. Thus was sacrificed to the general unreason a Bill which concerned, as much as any Bill possibly could concern, the happiness of the people and the strength of the State.

Only in one quarter had Peel's Ministry done nothing to lighten the difficulties of the State. Whatever the other failings of Lord Melbourne's Ministry, it had always handled Irish affairs in a conciliatory spirit. It had shown a disposition to meet the wishes of the Irish Catholics, and it had maintained a loose alliance with O'Connell. The dissolution of the Whig Government had freed O'Connell from any ties to an English party, but the general election had proved his weakness in Ireland. Although he renewed his agitation for the repeal of the Union, he would hardly have done much without the help of the Young Ireland party, which had high ability, youthful energy, and overflowing enthusiasm. The time was favourable to the spread of their views. Peel was no bigot, but his Irish connection was made up mostly of aggressive Protestants. Under his administration, although there might be no specific acts of tyranny, the Irish Catholics felt that they were not liberally treated, and discontent readily took form and shape in the national movement. The agitation attracted so much notice that in the session of 1843 the Government was formally asked in each House what it meant to do. Peel in the one House and Wellington in the other replied that they were resolved to maintain the Legislative Union. With regard to the Irish Arms Act, which had been passed in 1838, the Cabinet decided, instead of merely continuing it, to strengthen it with fresh provisions. This decision caused them a great deal of trouble. The new Arms Bill led to long and angry debates, in the course of which Disraeli first ventured to announce his rebellion against Peel's authority. Meantime the Government could offer no remedy for any of the deep-seated miseries of Ireland. This year saw, indeed, the appointment of the famous Devon Commission, whose report first went to the root of the matter. But the debates initiated by moderate men like Ward and Smith O'Brien had no result. When the session ended, the agitation was more angry and formidable than ever. A series of immense meetings culminated in the announcement of a meeting more enormous still, to be held at Clontarf on the 8th of October. A proclamation in the *Gazette* forbade the meeting, and O'Connell yielded to the prohibition. He was, notwithstanding, arrested on a charge of conspiracy and sedition. His trial was deferred until February of the following year; but the agitation subsided with the arrest of its chief.

By this time the poverty and depression which had prevailed when Peel first took office were giving place to abundance and activity. The harvest of 1842 had been good, it was equalled by the harvest of 1843; the farmers were again flourishing and the manufacturers again had plenty of orders. The rates were relieved by the decrease of paupers, and the revenue flowed in beyond Goulburn's hopes or calculations. Peel regained his ascendancy over men's minds as his policy began to show its effects.

How successful that policy had been appeared by the financial statement made in the session of 1844. The revenue of the past year had been estimated at £50,150,000 ; it actually rose to £52,835,000. The actual expenditure had been £48,669,000, whilst the estimate had been for £49,338,000. The surplus thus amounted to £3,400,000. This and a smaller surplus from the year ending in April of 1843 was enough to clear off the deficit of the year before, and to cover the sacrifice of the import and export duties upon wool, as well as the reduction of the duties on glass, coffee, foreign sugar produced by free labour, and sundry articles of less consequence. At the same time the conversion of a great part of the National Debt attested the confidence inspired by Peel's government. In the course of his three years of office the price of Consols had risen from $89\frac{3}{4}$ to $99\frac{3}{4}$. But nearly £250,000,000 of the National Debt still bore interest at the rate of $3\frac{1}{2}$ per cent. This sum was now converted into a stock paying $3\frac{1}{4}$ per cent. for the next ten years, and 3 per cent. after that date. Although Goulburn did not increase the capital of the National Debt, he needed only £250,000 to pay off those who declined to take the new stock, whilst he got an immediate relief of £625,000 and a prospective relief of £1,250,000 a year. This was the largest and most successful conversion of the National Debt effected before our own time.

The Budget was less noticed than the Bill brought in by Peel himself on the occasion of the renewal of the charter of the Bank of England. The growth of commerce, and in particular the establishment of numerous joint-stock banks had given a dangerous impulse to issues of paper money, which were not then restricted by law. Even the Bank of England did not observe any fixed proportion between the amount of notes which it issued and the amount of bullion which it kept in reserve. When introducing this subject to the House of Commons, Peel remarked that within the last twenty years there had been four periods when a contraction of issues had been necessary in order to maintain the convertibility of paper, and that in none of these had the Bank of England acted with vigour equal to the emergency. In the latest of these periods, from June of 1838 to June of 1839, the amount of bullion in the Bank had fallen to little more than £4,000,000, whilst the total of paper in circulation had risen to little less than £30,000,000. It was clear, therefore, that the paper which professed to be convertible might, in a crisis, prove inconvertible, and that there was no security for the making of those cash payments which Peel's own Act of 1819 had required. That the danger was not imaginary was shown by the catastrophe which took place in the United States in the year 1837, when every bank stopped payment, and one hundred and eighty banks were totally ruined. This country itself had not escaped an experience similar, although less terrible.

In this instance again Peel was not the first to devise the methods which he adopted. Mr. Jones Loyd, afterwards Lord Overstone, who impressed the learned with his tracts and the vulgar with his riches, had advised the principal changes in the law relating to the issue of paper money which Peel effected by the Bank Charter Act. These changes were three in number. The first was to separate totally the two departments of the Bank of England, the banking department and the issue department. The banking department was left to be managed as best the wisdom of the directors could devise for the profit of the shareholders. The issue department was placed under regulations which deprived the Bank of any discretion in its management, and may almost be said to have made it a department of the State. The second innovation was to limit the issue of paper by the Bank of England to an amount proportioned to the value of its assets. The Bank was allowed to issue notes to the amount of £14,000,000 against Government securities in its possession. The Government owed the Bank a debt of £11,000,000, besides which the Bank held Exchequer Bills. But the amount over £14,000,000 which the Bank could issue was not, henceforwards, to be more than the equivalent of the bullion in its possession. By this means it was made certain that the Bank would be able to give coin for any of its notes which might be presented to it. The third innovation was to limit the issues of the country banks. The power of issuing notes was denied to any private or joint-stock banks founded after the date of the Act. It was recognized in those banks which already possessed it, but limited to a total sum of £8,500,000, the average quantity of such notes which had been in circulation during the years immediately preceding. It was provided that if any of the banks which retained this privilege should cease to exist or to issue notes, the Bank of England should be entitled to increase its note circulation by a sum equal to two-thirds of the amount of the former issues of the bank which ceased to issue paper. The Bank of England was required in this contingency to augment the reserve fund.

By Acts passed in the succeeding year, the principles of the English Bank Charter Act were applied to Scotland and Ireland, with such modifications as the peculiar circumstances of those kingdoms required. The Bank Charter Act has ever since been the subject of voluminous and contradictory criticism, both by political economists and by men of business. Without presuming to offer any confident opinion on questions which learning and experience seem not yet to have decided beyond dispute, a plain man may think that, in principle, a statute which limits the issue of notes to such an amount as will certainly be convertible must be sound, and that, in practice, it must have proved on the whole advantageous, since after more than forty years' trial it has been left in force ; and to the objection that its suspension has at certain times been found necessary, he may reply that a possible need for suspension was foreseen by those who recommended the measure, that it has been suspended only for three brief periods, and that only in one of those periods has the Bank made any use of the powers thus bestowed. In the crisis of 1857, the Bank did exert these powers by issuing notes to a considerable amount. In the crisis of 1847, as in the crisis of 1865, the mere knowledge that the Bank possessed them was enough to restore the confidence of the commercial world.

Early in the session of 1844 Graham introduced anew his Factory Bill of the year before, without the education clauses which had caused so much bitterness. The Bill passed the first and second reading quietly enough ; but in committee it encountered new perils. Lord Ashley's amendment, fixing at ten the hours of labour for young persons and for women, was so numerously supported that Graham withdrew his Bill. He then brought in a second Bill, which differed rather in form than in substance from the first. Ashley again moved an amendment in favour of the limit of ten hours, and

Fielden, the member for Oldham, went farther, and declared that a day of eight hours was as much as should be allowed. But the Ministry were obdurate. Sir Robert Peel himself argued that any further limitation of the hours of labour would disable our manufacturers from competing with the manufacturers of other countries, would reduce the sum available for wages, and would end by putting the operative class in a worse than their actual condition. Subsequent experience has not confirmed these fears. The improvement in strength, character, and intelligence which has followed upon the abridgment of the hours of labour seems to have made good the loss which might have been expected to follow that abridgment. Sir Robert cannot be severely blamed, however, for a miscalculation common to so many of the most competent authorities. His reasons prevailed somewhat, and his authority more, with the House, which rejected Ashley's proposal by an immense majority. In these divisions the ties of party were little respected. Many manufacturing Liberals, and some economic Radicals, offered the most obstinate resistance to that which we should now consider the popular cause. Many Conservatives who had no unconscious bias of interest, did not love the manufacturers, and did not dislike a paternal government, supported Ashley against the Ministers of their choice. The Bill which had caused so much heat in the House of Commons passed quietly enough through the House of Lords. It was a defective measure, but we should not have secured even so much if the Manchester school had not been counterpoised by the landed interest.

The spirit of fairness which Peel had infused into the

councils of his party was illustrated in this session by
a series of Acts designed to protect unpopular religious
persuasions. The Act which secured their chapels to
the Unitarians had a curious history. A certain Lady
Hewley, who died at the end of the seventeenth century,
had devised her estates to trustees for the purpose of
supporting godly preachers of Christ's gospel. In the
course of time the trustees came to be mostly Unitarians, who gave effect to Lady Hewley's wishes by
spending the revenue of her trust in the maintenance
of Unitarian chapels and clergymen. Their action was
impeached in a court of equity, and at length came
before the House of Lords. The Lords pronounced
that there had been a misappropriation of Lady
Hewley's trust. Lady Hewley had not been a Unitarian ; she believed in the Trinity as firmly as did
St. Athanasius. Even if she had been a Unitarian it would not have availed; for she died more
than a hundred years before toleration had been extended to a sect so remarkable for virtue and piety ; and
it could not be supposed that the State would enforce
a trust for the benefit of those whom it would not
tolerate. Thus the judgment of the House of Lords
was as certainly right in law as it was vexatious to the
Unitarians. But the Unitarians were not the only
dissenters to take alarm. The Chancellor, therefore,
brought in a Bill providing that in such cases an unbroken enjoyment of twenty-five years should secure
the trustees against molestation. When the Bill came
down to the House of Commons it was welcomed by
the best men of all parties, and rapidly passed through
all the stages.

Another Act quieted all doubts respecting the legality
of marriages celebrated by Presbyterian ministers in

Ireland.   A third redressed a grievous wrong which had
been done to the Irish Catholics.   Until the time of
which we are speaking, all bequests to charitable uses
made in Ireland had been administered by a body which
was wholly Protestant.   Catholics had been unable to
devise real property for the benefit of their clergy.   They
were now empowered to do so, and the control of charitable bequests was transferred to a body consisting of
Catholics and Protestants in equal numbers, assisted by
a Catholic secretary.   Finally, a number of obsolete
penal laws which still appeared in the statute book, a
disgrace to the nation and an insult to Catholic citizens,
were formally repealed.

About this time a difference between England and
France threatened nothing less than war.   The adventures of Mr. Pritchard have long since been overtaken by oblivion.   Here it is enough to say that
Pritchard was a missionary and English consul at
Tahiti; that when a French officer annexed Tahiti,
Pritchard, with the help of a man-of-war, restored
the native Queen; that the French disavowed their
officer; that the English disavowed Pritchard; that
Pritchard, after resigning his consular function, went
on giving the French what trouble he could; that
the French roughly arrested Pritchard, imprisoned
him, and at length sent him back to England; that
England was in a flame; that France was in a flame;
that Peel demanded the restoration of Pritchard to
Tahiti and the recall of the French consul and com-
mandant; that Guizot neither could nor would consent
to this demand; that Pritchard hinted he would prefer
a round sum of money to any other satisfaction, and that
the King of France was so pleased to end a foolish
quarrel that he paid the suggested compensation out of

his own civil list. When Parliament was prorogued the Chancellor was able to announce that our grievances had been redressed. About the same time the French, by a series of·speedy and successful operations, brought to a close their war with Morocco, which had awakened suspicions of a design to subdue that country. As they annexed no territory no cause for umbrage remained. King Louis Philippe returned in October the visit which he had received from Queen Victoria in September of the preceding year. He was made welcome by the public, and nobly entertained at Windsor. These royal civilities gave opportunities of intimate conversation to Guizot and Aberdeen, which strengthened their mutual understanding.

This year did not pass without some incidents extremely annoying to the Cabinet. Lord Ellenborough had quieted Gwalior, annexed Scinde, and restored the authority of the British name; but he provoked so much criticism and gave so much offence to the Board of Directors that he had to be recalled from India. In his stead Hardinge became Governor-General, whilst Sidney Herbert took Sir Henry's place as Secretary at War. O'Connell had been tried and convicted for sedition, but the circumstances of his trial threw doubt on its fairness, and his conviction was quashed by the House of Lords. The public had been thrown into a ferment by Mazzini's petition to the House of Commons, complaining that his letters had been opened by order of the Home Secretary. Such a stretch of authority was made more odious by the general belief that Sir James Graham had acted in the interest of the Austrian Government and in concert with the Austrian police. Graham was able to show that the right of opening letters which passed through the Post Office had been

claimed and exercised by all his predecessors at the
Home Office. He also satisfied secret committees of
both Houses that he had not abused this right in the
interest of any foreign power. But the use of such
a right must always be open to suspicion. Lastly,
Peel himself had put the deference of his followers
to a sharp trial. We have seen that he made the
House reverse its decision on one of the principal
questions relating to the Factory Bill. Soon afterwards he obliged it to recall a vote on the Sugar
Duties. The advocates of Protection had persuaded the
Whigs to vote for a resolution in favour of lessening
the duties on sugar raised by free labour, whether in our
own colonies or elsewhere, and the resolution had been
carried against the Ministers by a majority of twenty.
The Ministers resolved to insist upon a reversal of this
vote, and if unsuccessful then to resign. Peel announced
their resolve in a speech much too masterful in tone,
which provoked a clever and insulting retort from
Disraeli. He carried his point, but not without a wrench
to the feelings of many Conservatives. A little later he
tried with imperfect success to soothe them. Yet in
spite of mistakes and misfortunes he had gained in
authority during this year. The Bank Charter Act had
added to his great reputation as a financier. The
development of railways, so warmly recommended by him,
had created a prosperity too exuberant to last, but,
whilst it lasted, conducive to the peace and contentment
of the kingdom. All agitation, whether for the repeal
of the Union, the repeal of the Corn Laws, or the
enactment of the people's charter, seemed to have lost
much of its former energy. Abroad it was generally
believed that Peel would retain office as long as his
bodily strength should prove equal to his labours. At

home Peel was not popular; but he was felt to be the fittest man for his place.

In 1845, as in 1842, Peel took charge of the Budget. Such had been the thrift of the administration, and such the prosperity of the nation, that he was able to promise a surplus of £5,000,000. With this surplus he might have remitted the income-tax, but he preferred to ask for its renewal and apply the proceeds to fiscal reform. He calculated that for the incoming year the revenue would be £53,100,000, whilst the expenditure would be £49,690,000, bearing a surplus of £3,409,000. Even in the reduced tariff no less than 813 distinct kinds of commodities were numbered; 430 of these were struck out at one blow, and so insignificant were most of them, that the total loss to the revenue was only £320,000 a year. The duties upon sugar were reduced at the estimated cost of £1,300,000. The duty on raw cotton, which in the preceding year had brought in £680,000, was abolished altogether. Two alterations in the excise duties contributed, the one to the promotion of commerce, and the other to the spread of comfort. The auction duty was so oppressive that exemptions from it had been granted in thirty-two different classes of cases, and evasions intercepted most of the revenue which exemptions had spared. It was now abolished, at a loss of £300,000. A like fate overtook the duty on glass, which had been doubled since 1815, and amounted to upwards of 200 per cent. on the value. Even the window tax had done less harm to the poor than was done by the glass duty. Yet it produced only £640,000 a year. By the reduction or extinction of so many imposts, Peel had used up almost all the surplus assured by a continuance of the income-tax. Although it was impossible to lessen our army and necessary to increase our navy, Peel trusted that the encouragement given to industry and expenditure would put the State in a position to meet all its charges.

Once more the great Minister overbore all criticism and obtained the acceptance of all his proposals. From the first moment of the session, however, he found that his enemies were taking heart. No reform could disarm the Whig opposition, whose vocation was censure. No concession could appease the League politicians, whose one idea was absolute free trade. But every concession and every reform alienated some obstinate or timid or interested or stupid follower. And there was one politician more dangerous to Peel than any ancient foe or vulgar malcontent; a politician of genius sharpened by ambition and envenomed by antipathy, who knew exactly when and where and how to deliver his penetrating blow. Disraeli's revolt against Peel was prompted not merely by the desire of filling Peel's place, but also by the utter contradiction between Peel's nature and his own. Had Peel shown civility to Disraeli, he might have delayed, he would scarcely have averted, the breach. As he neglected Disraeli, it began to be felt less than two years after the Conservatives had regained power.

Early in this session Mr. Duncombe renewed his complaints as to the opening of letters in the Post Office. Disraeli supported Duncombe on this occasion. From a defence of his own conduct in this matter he artfully passed to an impeachment of the general conduct of the Minister, and ended with a passage of the most cutting sarcasm. In a previous encounter Peel had applied to Disraeli Canning's familiar lines:—

> Give me the avowed, the erect, the manly foe,
> Firm I can meet, perhaps may turn the blow;

> But of all plagues, good heaven, thy wrath can send,
> Save me, oh save me from the candid friend.

Referring to this quotation Disraeli said :—

The right honourable gentleman knows what the introduction of a great name does in debate, how important is its effect and occasionally how electrical. He never refers to any author who is not great and sometimes loved—Canning, for example. That is a name never to be mentioned, I am sure, in the House of Commons, without emotion. We all admire his genius ; we all, at least most of us, deplore his untimely end ; and we all sympathise with him in his fierce struggle with supreme prejudice and sublime mediocrity, with inveterate foes and with—candid friends. The right honourable gentleman may be sure that a quotation from such an authority will always tell. Some lines, for example, upon friendship, written by Mr. Canning and quoted by the right honourable gentleman. The theme, the poet, the speaker, what a felicitous combination ! Its effect in debate must be overwhelming ; and I am sure, were it addressed to me, all that would remain for me would be thus publicly to congratulate the right honourable gentleman, not only on his ready memory but on his courageous conscience.

The accusation was unjust; the sarcasm was admirable. Peel paid his assailant the compliment of a reply which, however sound in substance, was not effective in form. For bitter personal contention he was at no time well fitted. Now that he was far advanced in middle life, laden with countless labours, and habituated to that profound respect which the House generally pays to the consummate man of business, he was almost helpless against a young, vigorous enemy, who was withheld by no feeling of remorse, and gained both influence and reputation by every fresh attack.

Such an enemy never wants opportunity to renew his assault. A motion by Mr. Miles, the member for Bristol, to the effect that the relief of the agricultural interest should be regarded in the application of surplus revenue, was opposed by the Prime Minister in a speech

11

which showed how little he really dissented from the doctrine of the Manchester school. The only question on which they were really at issue was a question of time. Disraeli tried to alarm the party of Protection in that famous speech which described Sidney Herbert as Peel's valet, and the Conservative Government as an organized hypocrisy.

Peel's fiscal measures were bold and ample; his Irish measures modest and timid; but the resistance provoked by his Irish measures far exceeded the resistance provoked by his fiscal measures. He had always concerned himself in the progress of enlightenment, and during his administration the annual grant for elementary education in England had been raised from £30,000 to £100,000 annually. He now wished to improve the education of the Catholic clergy and middle class in Ireland. His first step was to recommend an increase in the grant from the Treasury to Maynooth College. That college was the place of education for the great majority of the clergymen who were to serve the Church of the great majority of the people of Ireland. If the Established Church were not to be disestablished, nor even remodelled —and indefensible as was the position of that Church, neither disestablishment nor remodelling would have commended themselves to Peel, or could have been suggested by the leader of the Conservative party—then surely no man could complain that the State was to do something for the education of the Catholic clergy. So forcible was this consideration that as early as the year 1795 an annual grant had been made to the college at Maynooth. But this grant of £9,000 a year, although supplemented by the pious efforts of the Irish Catholics, was too little to maintain the college in a proper state. The buildings seemed mean to Englishmen familiar with the regal magnificence of Oxford and Cambridge; a stipend of £120 a year belied the title of professor, and an allowance of £23 was equally unsuited to the wants of a simple student. Peel proposed to raise the annual grant from £9,000 to £26,000, and to place it upon the Consolidated Fund instead of letting it depend on the chances of an annual vote. He also proposed to give £30,000 towards the erection of new buildings. These proposals raised a storm of fanaticism. The blind and bigoted Protestants of every denomination and of every class took up arms. Never since the agitation in favour of the Reform Bill was there known such holding of meetings, such declaiming, such signing of petitions, such contagious and effusive madness. For it was the mad element of the solid British character which manifested itself then, as on the occasion which prompted the Ecclesiastical Titles Bill. But the popular frenzy was unavailing against the resolution of the minister. Although some of his party rebelled and others would have liked to rebel, the main body still felt attachment for Sir Robert Peel, or at least felt the need of his services; and the Whigs could not do otherwise than support a measure in harmony with that tolerant and humane spirit which had inspired their best statesmen. The proposal could not be defeated, but the proposer could be worried.

To follow in detail the agitation provoked by the Maynooth Bill would be waste of time; but the utterances of one or two eminent men respecting it are remarkable. Mr. Gladstone approved of the Bill, but thought that his former professions would not allow him to remain a member of the Cabinet which brought it in; so he resigned his post and gave the Bill his support. O'Connell took care to enforce the moral that it

11 *

was he who had extorted this concession.   Disraeli
acted his worst part.   However sincere he might be in
disliking Peel, he could not have been animated by an
honest fanaticism.   His novels disclose a sentimental
admiration for the Catholic religion.   His speeches show
a clear insight into the state of Ireland.   Yet he opposed
the Bill, not on its merits, but on Peel's demerits.   On
the second reading he made a merely personal and
altogether mischievous speech.   Macaulay took a more
manly course ; he supported the Bill without hiding his
dislike of its proposers.   He concluded a very able
argument in favour of the grant to Maynooth with a
very eloquent peroration against the ministers.   With
the help of Macaulay and the Whigs who agreed with
him, the Government had a large majority on the
second reading.

The augmentation of the grant to Maynooth was
accompanied by the foundation of the Queen's Colleges.
Trinity College had long since admitted Catholics to
partake in its studies and receive its degrees ; but
Trinity College continued to be a Protestant University,
with a Protestant governing body, a majority of Protestant students, a Protestant tradition, and Protestant
religious instruction.   Besides, Trinity College, altogether apart from its constitution, was inadequate to
the wants of the country.   It was remote from many
of the most populous districts of Ireland, and the
education which it gave was more costly than suited the
means of many who were desirous to benefit by a liberal
education.   These reasons were enough to justify a
scheme for the foundation of three colleges, situate
respectively in Belfast, in Cork, and in Galway, which
were to be affiliated to a central university in Dublin,
and were to give instruction in all the principal branches

of secular knowledge. A sum of £100,000 was to be applied in the establishment of these colleges, and an annual sum finally fixed at £7,000 was to be applied to their maintenance. This project was opposed by those men of extreme views who had opposed the foundation of the National Schools. But it encountered no general resistance.

Another Act relieved the Jews from a disability un-wittingly imposed upon them by the Act which repealed the Test and Corporation Laws. We have seen that the declaration, substituted by that Act for the sacramental test, had been made more emphatic by the addition of the words "on the true faith of a Christian." These words could not honestly be uttered by any Jew. The necessity of uttering them was now taken away, and Jews became eligible for municipal office, although not yet for seats in the House of Commons.

The events of this session had gone far to dissolve the Conservative Party. It was apparent that Peel's fiscal policy could end in nothing less than Free Trade, and people began to conjecture when he would get rid of the Corn Laws altogether. It seemed not improbable that the Maynooth grant was the first step towards making a provision for the Catholic clergy of Ireland, a measure often recommended, but hateful to zealous Protestants. The dullest or most faithful Conservative could no longer help seeing that the Premier was a Liberal; that the Ministry was one of Tory men and Whig measures; and that it was not fulfilling the purpose of the greater part of those who had placed it in power. This know-ledge naturally bred discontent, which often threatened open mutiny. At one time the ministers expected to be driven from office on the Maynooth question; and even after they had succeeded with the help of their enemies, they felt no assurance of prolonged safety. Yet they had one or two circumstances in their favour. Although half the House of Commons would gladly have displaced Sir Robert, nobody had a reasonable hope of being able to carry on the Government in his place. Although parties were fuming with rage, the country was listless. It had forgotten the excitement of talking politics in the excitement of getting money. It was possessed with the one idea of making new railways, and this idea found employment for all the labour and capital available. Such times of commercial enthusiasm are halcyon days for Cabinets ; and happy is the Cabinet which gets its dismissal before they end in bankruptcy, despair, and the blind passion of revenge.

Thus it happened that Peel's administration was, in the autumn of 1845, nearly as strong as it had ever been. The calamity which was to overturn it was then just beginning. In the beginning of August, Peel first heard of the disease among the potatoes, which had appeared in the Isle of Wight. A little later on Mr. Parker, a potato merchant, wrote to Graham to say that the potato crop had failed in Kent. Like news soon came in from all quarters, especially from Ireland, where four millions of human beings fed chiefly if not entirely upon potatoes. At first the ministers were slow to believe in the extent of the calamity. At the end of September, Graham expressed to Peel the hope that the failure of the crop in Ireland, although serious, would be by no means general. But in the second week of October the reports from Ireland became truly alarming. On the 15th of October, Peel wrote to the Lord Lieutenant respecting the remedy for the approaching evil. He suggested that the remedy must be " the removal of all impediments to the import of all kinds of human food—

that is, the total and absolute repeal for ever of all duties on all articles of subsistence."

As things continued to grow worse, a Cabinet Council was held on the 31st of October at Peel's house in Whitehall Gardens, where he was then confined by illness. When Peel had read to his colleagues all the information which he had received, the meeting adjourned till the following day. Peel circulated a memorandum, in which he declared that under this pressure the Corn Laws must be modified or suspended, by an act of the Crown or by an Act of Parliament. Differences of opinion appeared in the discussion which followed, and it was resolved to meet again on the 6th of November. Meantime the prospect grew more and more gloomy. A public meeting held at Dublin, under the auspices of the Duke of Leinster, passed resolutions declaring famine and pestilence imminent, and demanding that the ports should be opened. Unsought advice poured in upon the Premier from all quarters. Just before the Cabinet met he informed the Queen that grave dissensions were not unlikely. He circulated among his colleagues a second memorandum, which proposed at once to suspend the Corn Laws by Order in Council, and afterwards to summon Parliament for the purpose of obtaining an indemnity. It further proposed that they should recommend a modification of the Corn Laws to the extent of admitting maize and colonial corn free, and of revising the duties upon other kinds of corn. The majority of the Cabinet were willing to suspend the Corn Laws by Order in Council, but not to modify them permanently; and so the third Cabinet Council held in one week parted without doing anything. It had done nothing, but it had sealed the fate of the Corn Laws.

Without either resigning or withdrawing his proposals, Peel resolved to wait for fresh intelligence. His new ideas and the disputes in the Cabinet must have been guessed by the public. He was advised by one distinguished person to announce, in the last session of the existing Parliament, that he would propose to a new Parliament the immediate or remote repeal of the Corn Laws. By adopting this course Peel, his adviser wrote, would escape the imputation of betraying party attachments, and of inflicting a heavy, perhaps a deadly blow, upon constitutional government. Peel has told us what reflections were raised in his mind by the letter giving this advice.

> It appeared to me that all these considerations—the betrayal of party attachments—the maintenance of the honour of public men—the real interests of the cause of constitutional government—must all be determined by the answer which the heart and conscience of a responsible minister might give to the question, What is that course which the public interest really demands ? What is the course best calculated, under present circumstances, to diminish the risk of great suffering and the discontent which will be the consequence of that suffering, if timely precautions, which might be taken, be neglected ?

Peel had already commissioned two eminent men of science, Professor Lindley, and Dr. Playfair, to visit Ireland and inquire into the loss sustained. They reported that at least half of the potato crop had perished, and that a quarter of the residue would be required for sowing. Such bad tidings came from so many other quarters that Peel resolved, in concert with the Chancellor of the Exchequer and the Home Secretary, to order large purchases of Indian corn in America. These purchases were made on behalf of the Government, but through the house of Baring, lest publicity should heighten terror. Meantime the Anti-Corn Law League was roused to new life. Aided by all the feelings of fear, of pity, and of indignation which were excited by the inactivity of the State in the face of a danger so appalling, it strained every nerve to frighten the Cabinet, and to drive it into some measure more far-reaching than an Order in Council, which, by suspend-ing the Corn Laws, might enable them to outlive the crisis. Behind the Anti-Corn Law League the Whigs advanced to the charge. Lord John Russell was at length convinced that his plan of a moderate fixed duty on corn could not be carried out, and he declared in favour of absolute Free Trade in his famous letter to the electors of London, written on the 21st of November. Not all the skill of all the politicians of the United Kingdom could now have restored the Corn Laws to that security which they had when November began.

On the 25th the Cabinet met once more to settle instructions for the Lord Lieutenant and the Commis-sion which had been appointed to organize the relief of distress. Peel thought that before these instruc-tions were finally adopted, the Cabinet should be acquainted with his opinion as to further measures. In a memorandum which was passed round the Cabinet, he insisted that a suspension of the Corn Laws must lead to a complete reconsideration of them. In another memorandum he urged the necessity of a suspension. By this time Peel's colleagues began to be aware of the change in his views. Great was their alarm and agitation. Even the faithful Goulburn argued against the repeal of the Corn Laws. Wellington inclined to agree with Goulburn, but he sacrificed his inclination to his favourite maxim that the Queen's Government must be carried on.

In respect to my own course [he wrote] my only object in public life is to support Sir Robert Peel's administration of the government for the Queen. A good government for the country is more important than Corn Laws or any other consideration, and as long as Sir Robert Peel possesses the confidence of the Queen and of the public, and he has the strength to perform the duties, his administration of the government must be supported. My own judgment would lead me to support the Cabinet. Sir Robert Peel may think that his position in Parliament and in the public view requires that the course should be taken which he recommends; and if that should be the case I earnestly recommend that the Cabinet should support him, and I for one declare that I will do so.

The Cabinet met again on the 2nd of December to consider a fresh memorandum, in which Peel reminded his colleagues that he had kept himself unpledged on the subject of the Corn Laws, and avowed that he was in favour of the gradual but complete removal of all duties on imported corn. During the next few days everything hung in suspense. So great was the authority of Peel, so impressive was the example of Wellington, that at one time the Cabinet seemed almost unanimous to accept the project of its chief; but Stanley and Buccleugh recoiled, and their recoil was decisive. Thinking that success was doubtful, and that failure must be pernicious, Peel went down to Osborne on the 5th of December, and asked Her Majesty to release him from her service.

Having accepted Peel's resignation, the Queen summoned Russell to her assistance. Russell came to Osborne on the 11th, and returned to town on the same day to consult his colleagues. In town he was visited by Graham, who also wrote him a letter promising that he and Peel would give their general support to the measures indicated in the Edinburgh letter. But Russell wanted more precise assurances of help. He wanted Peel to receive and consider the outline of a bill dealing with the Corn Laws, and to say whether or no he could bind himself to promote it. In default of this he went to Windsor to resign his commission of forming of a Cabinet. At his request the Queen wrote to Peel to inquire whether the dissenting members of his Cabinet would undertake to form an administration. Peel, after due inquiry, wrote to the Queen that they were not prepared to do so, and for himself declined to do what Russell had desired. Upon consideration of the altered state of affairs, Russell returned to Windsor and told Her Majesty that he was willing to undertake the Government in spite of Peel's refusal. He was then resolved upon immediate as well as total repeal of the Corn Laws. But an unforeseen obstacle arose. Earl Grey felt such an aversion for Lord Palmerston's policy as Foreign Secretary that he refused to join any ministry of which Palmerston was a member, and Russell, knowing how critical was the occasion, and how exclusive his party, did not venture to form a Government which should leave out either Palmerston or Grey. A second time within one week, Russell declared himself unequal to the task enjoined him. On the 20th Peel went to Windsor, and the Queen said: "So far from taking leave of you, Sir Robert, I must require you to withdraw your resignation, and to remain in my service." At the same time she offered him space to reflect; but he, thinking that what must be done should be done quickly, at once declared himself ready to serve, and on returning to town assembled his late colleagues that same night. All were there except Lord Granville Somerset. Peel declared his resolution to meet Parliament, Stanley persevered in resigning, Buccleugh wavered, but all the rest agreed to follow their chief. The die had now been cast, and the Conservative Cabinet was committed to the task of passing

a law repugnant to the Conservative party.   In a day
or two Buccleugh declared to Peel his resolution to
support the Government, although he could not approve its proposals.   He became Lord President; the
Earl of Haddington succeeded him as Lord Privy Seal;
Lord Dalhousie entered the Cabinet, and Mr. Gladstone took Lord Stanley's place at the Colonial Office.

On the 22nd January 1846 the Session of Parliament
was opened by the Queen in person.   The Speech from
the Throne scarcely satisfied the keen impatience with
which the public had awaited a declaration of the policy
of the Government.   Vague and cautious in its terms,
it turned chiefly on Ireland ; on the increase of crime
and the approach of distress.   It announced remedial
measures for both evils, and recommended to the consideration of the Houses the possibility of carrying
further the commercial legislation which had already
proved so successful.

When the Address had been moved and seconded, Peel
rose to make the most momentous statement which he
had made for seventeen years.   He began by saying
that the failure of the potato crop had been the immediate cause of the dissolution of the Government in the
preceding December.   But he hastened to add that the
importance of this cause must not be overrated ; that his
opinions on the subject of Protection had undergone a
change.   The natural presumption, he said, is in favour
of free and unrestricted importation.   Former concessions to the principle of Free Trade had resulted in a
remarkable growth of commerce, unattended with any
injury to the interests of agriculture.   Even after the
change in his own beliefs, however, he had not thought
himself the proper person to propose a change in the
Corn Laws.   He then explained the circumstances

which had led him to remain in power and to enter upon the course which he was taking. It cannot be said that this, the second part of his speech, was as luminous as the first had been. He next addressed himself to the accusation which had been made and was often to be repeated against him, the accusation of falsehood to the party which he led and to the interests which he was pledged to protect. Here personal feeling warmed him to unusual eloquence, and inspired a vigorous peroration.

I have over and over again attempted to define the relations in which I conceive myself to stand with respect to party, to my country, and to my Sovereign, and it is necessary that I should again describe that relation. I see it over and over again repeated that I am under a personal obligation for holding the great office which I have the honour to occupy, I see it over and over again repeated that I was placed in that position by a party, and that the party which elevated me to my present position is powerful enough also to displace me. I see constantly put forth allusions of the power of those men to remove me from office. I am afraid that with respect to holding the office that I hold there is a very material difference between the extent of the obligation and the amount of the penalty. I am not under an obligation to any man, or to any body of men, for being compelled to submit to the sacrifices which I have submitted to and to undergo the official duties and labours which I have undertaken. I do not underrate the distinction and importance of the position; but let us understand—and I am speaking not for myself, but for the many honourable men who have preceded me of different parties—let us understand what is the nature of the obligation we owe for being placed in office. As I said before, I do not undervalue the distinction and the power which are attached to the occupation of that offce; but what, I ask, is its real value? It does not consist in the power of distributing honours or conferring appointments. That power, it is true is inseparable from the office of Prime Minister and cannot be separated from it without injuring its authority; but the power of giving the highest rewards and the highest offices is constantly accompanied by the invidious duty of selection and the disappointment of those who may not have been selected. For my part, I value power not one farthing for any such privilege. I have served four sovereigns—George III. and his three successors. In the reign of George III. the office which I held was so subordinate that it was impossible my services could have attracted his notice; but, as I have said, I also served his three successors—George IV. as Regent and King, King William IV., and Queen Victoria, and during the reigns of those Sovereigns it has been my lot to hold some of the highest offices in the State. I served each of those Sovereigns at critical times and in critical circumstances. I did so with constant truth to each, and I constantly said to each of those Sovereigns that there was but one favour, but one distinction, but one reward which I desired that it was in their power to offer me—namely, the simple acknowledgment on their part that I had been to them a loyal and faithful minister. I have now stated my view of the obligations which are conferred on those in power; but let me remark that there is that valuable privilege in power, that it gives constant and favourable opportunites for exertion, and affords great facilities to the holder of it to render his country service according to his sense of the public good. That, in my mind, constitutes the real value of official power, and I can say with truth that I have never abused that power for any unworthy object. I have tried to use it for the promotion of the public interests and the advancement of the public good. I used it for the public advantage, and in doing so I cannot charge myself with any conduct at variance with the true and comprehensive policy of a Conservative Minister. . . .

Sir, believe me, to conduct the Government of this country is a most arduous duty. I may say it without irreverence, that these ancient institutions, like our physical frames, are " fearfully and wonderfully made." It is no easy task to ensure the united action of an ancient monarchy, a proud aristocracy and a reformed constituency. I have done everything I could do, and have thought it consistent with true Conservative policy to reconcile these three branches of the State. I have thought it consistent with true Conservative policy to promote so much of happiness and contentment among the people, that the voice of disaffection should be no longer heard, and that thoughts of the dissolution of our institutions should be forgotten in the midst of physical enjoyment. These were my attempts, and I thought them not inconsistent with true and enlarged Conservative policy. These were my objects in accepting office. It is a burden too great for my physical and far beyond my intellectual structure, and to be relieved from it with perfect honour would be the greatest favour that could be conferred on me. But, as a feeling of honour and strong sense of duty require me to undertake those responsible functions, I declare, Sir, that I am ready to incur these risks, to bear these burdens, and to front all these honourable dangers. But, Sir, I will not take the step with mutilated power and shackled authority. I will not stand at the helm during such tempestuous nights as I have seen, if the vessel be not allowed to pursue fairly the course which I think she ought to take. I will not, Sir, undertake to direct the course of the vessel by the observations which have been taken in 1842. I will reserve to myself the marking out of that course; and I must, for the public interest, claim for myself the unfettered power of judging of those measures which I conceive will be better for the country to propose. Sir, I do not wish to be the Minister of England; but, while I have the high honour of holding that office, I am determined to hold it by no servile tenure. I will only hold that office upon the condition of being unshackled by any other obligations than those of consulting the public interests and of providing for the public safety.

The sincerity of the professions made in this speech will hardly be questioned. But its flavour of pride, egotism, and insensibility to party ties, must have been eminently unpalatable to many of those who had hitherto fought Peel's battles. Taken by surprise, they now sat in sullen silence. Disraeli alone answered the Premier, in a speech described by a contemporary as " an hour of gibes and bitterness." After a brief debate, the House agreed to the Address with a facility which must have surprised the Ministers. In the House of Lords, Wellington explained the reasons which had determined him to stand by Peel. There, too, all was quiet as yet.

On the 27th of January the House of Commons went into committee on the Customs and Corn Laws, and Sir Robert Peel explained his fiscal proposals. Nothing could be more ingenious than his exposition. It was impossible to abolish protection for agriculture without abolishing protection for every other industry. Peel, therefore, began by enumerating the import duties on manufactured articles, which were to be reduced or abolished. "I am entitled," he said, "to call on the manufacturers to relinquish any protecting duties they may still enjoy." He proposed to reduce the duties on

cotton goods, woollen goods, silks, metals, and a variety
of less important articles, whilst he conciliated the manufacturers by reducing the duties still levied on certain
raw materials, such as tallow and timber.   Observing
that the manufacturers had been the first to call for
Protection, he said it was but justice that they should
set the example of doing without protection.   He gravely
quoted Adam Smith's saying, that " country gentlemen
and farmers are, to their great honour, of all people the
least subject to the wretched spirit of monopoly."   Then,
gradually approaching more weighty matters, he
announced a reduction in the duties on seeds and on
articles of food used for fattening cattle.   Thus praised
and petted, the farmers were prepared to receive other
changes.   The duties on butter, cheese, and hops were
to be reduced by one half.   The duties on meat were
abolished altogether.   Abolished, too, were the import
duties on animals of every kind.   The duty on corn was
to be reduced to 1s. a quarter from the 1st of February
1849.   In the interval the duty was to be 10s. whenever
wheat averaged less than 48s. the quarter, and to
diminish as the price rose, until, when the price was
53s. or upwards, the duty was to be only 4s.   Besides
the respite thus given the rural districts were to have
some relief from local burthens.   The expense of maintaining the highways was to be lessened by consolidating
into six hundred districts the sixteen thousand parishes
then charged with that duty.   The law of settlement
was to be so modified as to protect from removal any
person who became chargeable to the poor-rate after five
years' residence in any neighbourhood, and to save the
rural parishes from having paupers thrown back upon
them from the manufacturing towns.   Loans of public
money were to be made for the purpose of drawing and

improving agricultural land, on such conditions, however, as should secure the public from eventual loss. Lastly, the expense of prosecuting offenders and maintaining convicts was to be transferred wholly from the counties to the Treasury. Such were the proposals of the Minister now for the first time fully set forth ; and boundless were the alarm and anger which they aroused. A fortnight was to elapse before the commencement of the great debate.

In the course of this interval the Protectionists met together to consider what they should do. They were doubtful whether they should do anything. But their drooping spirits were revived by a man who now came into full view, and for the next two years played a considerable part in English politics. Lord George Bentinck had been Canning's private secretary; had sat for many years in Parliament; had voted for the Reform Bill, and had followed Stanley in the migration to the Conservative benches. But he had rarely spoken; he had never held office ; nor was he supposed to have either the industry or the capacity requisite to support a great public career. He was best known as a wealthy and eager sportsman. He was, in fact, rated far too low. He was able, and although habitually indolent, equal, when excited, to the most strenuous labour. Strung to the highest pitch by this crisis, and glowing with rage against the Minister who had betrayed the party and delivered over the landed interest into the hands of its enemies, he cared only to perish sword in hand and to involve in the general ruin the perfidious man by whom it had been wrought.

Lord George Bentinck was admirably seconded by Benjamin Disraeli; and they worked as one man to organize the party of Protection. It embraced about

12

two-thirds of the old Conservative party, about two hundred and forty members of the House of Commons. The remnant of the Conservatives adhered faithfully to Peel. By the 9th of February Bentinck's party was ready for action. It was resolved to oppose the ministerial measures at every stage, and as long as possible. Such a course, beside affording satisfaction to angry men, would give time for accidents which might displace Peel, or for a reaction in the country which might defeat his policy. When, therefore, it was proposed to go into committee on the Government resolutions, Mr. Miles, the champion of the agricultural interests, moved that the House should resolve itself into committee on that day six months. In the long debate which followed the friends of Protection spoke better than anybody had expected.

On the fifth night of the debate Sir Robert made a supreme effort of debating power. Nothing so roots a new conviction in the mind as having to argue in its defence. Nothing so endears a discovery as the ill-will which it brings upon the discoverer. These intellectual births are prized for the pangs which they cost. As the struggle went on, Peel became enthusiastic in the advocacy of the change which had long been growing familiar to his thoughts. This advocacy might be kindled into all the ardour of the missionaries of Free Trade.

This night is to decide between the policy of continued relaxation of restriction or the return to restraint and prohibition. This night you will select the motto which is to indicate the commercial policy of England. Shall it be " advance " or " recede "? Which is the fitter motto for this great empire? Survey our position; consider the advantage which God and nature have given us, and the destiny for which we are intended. We stand on the confines of Western Europe, the chief connecting link between the old world and the new. The discoveries of science, the improvement of navigation have brought us within ten days of St. Petersburg, and will soon bring us within ten days of New York. We have an extent of coast greater, in proportion to our population and the area of our land, than any other great nation, securing to us maritime strength and superiority. Iron and coal, the sinews of manufacture, give us advantages over every rival in the great competition of industry. Our capital far exceeds that which they can command. In ingenuity, in skill, in energy, we are inferior to none. Our national character, the free institutions under which we live, the liberty of thought and action, an unshackled press spreading the knowledge of every discovery and of every advance in science, combine with our natural and physical advantages to place us at the head of those nations which profit by the free interchange of their products. And is this the country to shrink from competition? Is this the country to adopt a retrograde policy? Is this the country which can only flourish in the sickly artificial atmosphere of prohibition? Is this the country to stand shivering on the brink of exposure to the healthful breezes of competition?

But in spite of the Premier's eloquence and enthusiasm the debate was adjourned once more. It was only after twelve nights of exhausting discussion that his resolution was carried by a majority of ninety-seven votes. It was only on the last day of February that the House of Commons went into committee to consider resolutions of the Government. It was only on the 20th of March that the House agreed to all the resolutions, and ordered that Bills should be brought in to give them effect. The Corn Bill was read a first time without difficulty; but before it could be read a second time another week was spent in debate. The discussion was marked by another great speech from Peel, remarkable less for its eloquence than for its display of perfect self-command under the most cutting or ferocious invective. Even Peel had never been so persuasive as in this speech. It seemed the utterance of a man really careless as to his own fate, if only he could confer a benefit on his country. When the Corn Bill had passed its second reading, the Home

12 *

Secretary introduced the Bill for the Protection of Life in Ireland, which had just come down from the House of Lords. To Bentinck and Disraeli it was a godsend, for it reinforced obstruction with half the Irish members and provoked such lengthy discussion that it had not been read a first time when the Easter recess brought a brief interval of silence.

Alleging that a stringent measure for putting down crime could be justifiable only if absolutely necessary, and that if absolutely necessary it ought to take precedence of all other legislation, the leaders of the party of Protection declared that they could support the Bill for the protection of life only if the Government gave it precedence of the Bill for the free importation of corn. The Protectionists and the Repealers discussed the Irish Bill at such length that it did not pass the first reading before May-day. But no subtlety, no efforts could much longer delay the progress of the Corn Bill. It went through committee; it approached the third reading. On the night of the 15th, the last night of the debate, the beaten side gave loose to all their passion. They made the roof ring with cheers when Disraeli reminded the House how the right honourable gentleman had ever traded on the ideas of others, described him as a burglar of others' intellect, and termed his life one great appropriation clause. When Peel rose to speak they hooted and screamed with fury. When he vindicated himself, and spoke of honour and conscience, they replied with shouts of derision and gestures of contempt. For a minute or more Peel had to stop, and for the first time in his life seemed to lose his self-possession. It seemed as though he were about to burst into tears; but he rallied and went on. Alas for the proud, sensitive man!

The Corn Bill was read a third time by a majority of ninety-eight, and when it went up to the House of Lords, the authority of Wellington secured its success. The Protectionists in the House of Commons saw that all was lost; but they remembered that revenge is sweeter than victory. They were resolved to hurl from power the chief who had deserted them, and they found an expedient which was sure to answer if they could make up their minds to use it. The Bill for the Protection of Life in Ireland had not yet been read a second time. On the first reading it had been opposed only by a certain number of Radical and Irish members. But the Whigs professed themselves dissatisfied with certain of its provisions, and the Protectionists declared that they could not vote for the second reading of a coercion bill which the Government had not treated as urgent. These considerations, or rather the desire for office and the desire for retaliation, were enough to make two great parties reverse on the second the vote which they had given on the first reading. Such a coalition, reinforced by those who objected to the Bill on its own account, left no doubt of the result. Late on the night of the 25th of June the Bill was thrown out by seventy-three votes. A numerous crowd was waiting to hear the result, and as Sir Robert Peel came out, they all uncovered in silence.

Peel now resolved to resign. Cobden, indeed, had written to Peel urging him to drop the Irish Bill, to dissolve Parliament, and to expect the verdict of the country. Happily for his honour Peel did not take this advice. Such a Bill as that which had been thrown out is no light matter. Exceptional measures cannot decently be brought in except under pressure of a dire necessity, which binds a Minister to push them forward at all costs, and to stake his authority upon their passing.   No abilities, however dazzling, no character, however lofty, can bear up against the inevitable dishonour which frequent and total changes of policy must bring upon a man who aspires to govern nations.   Peel announced his resignation to the House on the 29th of June.   After explaining his motives and intentions, he informed the House that the long-pending dispute with the United States respecting the Oregon boundary had just been settled.   He then paid a magnanimous compliment to his old enemies of the Anti-Corn Laws League. As he had formerly declared that the credit of Catholic Emancipation was due not to him, but to Grattan, to Plunkett, and to Canning, so he now declared that with the establishment of Free Trade would always be associated not his name, but the name of Richard Cobden. Last of all, in words which have become historical, he took leave of that great place which he had greatly filled.

In relinquishing power I shall leave a name severely censured, I fear, by many who, on public grounds, deeply regret the severance of party ties—deeply regret that severance, not from interested or personal motives, but from the firm conviction that fidelity to party engagements, the existence and maintenance of a great party, constitutes a powerful instrument of government.   I shall surrender power severely censured also by others who, from no interested motive, adhere to the principle of Protection, considering the maintenance of it to be essential to the welfare and interests of the country. I shall leave a name execrated by every monopolist, who, from less honourable motives, clamours for Protection because it conduces to his own individual benefit.   But it may be that I shall leave a name sometimes remembered with expressions of goodwill in the abodes of those whose lot it is to labour and to earn their daily bread by the sweat of their brow, when they shall recruit their exhausted strength with abundant and untaxed food, the sweeter because it is no longer leavened by a sense of injustice.

So the long struggle ended.   Now that almost all the combatants are in their graves, we can render to Peel, and even to Peel's opponents, the useless justice of posterity. Free Trade has, on the whole, been justified by results, although it has not fulfilled the dreams of its apostles. Peel thought that Free Trade once adopted by England would soon become general. Even in its native land it is now assailed, and from other lands it has almost entirely disappeared. Nor even in this, its chosen seat, has Free Trade made well-being secure or universal. Some valuable industries have failed to withstand competition. Agriculture especially began to decline as soon as improved means of transport enabled foreign producers to take full advantage of the repeal of the Corn Laws. The country population finding more and more difficulty in living at home, has been passing into the great towns or away from the shores of the United Kingdom. We have come to depend more and more upon distant supplies of food. Not only the honour and greatness but the very life of the nation now depends on the superiority of a navy which has never been tried. Yet these enormous disadvantages are more than balanced by the advantages which Free Trade has procured. From the time of Peel's fiscal reforms the manufactures and commerce of these islands, developing at a rate unknown before, have helped a growing population to find employment at high wages which cheapness of food has made more valuable still. With the improvement in their material condition the people have improved in health, knowledge, and morality. Since that time there has been much suffering even in periods of prosperity, and periods of depression have not failed to recur; but upon the whole there has been a social amelioration vaster than will be believed by anybody who has not studied the subject. The spread of material prosperity was speedily felt in the greater stability of the commonwealth. Old fallacies lost somewhat of their hold upon the people; acrid discontent became less rare, and when the tempest of 1848 overturned a score of thrones the ancient monarchy of England stood erect and unshaken amid a world of ruin. The political calm which followed 1848 was succeeded by an age of rapid reform, propitious to fevered hopes and crude projects; but no revolutionary party has yet struck really deep root in English soil. The majority of Englishmen are moderate in their political expectations, and peaceable in their political methods. For this sanity of public opinion, as well as for the solid wellbeing on which it depends, we are largely indebted to Free Trade; and for the attainment of Free Trade we are indebted to many eminent men, but chiefly to Sir Robert Peel.

The process of Peel's conversion to Free Trade was gradual but steady. The principle of Free Trade had been accepted by many English statesmen from the time of Adam Smith onwards. It had never been the exclusive property of a party. Fox had been less friendly to Free Trade than Pitt. Lord Grenville, a Whig who was almost a Tory, and Mr. Huskisson, a Tory who was almost a Whig, had been practically Free Traders. Even Lord Liverpool had professed a speculative preference for Free Trade; whilst Lord Melbourne had declared that Free Trade in corn was sheer madness. Thus it was not necessary for Peel either to discover the principle or even to overcome that disgust with which we borrow a principle from our political adversaries. Himself a man of mercantile origin, with a strong taste and faculty for economic study, he was from the first much influenced by the writings and speeches of the economists. Had he been free to form and to express the

opinions most congenial to his own mind, he would probably have joined the Free Traders at an early point in
his career. As it was, he no sooner obtained power in a
crisis of extreme difficulty than he risked a loss to the
revenue and strained the allegiance of his party, for the
sake of trying a great experiment in Free Trade. That
experiment succeeded beyond his hopes. The revenue
after a brief interval became more plentiful than ever.
Industry developed faster than it had done within living
memory. The exports and imports increased enormously.
Employment became general, and sedition grew tame.
This success emboldened Peel three years later to try a
second experiment; and this experiment answered also.
Meantime a political organization, powerful in numbers,
in resources, in tenacity, and in talent had been everywhere at work, and had ended in making a public
opinion which promised to become irresistible. The
incessant growth of population convinced Peel that no
system of Protection would enable this country to feed
all its inhabitants. The experience of recent years
satisfied him that high prices did not mean high wages,
and that wages might rise whilst prices fell. Thus whilst
Protection daily grew more difficult to maintain, the
value of Protection daily grew more doubtful to Peel.
When he was more than half converted, the failure of
the potato crop and the prospect of famine brought to
its consummation an intellectual change which otherwise might have needed a few years more.

Many persons, however, who approved of freedom of
trade could not approve of the method by which it had
been established. They could not reconcile themselves
to the conduct of a Minister who had been entrusted with
power partly in order to preserve that very system of
Protection which he used his power to destroy. They

felt that Peel had not dealt openly either with his friends
or with his adversaries ; that he had concealed from
his own party the revolution in his mind, whilst he had
defrauded the other party of the credit due to them.
They thought that Peel had shaken the confidence of
party and lowered the morality of public life. The charge
is grave ; the evidence looks plausible; let us hear Peel's
defence.

It was my intention, but for the unforeseen events of the autumn of
1845, to enter into that friendly communication, the omission of which
is blamed and lamented, to apprise the Conservative party before the
Corn Laws could be discussed in the Session of 1846, that my views
with regard to the policy of maintaining that law had undergone a
change, and that I could no longer undertake as a Minister to resist a
motion for the consideration of the whole question.

That unreserved communication which I had thus contemplated—
which is possible and most desirable under ordinary circumstances—
was in this case unfortunately precluded by the peculiar character of
the unforeseen emergency for which it was necessary to provide and
the peculiar position of the Cabinet in respect to the measures to be
adopted.

There was no period between the first alarming indications of the
failure of the potato crop, and the resignation of the Ministers on the
9th of December 1845, at which I could with propriety have given the
slightest intimation to the supporters of the Government with regard
either to my own course or to the probable decision of the Cabinet. I
could not have alluded to the differences which prevailed among the
members of the Government without extinguishing whatever degree
of hope there might be that those differences would be ultimately
reconciled.

The course of events subsequently to the resignation of the Government on the 9th of December equally precluded any confidential communication on my part with the supporters of the Government which
would have had a tendency to soothe irritated feelings or to mitigate
hostility to the measures about to be proposed.

It was a matter of public notoriety that the Government had
resigned on the 9th of December in consequence of differences on the
subject of the Corn Laws ; that Lord John Russell had attempted
and had failed in the attempt to form a Government ; that the Queen
had therefore appealed to her former servants, and that they had

resumed power with the full intention of proposing measures with regard to the import of food to which Lord Stanley had refused to be a party.

To assemble the supporters of the Government under such circumstances for the mere purpose of communicating to them facts which were notorious to the whole world, would have given offence rather than have calmed irritation.

Had a meeting taken place, there would naturally have been the demand for a full explanation not only of the grounds on which the decision of the Government had been taken, but of the peculiar nature of the measures which it was intended to propose.

Explanation could not have been given on the first point without serious prejudice to the Government by anticipating the Parliamentary discussion which must shortly follow. It could not have been given on the second, namely, on the precise mode in which the duties on corn were to be dealt with, without disturbing all commercial operations connected with the corn trade, and incurring the risk of giving to some parties an unfair advantage over others.

There is no security against these evils in cases wherein the imposition or repeal of duties is concerned, excepting entire silence and reserve on the part of a Minister until the hour when the intentions of the Government can be publicly declared in Parliament.

For these reasons I found it necessary to abstain on this occasion from those communications with the friends and supporters of the Government which, under ordinary circumstances, might to a certain extent have taken place, and to reserve for the meeting of Parliament a full explanation of the grounds on which the Ministers of the Crown had formed their decision, and of the measures which they felt it to be their duty to propose.

Most readers will feel that this defence is a little too technical. It is able and was made doubtless in good faith. But it does not remove the impression made by other passages in the Memoirs, that in the autumn of 1845 Peel was willing to propose the total abrogation of the Corn Laws, and would have proposed it if he could have got the assent of his whole Cabinet. It was apparently the dissension within his Cabinet rather than the reluctance to surprise his party which led him to offer to make way for Lord John Russell. Had circumstances allowed of delay, Peel would probably have gone on as theretofore, advancing gradually towards freedom of trade, carrying his followers along with him and preparing the whole public for the inevitable end. But this reconciliation of conflicting duties the pressure of events made inevitable. Finding himself possessed of power to carry out an urgent reform, he would not let scruples of delicacy stand in the way of the public service. In comparison with the glory of executing such a reform, he slighted the reproach of disloyalty and dissimulation. We may admire a sacrifice of this kind, but we would rather that a great man had not been summoned to make it.

CHAPTER IX.

LAST YEARS AND DEATH.

1846–1850.

Peel's Position after his Resignation—Progress of his Opinions—He
supports Russell's Administration—French Revolution of 1848—
Peel and Louis Philippe—Peel's last Speech—Peel is thrown
from his Horse—Last Days and Death—Honours paid to his
Memory.

PEEL's ministry once dissolved, the Whigs returned to
power, not because they were strong, but because other
parties were weaker. The Whigs, strictly so called,
were not much more numerous than the revolted
Tories; and they could not put absolute confidence
either in the Manchester party or in the party which
still adhered to Peel. The force of old connections
and the multiplicity of old claims to reward, hindered
Russell from making a serious endeavour to enlist in
his administration the men who had done most to
bring about a repeal of the Corn Laws. With Peel he
could not have coalesced. He sought to gain Dalhousie, Lincoln, and Sidney Herbert; but they all
refused to forsake their chief. Russell's ministry was,
therefore, composed solely of orthodox Whigs. As

such it was in a minority of the House of Commons, and consequently weak. At a time when the United Kingdom was threatened with great calamities, the weakness of the Cabinet was a public misfortune.

It was the general belief that one day or another, perhaps soon, Peel must take office again. In ability, in experience, and in reputation, he was the first of living English statesmen. He might be reckoned young, for he was only fifty-eight years old and could look forward to many more years of labour and of glory. Within our own time three statesmen, far older than Peel was in 1846, have formed governments and controlled the course of the State. But Peel had no wish to be Minister again. It is said that when he resigned office, he took a promise from the Queen never again to lay upon him such a burthen. Early accustomed to office and long since vested with power, he asked for nothing better than repose. Although still vigorous, he began to feel the effect of his protracted and intense toil. A little anxious about his health, he was forcibly struck with Macaulay's remark that no man had ever led the House of Commons after attaining the age of sixty years; he remembered the untimely fate of so many illustrious men who before him had filled that high station; and he readily listened to the anxiety of an affectionate wife, with whose happiness his own was bound up. Even if he had wished to resume power, where could he find a party to confer it? The Whigs he had opposed all his life; in their ranks there was no place for him. The Tories were no longer his own. He had kept almost all his personal staff, but he had lost almost all the rank and file. Two-thirds of that great array which had been so proud of him; two-thirds of

those country gentleman whom he had been so proud to
lead, now regarded him as a double-dealer and traitor,
whilst he wondered at their perversity and chafed
against their ingratitude.   No lifelong enmity could
be more bitter than that fresh alienation.   His old
friend Croker had turned against him in the last crisis,
and Peel haughtily rejected Croker's approaches to a
reconciliation.   Even the sensible Lockhart could believe
that Peel's faculties were failing when he proposed the
repeal of the Corn Laws.   All this personal suffering
awoke in Peel the remembrance of a like surrender,
followed by a like obloquy at the time of the removal of
Catholic disabilities, and set a lasting barrier between
him and his old followers.

It did more; it almost effaced Peel's early impressions, and brought him to a more vivid knowledge of
his own mind.   Late and sad for most men is the
coming of that knowledge.   Peel began to feel that
he was as much a Liberal as a Conservative.   "At
sixty," Disraeli wrote with some truth, "he began to
comprehend his position.   The star of Manchester
seemed, as it were, to rise from the sunset of Oxford,
and he felt that he had sacrificed his natural career to
an obsolete education and a political system for which
he could not secure even a euthanasia."   This is too
strongly said; yet it is true that Peel's life was one
long course of action and reaction between a cramping
education and an expanding nature.   The memorable
victory which deprived him at once of power as a
Minister, and of authority as a party chief, decided
this inward struggle.   For the first time in his life he
was a free man.   He had ceased to live for his party;
he henceforward lived for his principles.   Nor did he
lack the means to enforce them.   Although his fol-

lowing dwindled, as a small party standing between two great ones must dwindle, his popularity with the mass of his countrymen was at its height. The public generally felt that Peel had made a painful sacrifice to the common good, and honoured in him a patriot as well as a statesman. Then, too, his personal weight in the House of Commons was such as no other man could command. Thus he was still powerful enough to be of the utmost use to an administration which needed help wherever it could be found. Inasmuch as Peel no longer wanted anything for himself, he was ready to assist any administration which would adopt his latest policy and develop his latest legislation. As the Whigs were willing to do this, he gave a general support to the Whigs, often criticising them with the freedom and sincerity of a friend, never assailing them with the pique or malice of a rival. He continued to enjoy much of the influence without any of the cares of a party leader, and filled a great place in the general view without foregoing any of those pleasures which a happy home and an immense fortune could afford. The position was dignified and agreeable, although seducing, and Peel gained a new title to respect by the spirit in which he filled it.

Nor was it long before Peel had his generosity tested. Unwilling to let the session of 1846 end before they had contributed something of their own to the new policy of Free Trade, the ministers proposed to equalize the duties on sugar. The differential duties were upheld by the colonial interest, and by the enemies of slavery as well as by those who accepted the principle of Protection. They had been ratified, as it were, by the action of Peel in the preceding year. Even now Peel acknowledged that he was in favour of the differential duties, yet since the Government had resolved to stand or fall by the repeal of these duties he voted for the repeal on the ground that no new Government could be formed under the actual circumstances. His influence turned the scale, and the Whigs, who had contradicted themselves in order to turn Peel out, saw Peel contradict himself to keep them in.

At the end of the session it was seen that all parties had been hasty in their fears. The price of corn had varied so little that the farmers could not be roused by any efforts of eloquence. The famine, which by its mere report had destroyed Protection, still lingered on its way. What unusual distress there was in Ireland was still pretty well met by the joint efforts of public and private charity. But in the autumn of 1846 the potato crop failed a second time and more completely than before. With the spring of 1847 all the horrors of famine came to Ireland. The Government did what it could to mitigate these horrors, and at one time had 735,000 persons employed upon the relief works. But no sudden effort could undo the result of ages of neglect. Seeing how much remained to be done, Lord George Bentinck proposed to employ those who wanted food in the construction of a great system of railways, and to raise two-thirds of the necessary funds by pledging the public credit. On the second reading Bentinck's Bill was opposed by the Government. Peel supported the Government, arguing that it was not desirable to increase the National Debt by a sum of £16,000,000 ; that if the railways could be worked at a profit, private enterprise would make them ; and lastly, that their construction would not benefit those parts of Ireland which most needed relief. Bentinck's Bill having

13

been thrown out, the Government brought in another of the same kind, but petty in scale, which Peel opposed also. Yet Peel deeply felt, not only the passing desolation of the famine, but even more the standing misery of Ireland. Such palliatives as he could recommend were indeed imperfect. He spoke in favour of Lord Lincoln's motion that the State should assist those who could find no livelihood in Ireland, to settle in our thinly-peopled colonies. He insisted that the State should at least inspect and control the vast spontaneous emigration which went on without any suitable provision for the comfort, the health, or the morals of the emigrants. He recommended the establishment of agricultural schools throughout Ireland. But he laid most stress upon a measure which he may be said to have forced upon the Russell Ministry—the Encumbered Estates Act of 1848. He suggested the amendment of the Act adopted in the following year, which transferred its administration from the Court of Chancery to a special court. Peel, who was better acquainted with the English than with the Irish system of tenure, built great hopes on the transfer of land to owners with a large capital. But the Act has not realised his anticipation.

About the same time that famine began to rage in Ireland, an acute depression of trade began to be felt in Great Britain. A severe financial crisis due to extravagant speculation in railways was by many persons ascribed to the provisions of the Bank Charter Act; and Peel shared in its unpopularity. The Ministers, who were convinced of the wisdom of the Act, long resisted every inducement to its repeal. But, finding in October that the crisis continued, and the panic got worse, they authorized the Bank of England to enlarge its discounts and advances, and then summoned Parliament to indemnify them for this stretch of power. The mere knowledge that such advice had been given by the Government was enough to subdue the panic, and the Bank had no occasion to exceed its lawful authority. When Parliament met, Peel defended every particular in the conduct of the Ministers, and declared his cordial approval of their letter to the Bank, on the ground that it was necessary to soothe an alarm which reason could not dispel. He had the pleasure to see his Bank Charter Act approved by select committees of both Houses which had been appointed to examine the whole subject of commercial distress. Yet a few months later he thought it necessary to defend the Act from a new assault by Herries.

In his ideas of religious toleration Peel continued to display a strange mixture of narrowness and liberality. Even in the year 1847 he argued against the repeal of the so-called securities for Protestantism given by the Act for Catholic Emancipation. In the same year he spoke in favour of Russell's scheme for extending to the schools of every persuasion the benefit of the annual grant from the Treasury. In the next year he warmly advocated the claims of the most unpopular of churches. Many years previously Croker had noted Peel's faint resistance to measures of relief for the Jews. He had complained that Peel gave up the principle of connection between Church and State. Whilst still a Minister, Peel had admitted the Jews to municipal office. He now favoured their admission to Parliament. On this occasion he was in harmony with Bentinck, who held to the Whig tradition of religious liberty, and with Disraeli, who had the manliness to glory in his persecuted race. The Bill, thrown out by the House

13 *

of Lords, was brought in again the following year, when Peel's second son, Frederick, the member for Leominster, supported it in a maiden speech.

In this session Peel took part with the Government on its Bill to repeal the Navigation Laws. These laws, approved even by Adam Smith, constituted the chief remnant of our old Protective system. They had been almost annulled by a series of modifications, and they had been totally suspended in order to encourage the importation of food into Ireland during the famine. Yet their repeal was a signal incident in the triumph of Free Trade, and would not have been recommended by anybody but a Free Trader on principle. Peel's entire acceptance of the maxims of Free Trade was declared more than once in this and in the next session. He spoke and voted in favour of renewing the income-tax, which was still imposed only for short periods. He resisted the attempt to restore protection to colonial sugar, and the attempt to reduce the rates levied on real property. He steadfastly maintained that the policy of Free Trade was for the benefit of the whole community, and had improved the market even for native produce. He lived to see the final extinction of the corn duties in January of 1849, and to read of the banquet in honour of that event given by the chiefs of the Manchester party.

Whilst the British Parliament amused itself with endless discussions about convertible paper and colonial sugar, the states of the Continent, one after another, were overturned by the general revolution of 1848. The reigning dynasty of France fell with a suddenness which compelled wonder, and an ignominy which almost extinguished pity. Peel had always been friendly to the House of Orleans, but he had always claimed for every

country the right to manage its own affairs. When the
Whig Ministry made haste to recognize the French
Republic, Peel was among the foremost to justify their
action. But he reconciled goodwill to the victors with
friendship to the vanquished. When Guizot took refuge
in England, Peel entertained him at Drayton Manor
with a hospitality which left the most agreeable memories
in the mind of his guest. In the following year, when
it was doubted whether Claremont was a fit residence
for the Queen Marie-Amélie, then suffering in health,
Peel wrote a letter to King Louis Philippe, making
a tender of his house at Drayton. The King declined
this offer, but came to pay his thanks in person. It
was a singular meeting. Each of these men had
governed a mighty people; each had regarded the
other as the ablest politician in their respective countries;
each had seemed to the world secure in the enjoyment of
power; each had swiftly and irrecoverably fallen; and
now the fallen Minister welcomed the fallen King. A
common interest united them in every change of fortune.
Peel paid a just compliment to that love of peace, which
was the most amiable quality of Louis Philippe. Louis
Philippe gravely replied that his endeavours to maintain
peace had been made easy by Peel and Aberdeen. Then
they parted, not to meet again.

Peel had spent most of the autumn of 1849 in Scotland, where he had received the freedom of the city of
Aberdeen, an honour once conferred upon Dr. Johnson.
He returned to London for the Session, and was regular in
attendance at the House. Not until June did there occur
any debate of historical interest. Then the Lords signi-
fied their disapproval of the foreign policy pursued by
Palmerston, who had given repeated offence to our
neighbours, and had almost quarrelled with France and

Russia in his zeal to get redress for Don Pacifico from the Greek Government. By way of counterblast to the vote of the Lords, Mr. Roebuck moved in the Commons a resolution approving the foreign policy of Her Majesty's Government. In the course of his speech Mr. Roebuck reflected severely upon the foreign policy of the late Cabinet. After midnight Peel rose to vindicate the policy of Aberdeen and to criticize the policy of Palmerston. Without acrimony, but without hesitation, he pointed out the embarrassment which must result from Palmerston's well-meant interference with foreign nations. He had no desire to make up a majority against the Government; yet his dissent from their views, had so much influence that the majority in favour of Roebuck's motion did not exceed forty-six votes. The midsummer morning was bright when the House broke up, and Peel, returning to Whitehall Gardens, might enjoy for the last time the stillness and the freshness of that delightful hour.

He retired to take a brief rest. In the forenoon he attended a meeting of the Commission for arranging the preliminaries of the Industrial Exhibition of 1851. In the afternoon, shortly before 5 o'clock, he went out to take the air on horseback and called at Buckingham Palace, where he entered his name in the Queen's visiting book. Going up Constitution Hill, he had come nearly opposite the wicket gate into the Green Park, when he met Miss Ellis, daughter of Lady Dover, also on horseback, and had just exchanged salutes with her, when his horse became slightly restive, turned sharply round, and threw him over its head on his face. Two gentleman, who saw the accident, ran forward and raised Peel into a sitting posture. Then a Dr. Foucart, of Glasgow, stopped to give help, and asked Peel whether he was hurt. " Very much," replied Peel, and immediately became unconscious. He was placed in a passing carriage belonging to a Mrs. Lucas, where he slightly recovered, and was driven slowly towards Whitehall Gardens. The carriage had not gone far 'before it was met by Sir James Clark, the Queen's physician, who, hearing what had happened, offered his assistance. When brought home and lifted out of the carriage, Peel revived so much that he was able to walk into the house, where he was met by his wife and family, who had heard the bad news. Almost immediately Peel swooned again in Foucart's arms, and was laid upon a sofa in the dining-room. With much difficulty he was removed from the sofa to a hydraulic bed ; but it was found impossible to remove him from the room.

The most eminent surgeons in London were at once called in, but all their skill was made unavailing by an unfortunate circumstance. Peel was of a gouty constitution and a sensitive temperament, which a life of sedentary labour had made more and more acute. For some time past the report of his own gun had been so disagreeable to his nerves, that he had given up shooting, once a favourite pastime. A few weeks before his accident, when he was visiting the Zoological Gardens with his children, a small monkey suddenly jumping on the palm of his hand had caused him to faint for several minutes. Now this morbid sensibility so much enhanced his pain, that he could not be minutely examined, nor could all his injuries be known. The surgeons could only be sure that his collar-bone was broken. When they tried to reduce the fracture, Peel's agony was such as to hinder them from completing the operation, and after a few hours the bandages, at his entreaty, were removed. He remained in a doubtful state, but grew more and more sensitive and restless.

Meantime the news of the accident spread all over the town. The Prince Consort and many other distinguished persons, amongst them Mr. Disraeli, came to make inquiries after Sir Robert Peel's condition. But the great crowd of poor and humble people who gathered in the approaches to his house, and eagerly waited for every fresh announcement by the surgeons, was a rarer and more striking testimony to the regard which Peel had inspired. When the courtyard was closed in order to give the patient that quiet which he absolutely needed, the bulletins were posted on the gates. But the number of those who could not come close enough to see was so great that the policeman on duty had to read each bulletin aloud as it came out. Then a second copy had to be given to the policeman at the entrance to Whitehall Gardens to be read to those who could come no nearer.

All through the Sunday and the Monday Peel grew steadily worse, and on Monday night he became delirious. In the intervals of delirium he was so feeble that the surgeons doubted whether he could last until day, but at four o'clock on Tuesday morning he fell into a sleep which lasted some hours, and woke refreshed and calm, although quite exhausted by suffering and want of nourishment. Early in the afternoon he lost speech and became stertorous in his breathing, whilst his pulse mounted up rapidly. All hope was now over. His old friend, Dr. Tomlinson, the Bishop of Gibraltar, came to administer the Sacrament, which Peel was just conscious enough to receive. With Tomlinson the family, who had hitherto been kept out, entered the sick-room. Peel knew their faces, and feebly extending his hand, murmured, "God bless you," in tones scarcely audible. Last came his old and trusty friends Hardinge and Graham, whose names he had often repeated in his delirium. His poor wife broke down altogether, and had to be carried out. But Peel's sufferings were over; he had ceased to feel pain; he soon became insensible, and at eleven o'clock he passed away.

After death it was found that the fifth rib on the left side had been broken, and pressing on the lung had caused effusion and engorgement which were fatal. As the family were unwilling to allow a complete examination, the total injury which he had sustained could never be exactly known.

On Wednesday it so happened that no member of the Ministry was present in the House of Commons. The adjournment of the House was moved by Mr. Hume, who had been one of Peel's stoutest adversaries, and was seconded by Mr. Gladstone, the most distinguished of Peel's younger lieutenants. Sir Robert Inglis expressed the sympathy of those Conservatives who had not been able to follow Peel, and the adjournment was voted unanimously. On the following day Lord John Russell, having brought up the Report of the Commissioners of the National Exhibition, took the opportunity of paying a generous tribute to the memory of the great man with whom he had so long disputed the possession of power. He concluded by saying that he should support any motion for bestowing on Peel the honour of a public funeral. But Peel had by his will directed that he should be interred in Drayton Church without ostentation or parade of any kind. Only a few weeks before his death he had pointed out to his wife the place, beside the coffins of his father and mother, where he wished that his own body should be laid. His friend and executor, Goulburn, therefore declined in terms of deep respect that honour which the House was impatient to grant. In the House of Lords all the leaders rose one after another to do honour to Peel's memory. The weightiest praise was paid by Wellington, who had known him so well and was himself so entirely honest. "In all the course of my acquaintance with Sir Robert Peel," he said, "I never knew a man in whose truth and justice I had a more lively confidence, or in whom I saw a more invariable desire to promote the public service. In the whole course of my communication with him I never knew an instance in which he did not show the strongest attachment to truth; and I never saw in the whole course of my life the smallest reason for suspecting that he stated anything which he did not firmly believe to be the fact. My Lords, I could not let this conversation come to a close without stating that which I believe to have been the strongest characteristic feature of his character."

On the next day after these words were spoken, a tribute of respect never before or after bestowed on any British statesman was paid to Peel. In the French National Assembly the President, M. Dupin, expressed the sympathy of France with the loss which England had sustained, and the high regard of Frenchmen for a statesman who, throughout a long and glorious career, had shown himself friendly in disposition and courteous in language towards the French nation. The Assembly unanimously adopted his words by ordering them to be recorded on the journals.

Agreeably to his own wish Peel was laid in the family vault in the church of Drayton Bassett. But the House of Commons resolved to honour his memory with a monument in Westminster Abbey. In moving an address to the Queen for this purpose, Lord John Russell mentioned that the Queen had desired to confer upon Lady Peel the rank of Viscountess, formerly conferred upon Canning's widow; but that Lady Peel declared herself unwilling to accept any style other than had belonged to her husband. Peel had, in his will, expressed a hope that no member of his family would accept any title or distinction in recompense for services which he might have rendered to the State. For himself he had always declined such a recompense, preferring to remain a simple commoner. In the same spirit he had declined the Garter proferred by the Queen. Although so wealthy, although so long powerful, so long the leader of the most splendid aristocracy in the world, he had never tried to cloak the humble origin of his family, or to distinguish himself from that great body of plain, industrious Englishmen amongst whom his father and grandfather were numbered. About Peel there was nothing resplendent; but neither was there any tinsel.

The statue voted by the House of Commons stands on the left hand of those who enter the north door of the Abbey, just where the transept meets the choir. Others were raised in almost all the chief cities of the kingdom by the respect of public bodies, by the liberality of nobles and merchants, and by the penny subscriptions of workmen, to whom Peel had given " abundant and untaxed food, the sweeter because no longer leavened with a sense of injustice." The circumstances of his loss of power had made him popular; the circumstances of his death had awakened compassion. The recollection of his early prejudices, of his mistakes in judgment, of his defence of causes justly lost was all effaced; and men remembered only his integrity, his industry, his

great and unquestionable services. They felt.that take
him all in all he had left no man more devoted to his
country or so well able to serve her.

Peel had seven children; five sons and two daughters.
Robert, the eldest son, succeeded to the baronetcy and
the representation of the borough of Tamworth. The
second son, Frederick, was Member for Leominster at
the time of his father's death. William ran a short but
glorious career as an officer in the navy. John Floyd
entered the army as an officer in the Scotch Fusiliers.
Arthur Wellesley gave himself to public life, entered the
House of Commons as Member for Warwick, and was
elected in the year 1884 to the office of Speaker, which
he still holds. Julia, the elder daughter, married Lord
Villiers, the eldest son of the Earl of Jersey; Eliza
married the Honourable Francis Stonor, son of Lord
Camoys. Lady Peel, their mother, died in the year
1859.

CHAPTER X.

CHARACTER AND ACHIEVEMENT.

Peel as a Statesman—Peel as an Orator—Peel in Private Life.

WHEN a man has lived forty years in public, when he has made the council chamber and the senate house his home, and has entwined his history with the history of the State, it might seem as though the exhibition of his character was complete, as though there could be no ground for suspense in appraising his real worth. But in judging Sir Robert Peel, a writer of the present day suffers from being at once too near and too remote. We are too remote in time from Peel to have that fresh and living knowledge of detail which belongs to contemporaries alone. We are too near in time to Peel to assign his place and measure his importance in English politics with the enlarged and impartial spirit of the historian. We have, indeed, the help of two or three assessors who combined the man of letters with the man of the world, and had a remarkable gift of seeing general characteristics under the complexity of practical life. Charles Greville, Bagehot, and Disraeli have exhausted their powers in the delineation of Sir Robert Peel. The portrait drawn by Disraeli in his *Life of Bentinck* is truly a masterpiece. The writer all but forgot the rancour of personal enmity in the delight of exercising his literary skill. He seized the salient features of Peel's character the more readily and distinctly because it was a character so unlike his own. Peel's singular combination of power and of weakness has never been hit off so happily as in the following passage :—

Nature had combined in Sir Robert Peel many admirable parts. In him a physical frame incapable of fatigue was united with an understanding equally vigorous and flexible. He was gifted with the faculty of method in the highest degree, and with great powers of application which were sustained by a prodigious memory, while he could communicate his acquisitions with clear and fluent elocution.

Such a man, under any circumstances and in any sphere of life, would probably have become remarkable. Ordained from his youth to be busied with the affairs of a great empire, such a man, after long years of observation, practice, and perpetual discipline, would have become what Sir Robert Peel was in the latter portion of his life—a transcendent administrator of public business, and a matchless master of debate in a popular assembly. In the course of time the method which was natural to Sir Robert Peel had matured into a habit of such expertness that no one in the despatch of affairs ever adapted the means more fitly to the end ; his original flexibility had ripened into consummate tact ; his memory had accumulated such stores of political information that he could bring luminously together all that was necessary to establish or to illustrate a subject ; while in the House of Commons he was equally eminent in exposition and reply ; in the first, distinguished by his arrangement, his clearness, and his completeness ; in the second, ready, ingenious, and adroit, prompt in detecting the weak points of his adversary, and dexterous in extricating himself from an embarrassing position.

Thus gifted and thus accomplished, Sir Robert Peel had a great deficiency; he was without imagination. Wanting imagination he wanted prescience. No one was more sagacious when dealing with the circumstances before him; no one penetrated the present with more acuteness and accuracy. His judgment was faultless provided he had not to deal with the future. Thus it happened through his long career that while he always was looked upon as the most prudent and safest of leaders, he ever, after a protracted display of admirable tactics, concluded his campaigns by surrendering at discretion. He was so adroit that he could prolong resistance even beyond its term, but so little foreseeing that often in the very triumph of his manœuvres he found himself in an untenable position. And so it came to pass that Roman Catholic Emancipation, Parliamentary Reform, and the abrogation of our commercial system were all carried in haste or in passion, and without conditions or mitigatory arrangements.

Sir Robert Peel had a peculiarity which is, perhaps, natural with men of very great talents who have not the creative faculty; he had a dangerous sympathy with the creations of others. Instead of being cold and wary, as was commonly supposed, he was impulsive, and even inclined to rashness. When he was ambiguous, unsatisfactory, reserved, tortuous, it was that he was perplexed, that he did not see his way, that the routine which he had admirably administered failed him, and that his own mind was not constructed to create a substitute for the custom which was crumbling away. Then he was ever on the look-out for new ideas, and when he embraced them he did so with eagerness and often with precipitancy ; he always carried these novel plans to an extent which even their projectors or chief promoters had usually not anticipated, as was seen, for example, in the settlement of the currency. Although apparently wrapped up in himself, and supposed to be egotistical, except in seasons of rare exaltedness, as in the years 1844–45, when he reeled under the favour of the Court, the homage of the Continent, and the servility of Parliament, he was really deficient in self-confidence. There was always some person representing some theory or system exercising an influence over his mind. In his " sallet-days " it was Mr. Horner or Sir Samuel Romilly ; in later and more important periods it was the Duke of Wellington, the King of the French, Mr. Jones Loyd, some others, and finally Mr. Cobden.

This brilliant analysis agrees with the judgment passed by Bagehot on Sir Robert Peel. "He never could have been a great thinker ; he became what nature designed—a great agent." Peel was pre-eminently what Bagehot calls the business gentleman. All his faculties were practical, and his political career was suited to his faculties. Early elected a member of the House of Commons, early admitted to high office, early regarded as a candidate for the highest, Peel became a partner in the counsels of grey-headed statesmen and in the cares of supreme power at a time when the ordinary profes-

sional man has scarcely completed his education. Thus
from the first Peel had as much business as he could
possibly do, and a life of incessant business exercised
the qualities in which he was strongest at the expense of
the qualities in which he was weakest. Bagehot has
shown, with rare delicacy and penetration, how the life
of a great administrator and great debater dulls the
reflective and imaginative powers. Always considering
how he shall perform the next bit of work which comes
to hand, and how he shall justify his performance to an
assembly like the House of Commons, always concen-
trating his mind upon this or that small but near object,
the ablest man impairs his range of intellectual vision,
and accustoms himself to think like common men.
Mankind in this respect resemble nature, that you can
prevail with them only by becoming their slave.

It is true that practice in affairs gives a kind of
wisdom which is hardly to be had in any other way.
Action as well as meditation tests our prejudices and
multiplies our ideas. An open mind derives from full
and varied intercourse with men and things not merely
a mechanical expertness, but also knowledge, prudence,
policy. All that a life of business could teach, Peel had
learnt and digested. Experience was his school; and
it is a sound, although a slow and a dear one. Hence
it was observed of him that his life was a perpetual
education, and that after every fresh defeat his mind
seemed to expand. Natural sense and professional training made him quick to see the meaning of facts, to judge
what was possible under any given circumstances, to
select and combine the best means of attaining it. At
times this talent in Peel rose to an inspiration of genius.
Nothing could be finer than his appreciation of the truth
that after the passing of the Reform Act every great

party must find its strength in the middle class—unless, indeed, it were the skill with which he suited the Conservative programme to their instincts, or the tact with which he subdued the more wilful Tories to the fulfilment of that programme. Nothing could be sounder than his judgment in renewing the Property Tax on his return to office in 1842. He thus made good the deficiency of the revenue without laying any new burthen upon the poor, displayed the owners of property in the character of useful and spirited citizens, and provided the means for carrying out a reform of the tariff which more than compensated their losses. On this occasion he showed one of the rarest qualities of a statesman, the power of making a temporary expedient subserve a lasting good. The man who was capable of strokes like these was more than a mere man of business, however adroit and diligent.

Yet Peel's talent, however admirable, was of a secondary order. It was a talent less for creating than for adapting, less for moulding than for regulating, less for discovering than for expounding. With such a talent, he was seldom much before the age or much behind it. He was swift to seize and cunning to execute the ideas floating in the mind of enlightened English society. But he could not construct in imagination the future growth of his own mind or the future course of human history. He lived on the intellectual earnings of his daily toil, but he had no large balance at the bank of thought. He was not one of those statesmen who from the rude heap of common business can distill the few precious drops of everlasting truth, and raise a speech or a pamphlet into a text-book of political wisdom. Nor was he one of those statesmen who in the turmoil of the present hour can detect the forces which will

14

shape the course of future ages, who have power to
qualify what they have penetration to foresee, and who
leave monuments more enduring than brass or marble
in those august institutions which preserve the fame of
the individual, because they satisfy the needs of the race.
Peel was sagacious, not profound.

Our virtues and our failings have one root, and from
the constitution of his intellect. came Peel's greatness
and littleness in politics. Scarcely any other English
statesman has procured the enactment of so many wise
measures.   The resumption of cash payments, the
amendment of the criminal law, the institution of the
Irish constabulary and the London police, Catholic
Emancipation, the emancipation of trade, and a crowd of
reforms only less beneficial than these, make up a record
of useful labour which has seldom been surpassed. That
most of them were not originally conceived by himself
matters little to his fame. Nobody would expect Peel
to have done, in addition to his own work, the work of
Adam Smith or of Bentham. What matters more is
that Peel spent much of his life in opposing several of
the reforms which he afterwards carried, and that he
could not have carried the most important without that
power which he had acquired by opposing them.   There
seems to be little doubt that he was honest in resistance
as well as in concession, that in each case he tried to
further what he believed to be the public good. But
this defence saves his integrity at the expense of his
judgment. A man who never modifies an opinion is simply
as stupid as he is unteachable. But a man who is always
shifting from one opinion to another, lacks something
which a man should have. Something must be amiss
with a statesman whom no experience and no means of
information can save from the necessity of constantly

yielding the position in which he has entrenched him-self, and of forsaking the followers who have put their trust in him.

Yet even in charging Peel with defect of insight, we must remember the peculiar circumstances of his education. Peel was brought up in that atmosphere in which Pitt had died, the atmosphere of terror and reaction. Pitt had been a Liberal before the French Revolution began, and Peel became a Liberal after the French Revolution had ceased to oppress the imagination of mankind. Had not the English middle class been frightened by the reign of the Jacobins, had not Peel's father imbued him with the prejudices of the time, Peel might have begun his career with a creed like the creed which he adopted at its close. Then he would have been spared the sorrow of so many separations and the shame of so many inconsistencies. The gratitude of a nation would not have been soured with the resentment of a party. Biographers would have celebrated a statesman as keen to foresee as he was skilful to execute. The man him-self would have been just the same. Whilst we allow all this, however, we must bear in mind that education has more power over some natures than over others. It had power over Peel because he had not a brooding medita-tive spirit. He took that which was given to him, and assumed that it was right until, by acting upon it, he was taught that it was wrong. Then he cheerfully sub-mitted to correction and began again. Whatever might have been his training, his course would probably have been thus flexible. He could not have been safe from repeated self-contradiction except by living in quiet times.

Peel's claim to political honesty will not now be seriously disputed. If he sometimes resisted in oppo-sition the measures which he adopted in office, we

14 *

must allow much for his peculiar cast of intelligence, and much for the laxity of public men even in his more upright age.   If he twice deceived the confidence of his own party, he did so to his own disadvantage, and in order to avert a national calamity which seemed imminent; civil war in the one instance, and in the other instance famine.   Whether in the autumn of 1828, or in the autumn of 1845, Peel did the thing which he ought to have done; whether he ought not to have at once avowed the change in his own ideas, resigned office, and been content to help his late rivals in carrying out his new views, is a question which can be answered only after full consideration of all the circumstances of each case.   In each case, Peel no doubt justified himself by the reflection that if the reform were necessary, the speediest and most certain way of bringing it about was the right way to choose. In each case Peel, unknown to himself, was probably biassed by the wish to link his name with a great measure.   In each case his party had some ground to complain of his behaviour.

The claims of party are certainly subordinate to the claims of country.   The necessity of State may certainly excuse a breach of party confidence.   But the necessity must be unmistakable.   It may be necessary that a change should be made, yet not necessary that it should be made by Peel rather than by Russell.   The mere inconvenience of a delay which does not threaten the public safety is not ground enough to justify a Minister in deserting his party without notice.   Party government cannot be sound unless parties represent principles, and parties cannot represent principles if the leader will not keep faith with his followers, if he will use to overthrow their principles the power which he derives from them. He is free to advise, to exhort, to remonstrate, and to retire when the variance between his beliefs and his situation becomes so great as to make retirement the more honourable course. He is not free to regard himself merely as an independent member of Parliament, or as a single disconnected servant of the Crown. These general maxims do not, indeed, remove the difficulties which are encountered in practice. Under very difficult circumstances Peel acted, we may believe, according to his conscience, but we must own that he showed a certain insensibility to party ties, and set an example which has encouraged the political profligacy of to-day.

In other respects Peel's public character was stainless. His industry it were superfluous to praise. His truthfulness was chosen for particular eulogy by the honest Wellington. Personal integrity might be easy to a man so rich ; but Peel disdained to job for friends, and used his patronage as honestly as the admitted claims of party would allow. Although naturally of a fiery disposition, he had schooled himself to almost perfect self-command and to a courtesy hardly ever ruffled by the coarsest or bitterest attack. Although sensitive and self-conscious, he was neither spiteful nor vindictive. His worst enemy owned that he was very free from rancour and had nothing petty about him. He grew softer all through a life of contention, and as time went on became more and more tender of human suffering.

Throughout his career Peel lost both in reputation and in influence by his shy, awkward, and embarrassed manner. Many anecdotes attest this failing so remarkable in a man of great powers who has always lived in the great world. When Hudson, after nine days of unceasing travel, reached Rome and greeted Peel with the invitation to return to England and to become Premier, Peel could only observe, " I think you might have made the journey in a day less by taking another route." Greville tells how in the House of Commons he forgot to bow to an Irish supporter, who, losing patience, exclaimed: "Damn the fellow! he's cut me again. I'll go and vote against him," and was with difficulty appeased by the skill of the Conservative managers. A still more curious illustration of Peel's unreadiness in little things has been given by the late Mr. Stapleton. "Mr. Hawes was chairman of a committee of the House of Commons before whom a certain witness gave important testimony. The committee expressed their opinion to their chairman that the Government ought to do something to reward the man. Mr. Hawes (who was in opposition) accordingly sought an interview with Sir Robert Peel, then Premier. A day being appointed, Mr. Hawes was ushered in, was very civilly received, and proceeded to state his case. When he had concluded, Sir Robert looked steadfastly at him without uttering a word, and continued to do so for so long that Mr. Hawes grew quite uncomfortable, and, taking up his hat, said, 'I beg your pardon, Sir Robert, I see that you think I have been taking too great a liberty in coming to see you as I have done. I wish you good morning.' On which Sir Robert started up and said: 'Good gracious! you are quite mistaken; I was only thinking how best I could comply with your request. It is my unfortunate manner which has been my bane through life.'"

This unfortunate manner had one very harmful consequence; it confirmed the impression of insincerity given by Peel's behaviour on various critical occasions. Like many shy men Peel took refuge in formality. He was so decorous and so plausible that he edged the tongue of malice. He was cold and crafty, men said;

he was always aiming at personal ends; he was always trying to make this rival ridiculous or that rival his catspaw; and he was always ready to flatter the prejudice or the passion of his inferiors. He lived to silence this gossip, to show that a warm heart beat under his chill exterior, and that he was patriotic as well as ambitious. But all through his prime it was loud and unceasing, and he was far from popular.

Peel was not a great orator. The four volumes of his speeches are seldom opened but by the conscientious student of history. Many of his utterances, it is true, suffer from their endeavour to satisfy the canons of a style which was not suited either to the author or to his age. Peel had formed his taste in the school of the orators of the eighteenth century. Like them, he understood by a set speech an elaborate work of art, a dignified composition which might sometimes lend itself to pathos or to humour, but must never stoop to be familiar; which might be adorned with well-chosen quotations, and should lead through long rhythmical periods up to a swelling and sonorous peroration. When delivered by the right speaker to the right audience, a speech of this kind may well be beautiful and effective. But in the speaker it requires a choice of words, a delicacy of ear, a turn for lofty sentiments and grandiose imaginations which may be improved by industry, but must come from nature. In the audience it demands at least freedom from drudgery and a love of art. Such an audience was not to be found in the reformed House of Commons, nor had nature created such a speaker in Robert Peel. Accordingly Peel's speeches are least pleasing when they are most ambitious. They constantly raise, but hardly ever satisfy, expectation. They

lack the something which everybody can feel and nobody
can define ; the something which distinguishes true eloquence, and which comes from the intense and glowing
mind of the heaven-born orator.   Only one felicity
brightens these laboured utterances, a felicity of quotation. Peel knew the Latin and the English poets well,
and could introduce with the happiest effect either a
majestic or a homely verse.

But when Peel forgot the grand style of another age
to use the common style of his own, when he gave up
art for business and set himself to abridge a bluebook
or to unfold a budget, then he was admirable, because
then he was spontaneous ; then his capacious memory,
his clear head and his untiring energy gave him a power
which has never been surpassed. "The oftener you
heard him speak the more his speaking gained upon you.
Addressing the House several times in the night on
various subjects, he always seemed to know more than
anyone else about each of them."*   The effect of this
overflowing knowledge was heightened by the tact
which might fail Peel in society but never failed him in
the House of Commons.   "He never seemed occupied
with himself.   His effort was evidently directed to
convince you not that he was eloquent but that he was
right."*   Such a speaker needed only long practice in
order to become a perfect debater ; and it has been
said that Peel played upon the House as a musician
would play upon an old fiddle.   The author of this
saying has given us an admirable criticism of Peel's
oratory.

As an orator Sir Robert Peel had, perhaps, the most available
talent that has ever been brought to bear in the House of Commons.
We have mentioned that both in exposition and reply he was equally

* Lord Dalling's *Sir Robert Peel.*

eminent. His statements were perspicuous, complete, and dignified; when he combated the objections or criticised the propositions of an opponent, he was adroit and acute; no speaker ever sustained a process of argumentation in a public assembly more lucidly, and none, as debaters, have united in so conspicuous a degree prudence with promptness. In the higher efforts of oratory he was not successful. His vocabulary was ample and never mean; but it was neither rich nor rare. His speeches will afford no sentiment of surpassing grandeur and beauty that will linger in the ears of coming generations. He embalmed no great political truth in immortal words. His flights were ponderous; he soared with the wing of the vulture rather than with the plume of the eagle; and his perorations, when most elaborate, were most unwieldy. In pathos he was quite deficient; when he attempted to touch the tender passions it was painful. His face became distorted like that of a woman who wants to cry but cannot succeed. Orators certainly should not shed tears, but there are moments when, as the Italians say, the voice should weep. The taste of Sir Robert Peel was highly cultivated, but it was not originally fine; he had no wit; but he had a keen sense of the ridiculous, and an abundant vein of genuine humour. Notwithstanding his artificial reserve, he had a hearty and a merry laugh; and sometimes his mirth was uncontrollable. He was gifted with an admirable organ, perhaps the finest that has been heard in the House in our days, unless we except the thrilling tones of O'Connell. Sir Robert Peel also modulated his voice with great skill. His enunciation was very clear, though somewhat marred by provincialisms. His great deficiency was want of nature, which made him often appear, even with a good cause, more plausible than persuasive, and more specious than convincing. He may be said to have gradually introduced a new style into the House of Commons, which was suited to the age in which he chiefly flourished and to the novel elements of the assembly which he had to guide. He had to deal with greater details than his predecessors, and he had in many instances to address those who were deficient in previous knowledge. Something of the lecture, therefore, entered into his displays. This style may be called the didactic.

Peel had the person of an orator. He was lofty in stature and large in make. His head was small and well formed; his features regular, the forehead broad rather than high; the brow almost beautiful; the nose slightly aquiline; but the mouth was compressed and the upper lip too long. In his youth he was of fair complexion with light hair and a radiant expression of face. Those who did not like him said that his glance was sly, and compared his movements to those of a cat. In later years he became portly, but always remained good-looking. The full effect of his comely presence, however, was lessened by faults of pose and gesture. A generation accustomed to the grace and majesty of Canning, thought him awkward, not to say vulgar in his bearing. His accustomed attitude, Greville said, was that of a dancing-master giving a lesson. In this, as in so many other respects, Peel was the homely man of business, without anything either of the noble or of the artist.

In private life Peel was admirable. He was a dutiful son, a loving husband, and an affectionate father. Those who knew him best liked him best. When Wellington said that Peel had no manners he was thinking of the graces which adorn a court, not of the amenities which sweeten a home. With intimate friends Peel would throw off all reserve, be gay and hearty, talk freely and tell a good story with great spirit. He was a liberal landlord who took pleasure in improving his estate and in ameliorating the condition of all who lived upon it. He used a vast fortune with judgment and with spirit; was never lavish but would spend freely for any worthy purpose. He preserved to the end of his life the literary tastes of his youth, and kept up a familiar intercourse with the great authors of Greece and Rome. Those who believe that a classical education unfits its subject for practical life may note that the greatest of English administrators and financiers revelled in classical literature. Upon the value of classical studies he insisted with ardour in the inaugural address which he delivered to the University of Glasgow in 1837, when chosen to the office of Lord Rector. But he did not neglect modern authors. Even an intelligent foreigner like Stockmar regarded him as a man of ripe culture and varied information. It is the more remarkable that he seems to have been scarcely touched by the stir of those religious controversies which became so clamorous in his later years. He remained a temperate Anglican of the old school. He shared neither in the High Church movement nor in the reaction which it provoked. " There is nothing," he wrote to Croker in 1835, "more intolerable than the tyranny of party, and nothing more insane than the excommunication of a man because he differs on some one point from those with whom he is disposed generally to act." We may conjecture that he would have also regarded in this spirit the liberal tendencies of men like Arnold and Maurice.

Peel was even fonder of art than of letters. As a minister he took a particular interest in improving and enriching the National Gallery, and, as a private person, he was one of the most liberal and judicious of connoisseurs. His collection of Dutch and Flemish paintings, although celebrated, was scarcely so interesting as his collection of English portraits. This latter is said to have been formed upon the model of the collection made by Clarendon and described by Evelyn. Beside portraits of many of our most distinguished statesmen it contained the portrait of Pope, by Richardson; of Butler, by Soest; of Samuel Johnson, by Reynolds; of Southey, by Lawrence; of Byron, by Phillips; of Wordsworth, by Pickersgill. Next to George IV. Peel was the most munificent patron of Lawrence. For Peel Wilkie painted his picture of John Knox preaching.

Many other painters of less note received from Peel their most valuable commissions. The pictures from Peel's collection which have found a place in the National Gallery attest the breadth and refinement of his taste.

Nor was Peel one of those critics and connoisseurs who praise the work and let the workmen starve. He was always prompt to befriend artists, men of letters and men of science. The small funds which an English minister can apply to this purpose were employed to the utmost advantage by Peel. At the end of his brief adminstration in 1835 he could write to a friend, " The pensions—the only pensions I gave—were to a Mrs. Temple, whose husband, an African traveller, died, I think, at Sierra Leone. She had £100 a year, Professor Airy £300, Mrs. Somerville £200, Sharon Turner £200, Robert Southey £300, James Montgomery (of Sheffield) £150. The Chancellor gave Crabbe a living. I gave Milman the only preferment I had to give, that of St. Margaret's and the prebend of Westminster." Milman's preferment illustrates that impartiality which brought upon Peel the reproach that he would help a literary man of the adverse party sooner than a literary man of his own. On his return to power he continued to follow the same course. He embraced in his kindness the children of persons distinguished in art or letters. The first appointment of his first administration was given to a son of Allan Cunningham. For the sons of Mrs. Hemans he found places under the Crown. One of his last official acts was to give a situation in the Customs Department to a son of Benjamin Haydon. This was only one of several acts of kindness to that unhappy painter and his family. For in such cases Peel was as liberal of his own as of the public means, and gave help in that thoughtful and delicate way which alone could make charity acceptable to a man of proud spirit.

The mention of these acts of pure beneficence may fitly close the record of a great career. They call to mind Peel's best qualities: his humanity and his zeal in the cause of civilization. To these virtues many mistakes of judgment, many frailties of nature, must always be forgiven. But when we retrace his long laborious public life, when we contemplate his steady endeavour to bridge the chasm between an old and a new age, when we note his fortitude in the hour of defeat, and his moderation in the hour of victory, when we enumerate the prejudices which he outgrew and the toils which he achieved, and remember that he, the pupil of Eldon, the successor of Sidmouth, having become one of the greatest of English reformers, was still growing and learning when overtaken by death, we shall own a debt not of forgiveness but of gratitude and admiration, and think ourselves happy to be citizens of a State in which the Conservative Party could be led by such a statesman as Sir Robert Peel.

INDEX.